BANKING ON LIFE

RICHARD KING

BANKING ON LIFE

Baraka
Books

Montréal

ISBN 978-1-77186-240-0 pbk; 978-1-77186-241-7 epub; 978-1-77186-242-4 pdf

Cover by Richard Carreau
Book Design by Folio Infographie
Editing by Elise Moser, Deirdre King, Robin Philpot
Proofreading by Blossom Thom, Rachel Hewitt

Legal Deposit, 2nd quarter 2021
Bibliothèque et Archives nationales du Québec
Library and Archives Canada

Published by Baraka Books of Montreal

Printed and bound in Quebec

Trade Distribution & Returns
Canada – UTP Distribution: UTPdistribution.com

United States
Independent Publishers Group: IPGbook.com

We acknowledge the support from the Société de développement des entreprises culturelles (SODEC) and the Government of Quebec tax credit for book publishing administered by SODEC.

CHAPTER 1

Friday – Where's Annie's Patient

Annie Linton had worked a double shift, sixteen hours with only a couple short breaks, the previous day, a normal occurrence in the chronically understaffed ED, Emergency Department, at the Gursky Memorial Hospital, and was not thrilled about having to be back at work at 7:00 on Friday morning. On the other hand, she had the weekend off and she would not work a double shift on this day no matter how many times she was asked. She was tired and wanted an early night. She and her boyfriend had plans for the weekend and she planned to be well rested for them.

She was pleased when she was assigned to her favourite service—Triage.

The staff of the Green Unit were switching into daytime mode. The nurses going off duty brought the day staff up to date on the patients, noting who would be released and who would be staying longer. Daniella Taddeo, the nurse assigned to the patient in room seven, Michaela Bédard's room, walked over to the bed and gently shook her by the shoulder. "Time to wake up, Ms. Bédard," she said. "It looks like you had a good night's sleep."

Getting no response, she pulled the flannel sheet away from the patient and gasped. In the bed was a man where she expected to find a woman. For a moment she thought she had the wrong room. She checked the chart to ensure she hadn't made a mistake and then checked the patient's carotid pulse. "Dear God," she exclaimed. She dropped the chart on the floor and rushed to the door. She realized she did not want to scream that she had a dead (and unknown) patient on her hands. Instead, she yelled, "Code blue in seven," the code for a life-threatening emergency. Not literally true but close enough. All the doctors on duty along with a couple of nurses rushed to where she was standing and pushed past her to get to the patient.

Dr. Rosen was the first person to get to the bed. "What've we got?" he called.

"Dead patient," Daniella said.

"What? What the hell are you talking about?" Dr. Rosen gave the body a cursory look and determined that he was indeed dead. "Where's the bloody chart?"

The nurse picked up the chart and handed it to Dr. Rosen. None of the other people who had charged into the room made a move to leave. They sensed that something exciting was about to happen.

The doctor flipped through the chart. Dr. Rosen was a tall man, overweight, bald and short-tempered. "What the fuck is this?" he shouted. "I'm supposed to be looking at a woman who suffered an asthma attack." He waved the chart at the poor nurse who was beginning to feel that she had done something wrong.

She regained her composure. "I didn't put the patient in the bed. I found him."

Dr. Rosen did not like backtalk from nurses. "Well, who the fuck put the patient here?" He consulted the chart and continued at volume, "Linton! Is Linton on? Someone get her in here."

The nurse nearest to the door poked her head into the work area and called to the Unit Agent to page Annie Linton.

The page went out over the PA system and a moment or two later Annie appeared, surprised to find a crowd of doctors and nurses surrounding Dr. Rosen, who was waving a chart at the assemblage.

"What's going on?" Annie asked.

"Good question," Dr. Rosen said. "Who are we supposed to have here?"

Annie grabbed the chart that Dr. Rosen was waving at her. She gave it a quick look and said, "Michaela Bédard. Asthma. I triaged her last night. I remember her because she was one of the last patients I saw before I left for the day."

"And who have we got?" Dr. Rosen asked, standing aside so Annie could see who was in the bed.

"Who's he? Where's my patient?" Annie asked.

"Yeah, my questions exactly."

Annie didn't have to take the patient's pulse to see that he was dead. "Did anyone call the police?" she asked.

"The police? Why call the police? Probably some nurse got the wrong patient into the wrong bed. I'd be more worried about malpractice." Dr. Rosen glared at Annie.

"Really?" Annie replied. "Did anyone check his wrists?"

Dr. Rosen picked up one of the corpse's lifeless arms and then the other and said, "There's nothing on his wrists!"

"Exactly," Annie said. "If there is no hospital bracelet it means he wasn't registered. Which means he's not a patient, he's a victim." Annie paused for a second or two and continued in a more conciliatory tone. "Perhaps we should call the police. I'll do it."

She walked to the desk of the Unit Agent and used her cellphone to call her boyfriend, Gilles Bellechasse, a detective in the Major Crimes Division of the Montreal Police Department.

Annie had met Gilles when he was the victim of a shooting and was brought to the Emergency Department of the Gursky. A couple of months after he was discharged and on the mend, he returned to the hospital to thank Annie for her quick thinking, which had saved his life. They went out to dinner and after a time fell in love and became a couple. Annie was instrumental in discovering the clue that helped Gilles solve a series of murders and attempted murders.

On the occasions that the police were needed at the Gursky, a call was placed to 911 or to a special phone number that went directly to the squad that dealt with criminal activity in hospitals. Annie knew she would get faster action if she called Gilles directly.

"Hi, Sweetheart," Gilles said when Annie's name appeared on his cellphone. "What's up?"

"Problem. A big one."

"Tell me," Gilles replied.

"We found a dead body in one of the beds in the ER."

"Is that a police matter? Wouldn't that happen from time to time?" Gilles asked.

Annie explained that the dead body was not a patient and that it was found in the bed of a patient who had disappeared.

"Got it," Gilles said. "Seal the room. I'll be there to start the investigation as soon as possible. Stat, I guess you'd say."

Annie returned to the room where the body was located and told all those there to leave without touching anything and to get security to make certain that no one entered the room until the police arrived.

The nurses and orderlies left the room. Dr. Rosen remained where he was and slowly looked around the room as if making sure *his* orders were the ones being obeyed. He was the last one to leave.

CHAPTER 2

38 Days Earlier – A Meeting

Rob Scroyle, CPA, the senior partner in the firm Scroyle, Caitiff, Rudisbe and Spavin, got to the office early that Tuesday morning in August. The firm occupied two floors of office space on boulevard René-Lévesque, the street where many of Montreal's prestigious professionals had offices. He was at his computer when his early appointment knocked on his office door. Rob Scroyle got up, straightened his tie, and smoothed the trousers of his navy-blue bespoke suit. He took his suit jacket from where he had hung it on the back of one of the visitors' chairs. He gave it a gentle shake, slipped it on and walked to the door of his office.

Of all the partners, Rob had the best office. It looked north, and he had an unobstructed view of Mount Royal.

Rob unlocked the door. Felix Nergal was standing in the corridor getting ready to knock again. "Felix," Rob greeted him warmly, "come in, come in."

Felix Nergal, at almost six feet three inches, was taller than Rob, and at close to three hundred pounds a lot broader. "Your receptionist isn't at her desk so I came directly to your office." he explained. "Why the locked door?"

Rob stood aside so his client could enter. "Privacy. Let's sit over here." He indicated a sofa with two upholstered chairs facing it, a coffee table between them. The furniture was placed to afford the person sitting on the sofa the view of

Mount Royal. Felix made himself comfortable and Rob made a detour to his desk to retrieve his cappuccino and sat down in one of the chairs. He adjusted his Hermès tie and arranged himself to crease his suit as little as possible. Felix was also expensively dressed, in a chalk-striped charcoal-grey suit which emphasized his height but hid his bulk. He crossed his right leg over his left, the side of his shoe resting against his trousers. Rob was certain that his guest's shoe would leave a mark on his pant leg.

"Can I get you a coffee?" Rob inquired. "I'll call down to the coffee shop. It'll only take a couple of minutes."

"Robbie. I didn't come to your office early in the morning to have coffee. I could have done that at home. Why am I here?"

"Good question. I've come across an opportunity that might be of interest to you."

"And not something you wanted to discuss on the telephone," Felix said.

"Exactly," Rob said.

Early in his practice Rob had had the insight that from a purely accounting point of view, there was no difference between legitimate and criminal businesses. Over his years in practice Rob had developed the ability to find business opportunities that were not always on the right side of the law. Sometimes the businesses started off on the shady side and in others, they started off in a perfectly legitimate way and ended up supporting an illicit enterprise. He developed techniques to legitimize the illegitimate for certain of his clients.

When Rob came across one of these opportunities, he took it to one of his select clients. Felix Nergal was one of the chosen few.

"Do you want to hear about it?"

"I wouldn't be here if I didn't."

"Okay." Rob shifted in his chair. "I've heard about an initial offering that will be made later this year. It's a high-tech business. Completely legit."

CHAPTER 3

Friday –
Gilles Begins his Investigation

Gilles went to the office of his boss, Captain Henri Lacroix, and reported what he had been told. "Sounds bizarre," Captain Lacroix commented. "Keep me posted." On his way out of the office Gilles called the Forensics Division and asked to have a team meet him in the emergency department of the Gursky. He also called the dispatch centre to have them get a squad car to the hospital as quickly as possible to secure the crime scene. He did not have a lot of faith in the security agency the hospital used.

Less than thirty minutes later Gilles strode through the door of the ER. He spotted Tom Andreadis, whom he knew from a previous case, and asked him to get Annie. It only took a moment or two for Annie to respond to the page, and she brought Gilles to the room that had been assigned to Mickie Bédard.

Gilles flashed his badge and nodded a greeting to the cops who had arrived fifteen minutes before Gilles and were standing by the door to the room. Gilles entered but was careful not to touch anything. He could see that there was a body lying on its side on the bed. A chair was lying on the floor but otherwise the room did not look any different than any other hospital room. There were a few other items, a table on wheels that could be brought to the bed for meals and an IV stand that would have been upended if there had been a struggle. The chair on the floor suggested that there had been some kind of a struggle.

"Has anything been touched?" he asked Annie.

"Just the patient and the bedding," she explained. "And the door, of course, and probably the walls."

"Nothing else?"

"No, everything is just as we found it."

"Très bien. He's not the patient who is supposed to be here?" he asked, indicating the corpse on the bed.

"Exactly. We have no idea who he is." Annie gave her boyfriend a rundown of the events of the previous night, triaging Mickie Bédard and assigning her the room.

"We just wanted to keep her overnight to ensure that she did not have a relapse. She would have been discharged this morning," Annie concluded.

Just as she finished recounting events the forensics team arrived along with Dr. Charles Lapointe, the medical examiner. Dr. Lapointe and Gilles exchanged pleasantries. Gilles was about to introduce Annie when Dr. Lapointe extended his hand, smiled, and said, "I remember you from my last visit to this hospital. Annie, correct?"

Annie returned Dr. Lapointe's smile and shook his hand. "Correct. You have a good memory."

The forensics team got to work.

"There's not much I can do until these guys finish with the area around the body. Why don't you and Annie have a coffee or something? I'll call you when I'm done. You can start your investigation before I take the body," Dr. Lapointe suggested.

"Actually, I'll want Annie to get me the address, phone number and any other information about the patient she triaged. The person who was supposed to be in that bed,"

Gilles said. "But yeah, call me when I can have a closer look at the body and the rest of the scene."

Gilles and Annie walked back to the Triage/Registration area of the ER and Annie logged into one of the computers. She quickly located Mickie Bédard's file and gave Gilles the information he needed—her home and work phone numbers and addresses along with her cellphone number. As a precaution Gilles noted the name and phone number of the person to contact in case of an emergency.

Gilles also asked for Mickie's medical information and the reason she was a patient in the ER but Annie refused to provide it. "I'm pretty close to the line in giving you her contact information. I can't cross it by giving you her private medical information," she explained.

Gilles was not surprised by Annie's refusal. "Can't blame a guy for trying," he said. "Do you have time for a coffee while I wait to get access to the crime scene?"

"No, I'm working and my break is not for an hour or so. But I'm sure that Tom and Ursula and I would love coffees if you went over to the Second Cup to get them." Ursula, one of the other nurses working in Triage, was a close friend of Annie's.

Gilles smiled and went to the Second Cup to buy coffees for the staff.

By the time he got back with a large carton coffee urn and a dozen cardboard cups, sufficient for all those working in Triage and Registration and then some, Gilles had received a text from Dr. Lapointe that he was ready to remove the body. Gilles poured himself a coffee and one for Dr. Lapointe and headed back to the murder scene.

The forensics squad from the Identité judiciaire were still in the process of collecting evidence when Gilles got back to the murder scene, but Dr. Lapointe had completed his preliminary examination of the body. A couple of guys from the coroner's office were at the door with one of their stretchers, ready to take the body to the medical examiner's office for a complete workup.

Gilles handed Dr. Lapointe a coffee. "Can you give me any preliminary information?"

Dr. Lapointe used a pen as a pointer and, holding it over the bridge of the victim's nose, explained, "The murderer is either very lucky or very well trained. They were able to drive the nasal bone into the victim's brain, killing him instantly."

"The patient who occupied this room, a woman, is missing. I don't have her vitals, but is it possible that she had the strength to kill someone that way?"

"It doesn't really take a great amount of strength if the perpetrator knew what they were doing, if they were trained in self-defence or one of the martial arts," Dr. Lapointe replied.

Gilles took a notepad from an inner pocket of his blazer and made a note. Tapping his notepad with his pen he asked, "Any signs of a struggle?"

"Hard to say. I'll know more when I get the vic on the table. Frankly, it's hard to imagine someone walking up to him and popping him one on the nose. The room's a bit of a mess but if there was a struggle it was short."

Gilles returned his notepad to his inner pocket and pointed at the victim's body. "Can I check his pockets for ID before you take him?"

"Be my guest," Dr. Lapointe answered.

The body was now lying on its back on the bed where it had been discovered. Gilles remembered that when he came into the room it was angled more on its right side. Gilles reasoned that if the perpetrator had been able to search the victim they would not have had access to the pockets on his right. He pulled on a pair of purple latex gloves and searched there first. There was some loose change in the right front pocket. In the right rear pocket Gilles found a Tracfone pre-paid cell phone and a MetroCard for the New York subway system. Gilles gently pulled the phone and card out of the victim's pocket and slipped them into evidence bags provided by one of the technicians who were working nearby.

"Interesting," Gilles said, holding up the evidence bag so that the techs and Dr. Lapointe could see the card. "It appears that our victim was from New York."

Gilles handed the evidence bag holding the MetroCard to one of the techs to have it logged. He took the bag with the Tracfone and carefully removed the phone, holding it by the bezel. He tapped the home button to turn on the phone. As he suspected he needed a thumb print to activate it. Gilles placed the victim's right thumb on the home button and the home screen appeared. Gilles navigated to the Settings Menu and changed the code to 1-2-3-4. Gilles slid the phone back into the bag and handed it to the technician to be logged as evidence.

Gilles then searched the victim's other two pockets but found nothing else. Lastly, he patted the front pockets because he knew that items sometimes got lodged in the lower corners of men's pockets. Gilles felt something. He used one hand to pull the pocket open and with the other dug as deeply as he could. He pulled out a key ring with two keys on it. Holding the key ring in the crook of his little finger he held the keys aloft and asked, "Have any of you ever seen keys like this?" One of the keys was black and the other had a New York Giants logo at its head. "Unquestionably a New Yorker and a Giants fan," Gilles said.

The technicians examined the keys. Both of them shook their heads. "I've seen a lot of keys, but none like these," said one.

"Exactly," Gilles agreed. He slipped the keys into an evidence bag. "Get the phone and the MetroCard to Constable Suzanne Rigaud at Computer Crimes as soon as you can. We have a possible identification of the murderer. Now we need to know who the victim is. Tell her that I changed the password of the phone to 1-2-3-4. It's strange, though; there's something missing."

"Il ne manque rien. Nous avons tout," the forensics tech said.

"I don't mean something's been misplaced. I mean there's something we didn't find. The victim's wallet. I think the murderer must have it."

"Done?" Dr. Lapointe asked. Gilles nodded and the two men from the coroner's office wheeled their stretcher in. As they lifted the body, a watch fell to the floor. Either it had been removed from the victim and tossed onto the bed, or in some way pulled from the murderer's wrist.

"Careful," Gilles said. He stooped and, using his pen, picked up the watch. It too went into an evidence bag. A more thorough search of the bed in which the victim had been lying yielded no additional evidence.

Dr. Lapointe followed the coroner's men out of the room. "I'll get you a preliminary report as soon as I can," he said, "and please say goodbye to Annie for me."

"I will," Gilles promised. He turned to the technicians and said, "I'm done here, as well. Get me your report as soon as you can."

"D'accord," the tech responded. "Do you want the sheets and the other bedding?"

"Keep it in the evidence lock-up unless you find something significant on it. I'll tell them that you're taking it."

Gilles went back to the triage area to find Annie. "I'm heading off now," he told her. "But I have one more question. Are there closed-circuit cameras in the rooms?"

"You wish," Annie replied. "That would be a total violation of the patient's privacy—not to mention that of the staff. But the waiting area and the hallways are covered. Security can show you."

Gilles had the security guard paged and told him what he wanted. The security guard radioed his supervisor who told them to come to his office. Annie went along with them so she could identify the patient.

Gilles was able to review the security tape from the night before. He knew the time Bédard had been triaged and he checked that portion of the tape first. Annie indicated the patient being wheeled into the Green Unit. Gilles had the security agent advance the tape slowly and spotted the victim come in several hours later, but could not see his face. He had been careful to keep it out of sight of the cameras. Gilles recognized him from his clothing.

The security person again advanced the tape slowly until Annie told him to stop. She pointed to a woman, her face away from the camera, leaving the hospital. About fifteen minutes elapsed between the time the victim came into the ED and Bédard left.

Gilles walked Annie back to the ED. As they were both on duty, when they made plans for that evening, they did so quickly, each of them then returning to work.

CHAPTER 4

38 Days Earlier –
A Meeting (Continued)

Nergal crossed his legs and wondered why his accountant had dragged him to an early meeting to talk about a tech company. They were a dime a dozen and Scroyle should have known that most of them were of no interest to him; the few that were could have been discussed over the phone once he had seen the prospectuses.

Rob sensed that his client was not impressed with anything he had so far heard. Rob continued his pitch. "The product the company has, has great potential, and if I understand it correctly it allows those who wish to move funds to do so without being noticed."

The last five words that Rob spoke piqued Felix's interest. He leaned forward and made a motion for Rob to continue.

"The company has developed some amazing artificial intelligence. But what is more important for you, I think, is its password and communications product, which is totally unhackable. If, for example, you are writing about a private business plan, the competition, whether corporate or governmental, will not be able to break in, so to speak, and..." Rob paused, "...read your email. By extension, it can be used to move funds without leaving a trace."

"So can Bitcoin," Nergal pointed out.

"Well, yes and no, but that aside, this software can move any currency anywhere. You don't have to speculate in Bitcoin. Less risky."

"Are you saying that no one, not even someone with a warrant, can trace deposits?"

"That's exactly what I'm saying—with one possible caveat. A government can see the bank the funds were transferred out of—if, and only if, that bank is within its jurisdiction. If the funds are housed offshore then their movement is invisible to anyone but the person who makes the transfers. It works for any and all currencies."

"Great, what's the catch?" Nergal asked.

"Yeah," Rob said, "here's the thing. I don't know much about the company. The offering, the IPO, is being handled by a small Montreal firm, Stevens, Bédard. They have an office on Crescent and so far as I can tell they've never done anything like this before."

"Why not just call them up?"

"I did just that. The person handling the IPO is one of the partners, Michaela Bédard. She wouldn't tell me much other than what was in the prospectus, which she sent me. But she also told me that the first offering was fully subscribed. If the bank handling this was one of the large American firms, I would walk away. There'd be no chance of opening a door. But this is a local firm, an investment bank, if you can call it that, which no one ever heard of. I became more, not less, curious."

"And I become involved how?" Nergal asked.

"Here's the thing. They're going to list on the American exchanges, which means the value should skyrocket. But I'm more interested in the product. It's not like Apple or Microsoft, where you know pretty much what the company does. There's a lot of secrecy and the company itself is a company that makes a game, one of those internet things."

"You want me to invest in a web game?" Felix could not believe he'd come to an early meeting for that.

"Hardly," Rob said. "The IPO is for the security software. They created a second company. It holds the security software and it's the one going public. Not the related company, the gaming company. The security software is supposed to be foolproof."

"What about the AI?" Felix asked.

"Also divided into two parts. One part in the security company and the other in the gaming company. Again, I gather that there will be an IPO for that a little farther down the road. It's definitely worth investigating. There is real benefit to you in owning a piece of the security company."

"Got it. What's my next step?"

"As I said," Rob continued, "they're playing it pretty close to the vest. I need someone who would be interested in investing to manage ..." Rob paused, "...an approach. Bédard has information on the product and information on those who are in on the initial purchase, pre-market."

"Ah, I see. The kind of thing that a firm of accountants can't do."

"Exactly. That information is critically important in a case like this one where so little is known about the company."

"Yeah, I get it. I can't see myself even thinking about this unless I'm able to get my hands on the information that whoever is managing the IPO won't share." Felix paused for a moment and added, "Precisely because they won't provide it. I work with some guys in New York, who have shown themselves adept at getting in on deals that might otherwise be exclusive, if you get my meaning. They'll provide the personnel to get the information we need."

"Why not someone local?" Rob asked.

"I like to get my information in a way that can't be traced back to me. Keep my fingerprints off deals, if you get my meaning. You know very well I'm a deep-background kind of guy. Very deep background."

"And they get what we need how?"

"Not a question I ask," Felix replied. "All you have to know is that the Americans will be doing the work and we'll reap the benefits."

"If all goes well," Rob concluded, "you'll be able to buy in and get access to the product before anyone else. You may even be able to have it adapted to your particular needs. Who knows?"

Felix leaned back in the sofa and spread his arms out to their full length along the back of it. He didn't say anything for a while and Rob knew better than to interrupt him. Rob turned to look out the window. After several minutes Felix suddenly got to his feet, startling Rob out of his reverie. "Listen to me," he said. "I'll probably do it, but I have a condition. I want to talk to a couple of my associates. It's something that I think they'll be interested in. And if they're interested, I want to be able to tell them that we can go in big. No penny-ante bullshit."

"Clearly," Rob agreed. "When will you let me know?"

"Later today. If it's a go, you'll fill me in on the details then," Felix strode to the door of Rob's office and Rob had to walk quickly to get there before him.

He waited at his office door until he saw Felix turn down the corridor to the front door of the offices. Rob smiled to himself, closed his office door and returned to his desk. He rocked back and forth in his chair. He was all but certain that Felix Nergal had taken the bait, and that at some point in the near future a large amount of money would be changing hands.

Rob's fee would ensure that some of that large amount would flow into his firm's coffers.

Felix waited until late in the day to get back to Rob but he didn't disappoint. He called a couple of minutes before six in the evening. "We're in. I'll let you know when I've got my hands on the information we need. New York is on it."

CHAPTER 5

Friday – Felix Has a Question

Felix Nergal paid his lawyers a handsome annual retainer to ensure that his money-making schemes were legal and well hidden. He was fifty-nine years old and hadn't spent so much as a minute in prison. He had spent many hours in court defending his practices, but he usually won the lawsuits and evaded any charges brought against him, and considered the few losses a cost of doing business. His business method, a form of piracy, was based on the simple practice of finding companies that were either undervalued or had hidden values. He bought his way into the companies and grabbed some of this unexploited wealth before the owners or shareholders could stop him.

He practiced his entrepreneurial alchemy by reading a large number of trade publications covering any and every kind of business, from agriculture to zoology. Nergal also stayed in the background, making his approaches and acquisitions through lawyers and accountants.

He had a second set of businesses, ones that provided the funds for his piracy. These businesses were the type of enterprise that dealt mostly in cash—convenience stores and car washes, to name a couple. Because a lot of cash flowed through these businesses it was impossible to know if the source of the sales was legitimate, or from other sources disguised as sales. Since no one thought to explore the ownership of individual car washes or convenience stores, Felix could own a large number of this type of enterprise through multiple layers of holding companies and prête-nom companies. The cash flowed back to him in an almost untraceable fashion. His partners were a little more at risk.

When he needed an American front organization, he worked with a couple of guys, Ben Taylor and Murray Richman, who operated in New York under the grand name of the Richman, Taylor Investment Bank. They in turn channeled any Canadian deals they had through Felix. Over the years this co-operation had turned a tidy profit for all three men.

Simon Connors had been sent to Montreal by the Richman, Taylor Investment Bank to get the documentation that Nergal needed for the deal that he and Rob Scroyle had set in motion a month earlier. Scroyle had been unable to get any information on the company in the normal way. Connors was sent to Montreal to get his hands on it in any way he could. Nergal expected to hear from him late Thursday night or early Friday morning. When he hadn't heard from Connors by ten on Friday morning, he assumed that something had gone wrong and he called Murray Richman in New York.

"Mur, it's Felix. I've not heard from your man."

"We'll look into it and send someone else if necessary. You've called my office number. It's not a secure line. Call me on my cell if you need to speak to me."

"No need," Felix said. "You have the relevant information." Felix ended the call thinking, why do these guys have a land-line if they don't want people using it?

There was nothing more that Felix could do on this deal until either Taylor or Richman did their part, so he hefted his bulk out of his easy chair and went to the room in his condo that he used as an office and got busy researching other prospects.

CHAPTER 6

Friday – Gilles Investigates

Gilles left the hospital and got into his car, but before he drove off, he consulted his notes and called in to the office to give his boss a report. He then called the phone number Mickie had given as her residential phone. He wanted to see if she was at home. His call went to her voice mail. He called her cellphone and this call too went to voice mail. He decided that his best course of action would be to visit Mickie's office. Even if Mickie was in the wind there would be someone at her office who might know her whereabouts.

He drove to Crescent Street and parked a couple of doors away from the address he sought. The building was a three-story greystone structure situated about a third of a block north of de Maisonneuve on Crescent Street under the watchful, poetic eye of Leonard Cohen whose portrait graced the side of a high-rise apartment building. A brass plaque to the right of the door stated: Stevens, Bédard, Banquiers et Gestion des Investissements. The front door was locked. Gilles pressed the bell next to the door. A female voice came over the intercom: "Oui."

"Mon nom est Gilles Bellechasse, je suis avec la police de Montréal. Je veux parler à quelqu'un concernant Michaela Bédard." Gilles held his badge and ID up to the camera that was placed above the door.

"Elle n'est pas encore arrivée," the voice responded.

"Oui. I want to speak to someone about her. Is there someone I can talk to?"

"Monsieur Stevens is here." The receptionist buzzed Gilles in.

He found himself in a small foyer. A glass door led to a reception area that was tastefully outfitted in better-than-average waiting room furniture. It held a small sofa and a couple of chairs, all of which looked to be very comfortable. Small tables had been placed on either side of the sofa and next to each chair. A counter on one wall held a Keurig coffee maker and half a dozen white coffee mugs.

A long desk occupied the width of the room at the back, and behind it sat the receptionist with whom Gilles had spoken. A large Riopelle painting hung on the wall above the receptionist. A hallway and a flight of stairs were to Gilles's left.

Gilles approached the receptionist but before he could say anything she said, "I'll announce you to Monsieur Stevens. Please have a seat."

Gilles strolled over to the seating area but chose not to sit down. It only took a moment for a young woman as pretty and well-dressed as the receptionist to come down the stairs. She introduced herself as Monsieur Stevens's administrative assistant and asked Gilles to follow her.

She knocked on an office door and opened it without waiting for a response. A distinguished-looking man in his early sixties got up from his desk and walked to the door to meet Gilles. "I'm Denis Stevens," he said using the French pronunciation of his first name. Denis Stevens was clean-shaven, with a full head of neatly combed grey hair. He was a little shorter than Gilles's six feet two inches and was dressed in an expensive, charcoal-grey suit with a blue-and-yellow-striped tie. Stevens had an air of self-assurance that comes from success.

Gilles introduced himself and Denis Stevens invited him to sit down in one of the chairs that were placed at a round table. His host took the other chair and offered Gilles a coffee, which he accepted. "Comment est-ce que je peux vous aider?" Denis Stevens asked, speaking with an Outremontais accent. "I'm afraid Michaela is late this morning."

Before Gilles could explain the reason for his visit, the administrative assistant came in carrying a silver tray that held china cups and saucers along with a carafe of coffee, a sugar bowl and a small pitcher with milk. She placed the tray on the table and left the room while her boss did the honours. The coffee ceremony gave Gilles a chance to look around. He admired the office, which was furnished in Quebecois pine furniture adapted to office use.

"I'm afraid I have some distressing news," Gilles said, matching his host's accent. "I'm investigating a murder."

Denis Stevens went white. He half rose from his chair and fell back into it. He reached for his coffee cup but his hand was shaking and he gripped the edge of the table instead. "Michaela? Something happened to Mickie?" he said in a quivering voice.

Gilles placed a comforting hand on Denis's forearm and explained, "As far as we know Ms. Bédard is fine. I'm investigating the murder of someone else, someone we think she knew."

Denis Stevens sighed audibly, relief bringing the colour back to his face. He took a sip of coffee.

Gilles provided a very brief explanation of events, being careful to give the impression that Mickie was a witness to a crime, not a suspect.

"You and Ms. Bédard, Michaela, are business partners?" Gilles asked.

"Oui. But more than that actually. The founder of the firm was her great-grandfather and my grandfather. So we're related. Doubly related, actually. We're third cousins or something like that, but I'm also her uncle. I was married to her mother's sister. Because my wife and I didn't have any children Mickie is a like a daughter to us."

Gilles noticed a photograph of the face of a beautiful woman on Stevens's desk, angled so that both men could see it. The woman had grey hair and delicate features, a straight nose, and intelligent eyes.

"Is that your wife?" Gilles asked pointing to the photograph. "She's very beautiful."

"Oui, that's Francine, my late wife. The photo was taken about a year before she died."

"I'm sorry. She looks so young," he added.

"Too young," Denis Stevens agreed. "She suffered from COPD and" –he paused and breathed deeply for a second or two– "and there were complications, and she was taken from me."

The conversation had taken a sad turn away from Gilles's investigation and he wanted to bring it back to the reason for questioning Denis Stevens. He allowed a short time to pass in silence as Stevens collected himself.

"I'll tell you why I'm here," Gilles said, "and then leave you in peace."

He explained that Mickie had been hospitalized due to a serious asthma attack and had disappeared. In her place they discovered the body of a man who had yet to be identified, but who appeared to be in his mid-thirties. Gilles had a photo of the victim on his cellphone, which he showed to Denis Stevens. "Do you recognize this man?" he asked.

"Non, pas du tout," Denis Stevens responded.

"Could he be a client?"

"Non. I know all of our clients."

"Can you tell me something about your business? Perhaps it will give some indication as to how this man came into your partner's life."

"As I told you," Denis Stevens said. "The business was started by her great-grandfather, who was also my grandfather. We handle investments for some of the oldest families in Quebec. We've been doing it for a very long time. When the original partners Bédard and Stevens started, the Stevens family brought Anglo business to the firm and the Bédards, the French families who had money to invest. Over time, through marriages, the names remained but the language changed. My grandfather and my father married French-speaking women. Mickie's side of the family married into the Anglo world. I guess I closed the circle when I married her mother's sister."

"And what you do is invest other people's money?" Gilles asked. The family history was interesting but not helpful in his investigation.

"Oui. Invest and manage. We would not be in business if we didn't make the rich richer." Denis Stevens chuckled at his joke.

Gilles could not see how investing money for old-line English- and French-Canadian families could lead to a murder. "This is what Michaela did as well?"

"Yes. But she wanted to try her hand at more exciting things. She recently started working with a group of people who were in a business that, frankly, I don't understand. Something to do with computer programs."

"Can you tell me the name of the company?" Gilles asked.

"It's a funny name, Diplomery."

"Do you mean DiplomRMY?" This was one of the gaming and AI start-ups that were located in Montreal's high-tech centre in the Mile End area of the city. DiplomRMY was probably the most famous of the tech companies. Even Gilles had heard of it and he was a long way from being a gamer.

"Oui, that's it."

"What was Mickie doing for it?"

"The company was going public and Mickie was working on the IPO," Denis Stevens said. "Frankly, I was opposed to getting into that line of banking and investments. It requires a lot of work and a big commitment of time and money on our end before we see a return. And we have to face competition from big players in New York and Toronto. It's not for me. But Mickie graduated from HEC and wanted to do the modern things."

"Have you heard from Mickie this morning?"

"Non. And that's very strange." Gilles gave Denis a couple of seconds to explain why he considered it strange that he hadn't seen or heard from Mickie. When he didn't offer an explanation Gilles asked, "Why is it strange?"

"Because she's usually here before me and she calls if, for any reason, she has to be away from the office."

This answered Gilles's question without providing any additional information. He realized he had reached a dead end in his conversation with Denis Stevens, for the time being at least. He got to his feet and said, "Thank you for your time." He took a business card from a card holder and wrote his cellphone number on the back of it. He handed the card to Stevens, who had also stood up, and concluded the interview. "Please have Mickie call me if you should hear from her. My cellphone number is on the reverse side." The two men shook hands.

Back on Crescent Street, Gilles took a moment to consider whether he had learned anything from Denis Stevens. The short answer was: not much. Gilles was certain that the victim was from New York; the MetroCard and the keys they found on him gave a clear indication of that. Stevens provided a connection between the victim and Mickie Bédard—an American bank or banks might have been interested in the deal she was working on.

Gilles's first order of business was to identify the victim. Then he would pay a visit to DiplomRMY and see if anyone there knew something.

Gilles returned to his car, which was parked under the Leonard Cohen portrait on the side of the building bordering the parking lot. He wasn't a big Cohen fan but Annie was. As far as Gilles knew she had all his CDs. He much preferred the blues.

Gilles attached his cellphone to his car radio with a USB cable and brought up one of his many blues playlists. He chose one devoted to Muddy Waters and turned up the volume. In spite of the lyrics, there was something about the four-four time signature and chord progression of twelve-bar blues that put Gilles in a good mood. He drove to his office, located on the second floor of the Place Versailles shopping centre in the east end of Montreal. He got comfortable at his desk and called Suzanne Rigaud, his contact in the Computer Crimes Division, which was located in a nondescript building in the northern borough of Ville Saint-Laurent.

Constable Rigaud got on the phone and said, "Salut, Gilles. I received the gifts you sent me."

"Always thinking about you," Gilles replied. Not for the first time he wondered what she looked like. "Did you get a chance to check them out?"

"Well, the phone was easy because I had the password. Your victim only called three numbers from the phone. One was a local number and he called it quite a bit. Short calls, though; none of them lasted more than, say, half a minute. Do you want the number?"

Gilles pulled a pad toward him and, pen in hand, said, "You bet." Rigaud dictated a phone number and asked, "Do you want to know who it belongs to?"

"I recognize it. It's the office number of a woman I'm looking for. The patient that was in the room where the vic was found," Gilles told Suzanne. "He couldn't have had much in the way of conversations judging by the short duration of the calls. What are the other numbers?"

"Both of them are New York City numbers, 212 area code for one and 718 for the other." Gilles wrote down the numbers.

"Do I have to ask?"

Suzanne laughed, "Of course not. The first one was to a bank, the Richman, Taylor Investment Bank."

"Makes sense," Gilles said. "And the second one?"

"A residential number, so far as I can tell. I couldn't find it in a data search so it must be unlisted, but I called it and the voice mail message made me think it was residential. I checked with AT&T and they wouldn't tell me much, wouldn't even say if the number was one of theirs without a court order. But I found out it was a Queens exchange. Queens is..."

"I know what Queens is," Gilles interrupted. "Anything else? What about the MetroCard?"

"It's a subway pass, like our Opus cards. I ran it through a reader we have. The programming on these things is pretty basic, and whoever owns the card has just over five dollars left on it. With a little work I can probably figure out where the owner went."

"Can't hurt and it might be helpful," Gilles said. "As usual, you've been terrific."

"Wait a minute," Rigaud said. Gilles sensed that she was suppressing a laugh. "Aren't you forgetting something?"

"Suzanne, you're killing me. What else is there?"

"The keys."

"How did you end up with the keys? They've nothing to do with computers...or do they?"

"To answer your second question first: they do. And I think Forensics sent them because they sent me everything they had."

"OK. What's the deal with the keys?" Gilles asked.

"Have you ever heard of a company called Itskey?"

"Itskey? Non."

"We don't have it here," Suzanne explained. "When I saw the keys, I knew that they were not made here. Wrong material. I took a closer look and there's a code stamped on each one, like a serial number. Then I checked locksmiths in New York and found Itskey. It's an amazing app. You take a photo of your keys and they're saved to the cloud. If you forget your keys or lose them you go to a kiosk in a dépanneur, or whatever they call them in New York, sign in with your password, and it makes copies of your keys. You can choose the kind of look you want. As our victim did."

"Brilliant!" Gilles exclaimed. "Do you know who our victim is?"

"No, I just know how to find him. Itskey is not going to give out information to a voice on the phone. I did speak to someone there and security is pretty tight. Worse than the phone company. You'll have to find a New York cop who can get a court order or something."

"OK." Gilles sighed. "Give me the Itskey phone number and send the keys to me if you're done with them and the rest of the stuff when you've finished with it. Good catch, Suzanne. I owe you."

"Well, then come to Ville Saint-Laurent so I can collect."

CHAPTER 7

Friday –
Gilles Finds a Cop in New York

Gilles placed the receiver in its cradle. He had to find a cop in New York who could help him. There were probably fifty thousand cops in New York. How was Gilles supposed to find the one he needed? He rocked slowly in his chair, pushing his lips in and out, as he considered the problem. It didn't take too long for a conclusion to present itself. He would find a precinct in Queens and get a cop there to understand that one of their residents had been murdered in Montreal and the police here needed help to identify the body.

Gilles sat up and pulled his keyboard to him. He Googled a map of Queens and saw that it was a bigger area than he had anticipated. He knew the population of New York was in excess of eight million people and he expected that Queens was a borough with the population of Montreal. His research told him that there were fifteen precincts of the New York Police Department in Queens and he had no idea which one to call. He decided to call one at random and hope that with the phone number he suspected was the victim's home number, he could find the correct precinct.

He called the 100th Precinct for no reason other than he liked the number.͏ He spoke to a desk sergeant and spent fifteen minutes convincing him that he was indeed a cop in Montreal investigating a murder. Gilles pried out of him the information that, based on the first three digits of the victim's phone number, it was likely that it was somewhere in the 114th Precinct's area.

Gilles called the 114th Precinct and spoke to another desk sergeant. This fellow flat out refused to provide information to a voice on the telephone. In spite of the inconvenience, Gilles thought that this was at least professional. Gilles convinced the sergeant to have someone call him. Gilles spelled out his name and gave him the phone number that went through the switchboard rather than his direct line. He thought this would confirm that it was a cop-to-cop conversation.

It only took five minutes for Gilles to receive a call from the receptionist that there was a long-distance call being transferred to him. Gilles identified himself when he answered the phone.

"My name is Chris Palmer. I'm a detective in Queens. Apparently you need help with a case?"

"Thank you for calling back so quickly," said Gilles, and he told the New York detective what little he knew about the murder victim, providing both phone numbers that had been taken from the cellphone.

"The phone number appears to be in this area. I should be able to track it and get back to you. Is there anything else?" Palmer asked. Gilles detected a slight New York accent.

"Yeah actually, there is. You have a key service of some kind called Itskey, right?"

"Yeah, it's an app so if you lose or forget your keys you can make a copy at a convenience store, like 7-Eleven," Palmer explained.

"We found some keys in the victim's pocket and we think that they were made by Itskey. We have serial numbers. Can you check them out as well?"

"Sure thing. Send me scans of the keys and I'll see what I can do. But I think I'll be able to get something from the phone company faster," Palmer told him and gave Gilles his email address.

Gilles gave the New York cop his cellphone number. He then put in a call to Suzanne Rigaud in Computer Crimes and asked her to send the key information to Detective Chris Palmer in New York.

Bellechasse checked with the cops who were keeping an eye on Mickie's condo to see if there had been any action there. Nothing so far, they reported. Gilles had also instigated a watch on Mickie's credit cards.

Gilles's next step was to visit the people at the game company, DiplomRMY, to see what they could tell him about Mickie Bédard. On his way out of the office he asked the receptionist to get in touch with him immediately should any information come from the credit card companies. Sooner or later she would buy something somewhere and Gilles would have her arrested and returned to Montreal.

CHAPTER 8

Friday –
Gilles Investigates DiplomRMY

The DiplomRMY offices were located in an old building on the corner of Park Avenue and Van Horne in the Mile End district of Montreal. Many years previously, the building had housed small needle trade companies. After they moved out, the building was only half rented to a series of sales agencies. Over time they too closed or moved and the building was all but empty as the twenty-first century began. And then Montreal, especially the Mile End area, became a centre for gaming and artificial intelligence companies, and the building with its high ceilings and large open spaces became repurposed as a centre for those companies. The previous tenants, tired old guys who complained about everything from business to the weather, were replaced by young men and women who came to work by bike and who were generally a very lively group. The men wore their hair in the inexplicably popular man-bun style and both genders demonstrated a predilection for flannel shirts in a variety of colours.

According to a signboard in the hall that led to the elevators, DiplomRMY was on the third floor.

Gilles expected to see some kind of lettering to identify the tenants on the doors that opened from the third-floor corridor. This was not the way it was done in the tech world. There was a small white card tacked to each of the doors indicating the unit number and occupant. He walked into the DiplomRMY office and found premises that occupied about a third of the space of the floor. Half of the space was taken up with long tables where the employees worked on laptops. Gilles looked around and noticed that there was a large space at the back of the office, separated from the rest of the room by a glass wall. This area held a ping-pong table, where a game was taking place, some exercise equipment, and a couple of workstations that appeared to be devoted to gaming hardware. Adjacent to this room, also separated from the rest of the work area by a glass wall, was a kitchen with a couple of microwaves, a Nespresso coffee maker, a fridge, cabinetry and a table where a couple of employees sat eating.

It was impossible for Gilles to determine which of the employees working at the long tables he could approach to ask to see someone in charge. He prepared the small leather case that held his badge and ID card and walked over to the young woman seated nearest the door. Gilles stood next to her for a moment or two and when the young woman did not acknowledge his presence, he cleared his throat and said, "Est-ce que vous êtes aveugle, mademoiselle?"

The woman looked up at Gilles and answered, "Oh, I didn't see you." She didn't say anything else and Gilles kept silent as well. She was not that much older than his daughter. Finally, she said, "What is it? A delivery? Do you want me to sign something?"

Gilles smiled, shook his head and flashed his badge. "I want to see someone in charge."

"Not that kind of place," she replied. "Do you mean one of the owners?"

"That's exactly what I mean," Gilles said.

The young woman half rose from where she was seated and called, "François, a guy here to see you. A cop."

François was at a smaller work table, near a window. He got to his feet and said, "Thanks, Beth," and waved Gilles over. Gilles approached and identified himself.

"François, François Royer." The men shook hands.

François was in his mid-thirties, about ten years older than the majority of the employees. He was a couple of inches under six feet tall and dressed in jeans, a blue cotton shirt and a red crewneck sweater. His dark brown hair curled at the collar but he eschewed the man-bun. He wore horn-rimmed glasses.

Gilles noticed that there were a couple of unused meeting rooms that ran along the wall behind François. "Is there somewhere we can talk privately?" he asked.

"Privately?" he asked, as if the concept was foreign to him. "Yeah, we can use one of the meeting rooms." He led the way to the closer of the two rooms.

He sat down at the table and indicated for Gilles to do the same. "How can I help you?" he asked.

"I'm making enquiries about Michaela Bédard," Gilles stated.

"Michaela? Oh, Mickie. Yeah, what about her?" François replied. Without waiting for an answer, he added, "I better get my partner in here. He worked with her as much as I did." François went to the door of the meeting room and called, "Éloi, can you join us?"

While they waited for Éloi to join them, François offered Gilles a coffee. He called out to Beth, asking her to bring three coffees to the meeting room. Beth gave François a long look and was about to say something but thought better of it and strode off to get the coffee. She was tall and slim. She wore her long blond hair in a ponytail and it swished from side to side as she moved across the large room.

Éloi Masson, who was about the same size and build as François, his sweater a green V-neck and his hair blond, joined the meeting.

"This is..." François paused.

"I'm Gilles Bellechasse. I'm with the Major Crimes Division of the SPVM. I'm investigating a murder."

"Murder?" François and Éloi said almost in unison. "I thought you wanted to know something about Mickie," François said. "Is she alright?"

"She's not the victim," Gilles said. "We need to question her as part of our investigation. It's routine. She seems to have disappeared. Her business partner told me she was working on a deal with your company."

"That's right," Éloi replied. "She's taking us public. You know, preparing the initial public offering, the IPO, arranging financing. That kind of thing. What's that got to do with murder?"

Gilles gave the two men a brief synopsis of the events that led to his looking for Mickie. "Is there something about your business that would be, I don't know, controversial, exceptional, something that would be dangerous? Why don't you tell me what it is that you do and how Mickie fits in?"

François and Éloi looked at one another for a moment. François was about to say something but gasped for air instead. He pulled an inhaler from his jeans pocket and gave himself a puff.

"Asthma?" Gilles asked.

"No, the other one. COPD."

Beth arrived with the coffee. When Gilles thanked her, she muttered a barely audible, "Yeah," and left the room.

Finally, François spoke. "We're a game company. We invented an online game, DiplomRMY, a play on the words diplomacy, army, and our names. It's based on current events. Did you play Risk when you were a kid?" Gilles nodded and François continued, "Well, that's the basic idea. Our game is much more complicated and it's played online. People can play individually or as a team."

"What makes your game more complicated?" Gilles asked. "Other than it's online instead of on a board."

"Very basically, there are two things that make it more complicated," François explained. "The first element that adds complexity is that the actions of the players change the game. An individual player or a team can trigger an event, a war, a border skirmish, a natural disaster, you name it. The only rule is that it is impossible to trigger World War III. That would end the game."

Gilles smiled. If only real diplomacy were that simple. "How do you stop it?"

"If the software that powers the game senses that a world war will be a consequence of a certain set of actions the game stops and won't start again until one or another of the teams does something to pull back from the brink."

Éloi took over. "The second is that, like in life, elements of the game change based on current events. For example, America gets into a trade war with China and the game changes accordingly."

"Is that what all those people are doing?" Gilles asked and waved in the direction of the room full of people working at computers.

"Some of them," Éloi continued. "Most of the changes are powered by the AI we developed to run the game. It is able to keep abreast of the news from a large number of sources. We have a team of people checking for information the software may have missed. In some cases, we have people translating articles that appear in sources such as Arabic- or Hebrew-language newspapers. Asian languages too, that kind of thing. Other teams make certain that the aggregated information is properly integrated. We have to avoid the AI paradox."

The conversation was getting pretty far away from the investigation, but Gilles was enjoying learning about the inner workings of the game. "What's that?" he asked and took a sip of his coffee.

François and Éloi looked at one another. With a jut of his chin Éloi indicated that François should make the attempt. He was quiet for a moment or two as he thought of the best way to explain it to Gilles. "Let's say you're in a car, a self-driving car powered by AI. There is road work and a construction worker with a flag stops the cars. The AI will see the obstruction, so to speak, and stop the car. But when the construction worker waves his flag indicating that traffic can continue, the AI won't understand that. It will always default to the safest option and in this case the safest option is not to drive, too many obstructions. Without the intervention of a human, the car will sit there..."

"...forever," Gilles completed the sentence.

"And simply put, that's the AI paradox."

"And there's enough money in this to become a publicly traded company? Like Amazon or Facebook?" Gilles asked.

"Not like Amazon or Facebook. Not yet, anyway," Éloi smiled. "Some of the people are working on aggregating information about the players. We sell them stuff. Some of it is game-related but we also sell the information to third parties who want to sell our members products. But what we think makes us a valuable company is our security software and the AI we developed that powers it. Our security software is totally secure. Impenetrable."

"Really?"

Éloi took a deep breath, thought for a moment, and said, "We charge a fee to play our game and you can buy extras. That's how we make money. We discovered that there were players who were able to get around our paywall, and when we discovered this, we set out to design a security system for our site so that this would be impossible. And we developed security software that cannot be hacked. It requires a login and password like all other websites. We invented an additional step that is unique to us. We built a company around it and that's the company we're taking public."

"And you can adapt this to other uses?"

"Exactly. Banks, online retailers, whatever. And that's why our company is valuable," Éloi agreed.

"A separate company? How many of your staff are working on that product?" Gilles looked in the direction of the room of workers.

"None of them," François said. "Our third partner, Daniel Yablon, is in charge of it."

"And where is Mr. Yablon?" Gilles asked. "I should talk to him."

"He works in a different office," Éloi explained. "We want to keep a Chinese wall between the gamers and the Fibonaclé coders—that's Danny's name for the product. Also, we continually test the software. Looking for holes and back doors. If such exist, we want to find them before black-hat hackers do."

Gilles pulled out his notepad. "Give me a number where I can reach Mr. Yablon. I'll want to talk to him." Éloi and François exchanged a look and then complied.

Gilles got to his feet but made no move to leave the conference room. "One more thing before I leave," he said. "Why use Mickie and Stevens, Bédard? I thought that IPOs were usually handled by Bay Street or Wall Street banks."

"You're right, they are," François said. "We didn't want to get involved with big players who might not always put our interests ahead of their own. And I knew Mickie from HEC. I liked and trusted her and she wanted to break into corporate banking. She found managing old ladies' trust funds boring."

"Got it," Gilles stated. "Did she deal with both of you or just you?" Gilles nodded toward François.

"Neither of us, actually," Éloi replied. "Danny was the point person with the bankers. They like numbers and he's a numbers guy."

"I'll get in touch with Daniel Yablon," Gilles told the two men. He handed each of them a business card. "I'll call you if I need more information and I would very much appreciate it if you would call me if Mickie reaches out to either of you."

François and Éloi slipped the cards into their jeans pockets and nodded. Gilles shook hands with the two men and left the office. "I'll walk you out," François offered. The two men walked to the front door of the DiplomRMY office and as Gilles was leaving François grabbed his elbow and said, "Please be frank with me. Is Mickie in any trouble, real trouble? I'm not so naive that I believe the 'routine enquiry' bullshit."

Gilles gave François a hard cop stare and told him, "My enquiries are not bullshit. Call me if you hear from Mademoiselle Bédard."

CHAPTER 9

Friday – Chris Palmer Investigates

Every experienced detective in the NYPD has a contact at the phone company, including all the cellphone providers, who would provide basic user information without the formality of a court order. Chris Palmer was too new to the squad to have developed that kind of relationship but he knew the cop who acted as his mentor would have such a contact.

A short off-the-record phone call with the contact at Verizon yielded the name, Simon Connors, and an address attached to the phone number. Palmer decided to pay a visit to the address before he called Gilles with the information.

He drove to 36th Street, parked in a no-parking zone, made certain that his police parking ID was visible in the windshield, and walked the short distance to the door of Simon Connors's building. The neighbourhood was a combination of small homes and low-rise buildings whose tenants were mostly construction and electrical equipment suppliers. There were garages covered in colourful graffiti. One of the larger factories in the area had been converted into the Museum of the Moving Image, which told Chris that the neighbourhood was on the verge of becoming desirable. All it lacked was a clever name.

Connors's building was two storeys. The red bricks had been painted beige at some point. It was now covered with urban grime. He rang the bell and after a moment or two a female voice came over the intercom. "Yeah. Who is it?"

"My name is Chris Palmer. I'm a detective with the NYPD. I'd like to ask you a question or two about Simon Connors."

"Oh, Christ," came the voice, "top floor." There was a buzz and Chris opened the door and made his way up the stairs.

Detective Chris Palmer was a tall black man with movie-star good looks. He spent enough time at the gym to keep himself in good shape and therefore looked well turned out even when wearing inexpensive off-the-rack suits and sports coats. He showed his badge and ID, smiled and extended a hand. "I'm Detective Palmer." Julia took the offered hand, looked up at Chris and blushed. She didn't often see a man this gorgeous off the movie screen. "I'm Julia. I walk the dog."

Julia was athletically slim and five-and-a-half feet tall. She had pale porcelain-like skin with a splash of freckles across her nose. Her strawberry-blonde hair, worn with bangs, was shoulder length. She was dressed in jeans, an oversize sweatshirt and running shoes.

"Can we talk inside?" Chris asked.

Julia turned and walked into the apartment. Chris followed. "You're the second person to come by today asking about Simon," she said when they were in the living room.

Chris sat down in one of the chairs and Julia in another. The German shepherd padded into the room and sniffed at Chris. The dog was rewarded with a pat and scratch between the ears. "Get over here, Duke," Julia called and the dog went to her, sighed, and lay down on the carpet.

Chris asked, "Do you mind if I get some personal information about you?"

Julia understood that it wasn't really a question. She nodded.

"Your full name and do you live here?"

"Julia Sutton and no."

"Then what's your address and a phone number where I can reach you?"

Julia provided both.

"And you're the dog walker?" Chris asked.

"That's right. The dog-sitter actually."

"That'll do for now. Can you tell me who else was interested in Connors?" Chris asked.

"A woman from Canada," Julia explained. "Her name was Michaela something. Who would name their kid that?"

Chris shrugged. "Did she say how she could be reached? A cellphone number?"

"No. She didn't offer and I didn't ask."

"Do you know where Mr. Connors is at the moment?" Palmer asked.

"Yeah, he's in Montreal doing some work."

"When was the last time you heard from him?"

"Yesterday or the day before, I'm not really certain," Julia replied. "Why?"

"I'm afraid he may have been the victim of an attack," Chris explained.

Julia blanched and stuttered, "A-a-an attack? What do you mean?"

The dog reacted to the worry in Julia's voice and got to his feet. She pulled the dog to her.

"I'd rather not say until I get confirmation from the Montreal police. What can you tell me about the woman who was looking for him?"

"I told you. She was from Montreal, and she wanted to know when I expected him back."

"I should talk to her. Did she say where she was staying?"

"No," Julia said. "What about Simon? What happened to him? I want to know."

"Let me check it out," Chris told Julia. "I promise to get back to you as soon as I get more information."

Julia and Duke walked Chris to the door. "Promise me," she said.

"Promise," he assured her.

Back at the office, Chris called the Department of Motor Vehicles to get a copy of Simon Connors's photograph from his driver's license. Chris also checked the FBI database and discovered that Connors had a record. He quickly reviewed it and saved it to the same file where he had saved the photo from the driver's license. He wanted to have the information so that Gilles could corroborate the identity of his murder victim.

Once he was satisfied that he had a complete file he gave Gilles a call.

"The man you're looking for is Simon Connors," he told Gilles. "You're not the only one looking for him. I discovered that a woman by the name of..." Chris flipped through his notepad until he found what he was looking for. "...Michaela. She's looking for him as well. Does the name mean anything to you?"

"Absolument," Gilles said. "As far as the police in Montreal are concerned, she's a person of interest in the death of Connors." Gilles explained how they had found the body of Simon Connors. Chris provided the details of his meeting with Julia and what he knew about the man.

"I've been trying to locate Mademoiselle Bédard," Gilles explained. "I don't suppose she gave any contact information to the person she spoke to?"

"No, she didn't. I asked," Chris reported. "In fact, she gave the impression that she was looking for Connors. Obviously, she didn't want the dog-sitter to know that Connors was dead."

"Tabernac," Gilles exclaimed.

"Huh?"

Gilles was about to curse in English so his colleague would understand when one of the cops on desk duty came over to Gilles's desk and signalled for him to interrupt his phone conversation. "As-tu demandé une trace de carte de crédit?" Gilles asked his American colleague to hold for a second.

"We got a hit. A hotel in New York."

"Fantastique," Gilles exclaimed, wrote down the information the cop provided, and gave her a thumbs-up sign. Gilles returned his attention to his phone call with Chris Palmer and told him, "We got a hit on Bédard's credit card. Do you know a hotel called the Paper Factory?"

"Yeah, it's in Queens, not all that far from where Connors lives...lived, I suppose," Chris said.

Gilles was pleased that things were moving along so efficiently. "That's terrific. I'm going to get a warrant for her arrest here and whatever I need for extradition purposes. Can I ask you to arrest her? I'll get the paperwork to you ASAP."

"Yeah, well, I can't arrest her without the paperwork but there's nothing to stop me from going to the hotel and, if I can find her, bringing her in for questioning. If she puts up a fuss, though...well, let's cross that bridge when we get to it."

"I can't thank you enough," Gilles told his colleague. "If there's ever anything I can do for you, you have only to ask."

"I'll give you a call when I have her or some news," Chris Palmer said, and provided the fax number to which Gilles was to send the paperwork.

Gilles called Manon Tremblay in the crown prosecutor's office to get the proper documentation so that he could have Michaela Bédard arrested and extradited to Canada. He told her why he needed the warrants, that Mickie's arrest in New

York would likely take place very soon, and asked if she could expedite matters. Manon promised to do her best.

Gilles's next step was to get Captain Lacroix to authorize the expense of a trip to New York to pick up his prisoner, assuming that all went according to plan.

Gilles got up from his desk, straightened his tie, buttoned his jacket and strode confidently into his boss's office. Without sitting down Gilles explained that thanks to excellent co-operation with the New York Police Department and the efficiency of the credit card trace, they had a very good chance of apprehending the suspect in the Connors murder case.

"Good work," Lacroix said.

"There's one more thing. If the New York police are able to arrest her I'll have to fly down there and bring her back."

Captain Henri Lacroix rocked back in his chair and looked up at Gilles. Neither man spoke for a minute. Finally, Captain Lacroix swivelled around to a credenza behind his desk. He flipped through some folders in a desktop file sorter and extracted a form. He returned to his desk, signed the form, handed it to Gilles, and said, "Fill this out and book a flight. There and back in one day. You're not getting a weekend in New York on the department."

"Merci, Chef."

Chris Palmer told his boss what he was about to do and with his grudging permission headed to the Paper Factory to try to locate Michaela Bédard. He pulled up in front of the hotel a little after four and walked into the lobby. The hotel occupied a red brick building and took its name from the fact that it had previously been home to a paper factory. It was a combination hotel and communal workspace. Guests could book a room for as long as they needed a place to work while in New York. The lobby was furnished with a long sofa upholstered in orange flanked by comfortable-looking chairs and a coffee table. There were a bunch of ottomans around a small conical table fashioned from dark wood. People were lined up at the check-in counter and there were some grumbles when Chris jumped ahead and went to the hotel employee who had just finished serving a guest. Chris again flashed his NYPD gold shield. This didn't stop the grumbling but it did get the attention of the employee.

"I'm looking for Michaela Bédard," he said. "I have reason to believe she's a guest here."

The employee tapped the information into her computer and said, "Yes, she just checked in."

"Room number, what's her room number?"

The employee gave Chris the room number and showed him where the house phone was located.

"Not necessary," Chris told the employee. "Nor should you call ahead to announce me. Get it?"

The employee nodded and Chris headed to the elevators. Exiting on the sixth floor he located Michaela's room. He knocked on the door. There was no immediate response so he pressed his ear to the door and heard the sounds of someone moving around. He knocked again, louder this time.

"Who is it?"

"My name is Chris Palmer. I'm a detective with the NYPD and I'd like to talk to Michaela Bédard. Please open the door."

There was a pause and then Michaela unlocked and opened the door.

"Michaela Bédard?" Chris asked and showed her his badge.

"That's me. What's this about?"

"May I come in? Or would you rather have this conversation in the hall?" Chris asked.

Michaela sighed and stood aside to give Chris space to enter her room.

Mickie's room was comfortably furnished but there was not a lot of room to move around. There was a queen-size bed with a bench at its foot and a desk and chair and a second chair in the corner near the windows. Chris indicated that Michaela should sit there. Chris sat at the desk and swivelled to face her.

"What's this about?" Michaela asked, hoping the cop would find her question disarming.

Chris Palmer said, "A Montreal colleague wants to interview you regarding a murder."

Michaela didn't say anything and Chris continued. "He's in the process of getting an extradition order and there is very little question that he'll be successful."

"But at the moment there is no extradition order, correct?" Mickie asked.

"No, there isn't."

"I'm free to leave if I wish, right?" Mickie continued.

Chris smiled. "Well, yes and no. If you leave the room, I'll follow you and maybe arrest you. All in all, I don't advise it."

Michaela was silent as she considered her options, which were not that many and none seemed good. "What's the plan?" she asked.

"Either we stay here and wait until Detective...," Chris paused to check the name of the Montreal cop in his notepad, "Bellechasse calls me with word that he has an extradition order, or we can wait at the station. Once I have the extradition order we can hold you until someone from Montreal comes to get you or until you get an American judge to void the order—not a likely outcome."

"I'd like to call my lawyer," Mickie said. "And I'd like some privacy while I do it."

Chris got to his feet and looked around the sixth-floor room. There were two windows that only opened halfway. Escape was impossible. "I'll wait outside. Let me know when you're done."

Mickie called the lawyer who handled her business dealings and quickly explained her situation. Her lawyer had trouble processing the information that his client was in New York and was about to be extradited back to Canada. Once he grasped the situation, he told Mickie to call Jay Berg, a criminal lawyer, and gave her the cellphone number.

Mickie had never met Jay Berg but knew about him from newspaper reports on some of his more noteworthy cases. She felt the stress of her situation in her fingers and it took a couple of tries to tap the ten digits into her cellphone. After three rings Mickie began to worry that she would not be able to reach the lawyer and would have to leave a message. Berg picked up on the fourth ring.

"Thank you," were the first words that escaped from Mickie's mouth followed by a sigh.

"You're welcome," Jay Berg answered. "Who is this?"

Mickie explained who she was and how she got the phone number. She didn't wait for the lawyer to ask how he could help. She launched into an explanation of the trouble she was facing.

"Murder?" Jay asked. "Are you certain that the New York cop said murder?"

"Absolutely," Mickie responded.

"Okay, I'm not going to ask you about that now, not on the phone," Berg explained. "Here are your options: the Montreal police will send someone to bring you back. You can waive your rights to a judicial hearing on the extradition order and return to Montreal with the cop or you can insist on a hearing, which you'll lose and then return to Montreal with the cop. It will take a couple of days for that process to run its course and you'll be in custody for all of them."

"Fuck!" Mickie exclaimed. "Sounds like my options aren't that great."

"There's more. If a judge affirms the order it will be on your record and you may have problems entering the United States in the future."

"Well, I don't have much choice but to agree to return to Montreal, right?" Mickie asked.

"Based on what you've told me, I would say so," Berg agreed.

"Can I go to the airport and fly back without waiting for an extradition order?"

"Maybe. I don't know how far things have progressed. I'd have to do some checking. You say a cop is with you? Let me speak to him to start."

Gilles was too nervous to do paperwork while he waited to hear from Manon Tremblay, the crown prosecutor. He decided to go down to the shopping centre and walk off his nervousness. He asked around the office to see if any-one wanted coffee, to make some use of the time he would be away from his desk. The reason for locating the Major Crimes Division above the Place Versailles shopping centre, so far from the courts and police headquarters, was lost in the mists of time. The cops who worked there liked the fact that parking was not a problem and they were not dependent on the sludge that passed for coffee in the squad room.

Gilles took the elevator and was on his second tour around the shopping centre when he got the call from the crown prosecutor. He breathed a sigh of relief when she told him that everything was in order and she would send him the extradition order. Gilles purchased the coffee and returned to his office. By the time he got the coffees distributed, the email with the PDF of the extradition order had arrived. He printed a copy and called Chris Palmer in New York to tell him that he had the extradition order and would email him a copy.

"Where are you?" Gilles asked when Chris answered his cellphone. "Have you spoken to Michaela Bédard?"

"Yeah, I'm just outside her hotel room. She's on the phone, talking to her lawyer."

"It won't do her much good," Gilles exclaimed. "I have the extradition order. The plan is for me to come to New York tomorrow morning to pick her up."

Mickie heard Chris Palmer's phone ring while she was talking to Jay Berg. When he asked to speak to him, she opened the door and beckoned him to come in. Chris barely had time to straighten up from leaning on it as Mickie pulled it open. Chris was talking to someone on his cellphone and said, "Give me a second," lowered the hand holding the phone and turned to Mickie. She backed into the hotel room and said, "My lawyer wants to talk to you."

He followed Mickie into the hotel room and took the proffered phone. "Yes," he said.

"My name is Jay Berg. I'm a lawyer and I represent Michaela Bédard. She's not going to fight the extradition order but I've instructed her not to answer any questions whatsoever. Please respect her right to keep silent."

"Got you," Chris agreed.

"Do you know the status of the extradition order?"

"I have Detective Gilles Bellechasse on my phone at the moment. He is about to send it to me. So, yeah, it's been issued," Chris explained.

"Damn," Jay exclaimed. "Okay, let me speak to my client."

Chris handed the phone back to Mickie. He turned his back to her and returned to his call with Gilles. "Do you know a lawyer named Jay, something, Berg, I think he said?" he asked in a low voice, hoping that Mickie could not hear the conversation.

"Yeah, everyone in Montreal knows him. She didn't waste any time," Gilles said. "I'll fly down tomorrow morning to collect her. What are your next steps?"

"I'll bring her into the station and book her, and she'll probably be sent to Rikers," Chris explained.

Gilles watched a lot of American television and the word "Rikers" made him think that it would be difficult to get Mickie out of there once she was in the system.

"Is there any way we can avoid that?" Gilles asked. "I'll be there by ten thirty or so. Can you keep her in a holding cell at the precinct?"

"I'll do my best and let you know," Chris replied. He gave Gilles the location of the precinct and told him it would probably take about thirty minutes to get there from the airport on a Saturday.

Chris put his cellphone back into his pocket and turned to Michaela. "I have to take you in now," he said. "Get your stuff together."

Mickie was still on the phone with her lawyer and held up her index finger. "The cop wants to take me somewhere," she explained.

"I'll talk to him in a minute," Berg said. "Do you want me to fly down and come back with you and the police?"

"Yeah, if you can," Mickie answered.

"Okay, I'll find out from Bellechasse when he plans to get there but my plan is to get there ahead of him. I'll probably fly down this evening. Let me speak to the cop again."

Mickie handed the phone to Chris. He and Jay had a brief conversation about what he planned to do with Mickie.

Once the phone calls were over it was time to leave. Chris picked up Mickie's suitcase and asked, "Do you have anything else?"

"I haven't been here long enough to unpack." She grabbed her purse and briefcase and allowed herself to be escorted from the room. Chris held her by the right bicep. It was uncomfortable but better than handcuffs.

CHAPTER 10

Friday – Julia Walks the Dog

Julia Sutton, Simon's dog-sitter, decided to take Duke out as soon as Detective Chris Palmer left. She wanted to be certain that he was not hanging around the neighbourhood spying on her. She saw Chris drive off and she immediately returned to the condo with a very disappointed Duke.

Julia recovered quickly from the shock of learning that Connors had been attacked. Experience had taught her to expect the worst and she assumed that "attacked" was a cop euphemism for murdered. Either way Simon was out of action and that meant Julia had things to do. Her fleeting thought was: our line of work is not without its risks.

Julia made herself comfortable in the easy chair in Simon's living room. Duke obediently lay on the floor at her side. Julia wanted to consider her next moves. Michaela Bédard had the information that Simon, and now she, sought. The question was: did she have the information with her and would she (Julia) be able to get her hands on it? Julia was certain that if she could find Mickie she could, one way or another, get what she needed. As she considered her options, she realized that she was in a race with the police, in the person of Detective Chris Palmer, to find Mickie Bédard, and that the cops had much better resources than she did. If Palmer found Bédard before she did—which was more than likely—then she would probably be sent back to Montreal.

Clearly, Detective Palmer didn't spontaneously decide to look for a woman from Montreal. He must have been asked by the Montreal police to find her. Therefore, Julia concluded, it would be best to get to Montreal ahead of her prey and finish the job Connors had started.

She used Simon Connors's desktop computer to do some quick research, printed the airline ticket she needed, and made a phone call to the client.

She explained that Simon had very likely been murdered in Montreal and discussed next steps. "Way ahead of you," she told the client as she got to the end of the call. "I'll be on my way on Sunday night and take care of things as soon after that as possible. I need the name of Simon's contact and the hardware supplier in Montreal." Julia wrote the information her client gave her on one of the pages she had just printed.

She found a tool box in Connors's hall closet—she knew that there had to be a tool box in the condo, all men, even the most inept, had one—and retrieved a Phillips head screwdriver. She removed the side panel of the computer, extracted both the hard disk and the motherboard and then screwed the side panel back into its original position. She placed the computer parts in her canvas Barnes & Noble book bag.

Connors didn't have that many paper files. Julia placed the few she found in her book bag. A quick search of the condo ensured there was no additional information that would be useful in an investigation. Finally, just before she left, she tore the second page of the printout she had made an hour or so earlier into eighths. She stuffed the bits of torn paper into her pocket with the intention of dumping them in a garbage receptacle on her way home. She didn't notice that one of the torn bits escaped her grip and floated to the floor near the front door.

She picked up her book bag, put the leash back on Duke and left the condo, locking the door behind her.

CHAPTER 11

Friday –
Gilles and Annie Check Facebook

Gilles left the office and had to make a detour instead of going straight to Annie's house for dinner. He lived in a condo in the east end of Montreal in the shadow of the Jacques Cartier Bridge. He didn't love the area but he chose it because his ex-wife and daughter lived in Longueuil on the South Shore, and being close to the bridge made it easier to get to his daughter when she preferred to be picked up rather than take the Metro. Annie lived about a dozen kilometres to the west on Park Row West, next door to her sister and her kids. In spite of the distance between their dwellings, neither Gilles nor Annie had any plans to move or to move in together. Each liked the comfort of living in their own place. It made their time together more special.

Gilles wanted to stop by his condo to change into jeans and to pick up a change of underwear, plus his passport and Nexus card for his trip to New York the following morning.

He interrupted the thirty-minute drive to Annie's house to pick up some wine and pastries. Annie's daughter Pamela answered the door when Gilles arrived. Pamela's father was Ugandan and she combined features of both her parents. Like her father she was tall, slim and graceful. She had her mother's charismatic, engaging smile. She wore her black curly hair naturally, letting it frame her face. Pamela also inherited brains and a strong work ethic from her parents. She was enrolled in pre-med at McGill University and placed in the top of her class.

"Hi, Gilles. Mom's in the dining room playing with Facebook."

Pamela had a healthy disdain for the digital world. Unlike most of her contemporaries she spent very little time on Facebook, Instagram and other social media. She saw her friends in person and left social media to her mother's generation.

Gilles deposited the wine and pastries in the kitchen and went through to the dining room. Annie greeted Gilles with a kiss. She leaned against the dining room table and asked, "Have you learned anything about my patient? I kept her overnight because I was concerned about her. Do you know what happened to her? Is she alright?"

"As far as I know she's fine. She's in New York." Gilles indicated the small duffle bag he had. "I'm going to pick her up tomorrow."

"New York? What's she doing there?"

"My question exactly. I'll find out when I get a chance to question her," Gilles said. He noticed that Annie had her Facebook page open on her computer. To change the subject he asked, "What's new on Facebook?"

"Ursula posted photos of a celebration that took place Thursday evening." Ursula was Annie's closest friend in the Emergency Department. She tilted the computer so Gilles could see the photo. There was a group of doctors and nurses along with the unit agent. They were smiling and displaying doughnuts for the camera.

"What was the event?" Gilles asked.

"One of the nurses became engaged and someone brought in way too many doughnuts in order to celebrate. I think the entire ER staff got a sugar high," Annie explained.

Something in the photo caught Gilles's attention and he pulled up a chair to take a closer look. "Wait a second. There's something there." Gilles pointed to the window of one of the rooms in the unit. "Is that the room where the murder took place?"

Annie bent forward to get a closer look. "Yeah, it must be."

"The blinds are up in this photo," Gilles pointed out. "Are there more?"

"God, yes. It's Facebook." Annie slowly clicked through the photographs that Ursula had posted. Gilles examined each of them. When Annie got to the fifth or sixth photograph Gilles covered her hand with his and said, "Right there. I can see into the room and the patient is in bed, probably sleeping. And it's clearly a woman. I can see her long hair."

Annie looked at the photograph. "You're right, but what does it prove? We knew that the patient in the room was a woman."

"Do you think there are other pictures that have not been put on Facebook? Maybe we'll be able to see when and how the patients were switched."

"There are no other pictures, but I'll post a message on my page asking anyone who has pictures taken on Thursday night to send them to me. I can almost guarantee we'll be inundated within a couple of hours," Annie told Gilles.

She pulled the computer to her and posted a message asking for all the pictures taken in the Green Unit on Thursday night. "Let's eat," Annie exclaimed and closed the lid of her laptop. She and Gilles went into the kitchen to put the finishing touches on the dinner Annie had prepared.

Pamela joined her mother and Gilles for dinner and a good deal of the conversation was good-natured teasing about Gilles's trip to New York the next day. Both Pamela and Annie loved the city and wanted to make a trip there in the

65

near future. They construed the fact that Gilles had to make his trip solo to mean that he owed them a weekend in New York. Gilles promised that as soon as both he and Annie had four consecutive days off, they would visit the city.

"You'll actually take time off from studying?" Gilles asked Pamela.

"For a trip to New York? You bet!"

After dinner, Gilles and Pamela cleared the table and did the dishes, following which Pamela returned to her studies and Gilles found Annie in the living room watching *The Crown* on Netflix. Gilles sat down on the sofa next to Annie and she snuggled in close to him, her legs curled under her, his arm around her shoulders. "Thanks for dinner," Gilles said and kissed her. Annie returned the kiss and pressed in closer. While Annie watched *The Crown*, Gilles thought about the murder he was investigating and his upcoming trip to New York.

When the episode ended and in the seconds before the next one began Gilles said, "I'd like you to check your email. I want to see if there are any more photographs of the murder scene."

Annie sighed and exited from Netflix. "You never take a break, do you?" She got up and Gilles followed her to her computer. Annie opened her email and saw that she had fifteen messages, all with attachments. "Told you," she said. "All these came in since I posted the request. I'll probably spend the weekend opening these things while you're running around New York."

Gilles replied, "I have to admit I didn't expect this much."

"Let's see what we have," Annie said. She opened the first email and scrolled through the six photos that were attached to it. None of them showed the room where the murder occurred.

Annie was about to open the second email when Gilles stopped her and said, "Can you save the photos in one or two folders? One for the photographs that are of no forensic value and the other for photos that might be useful?"

Annie smiled and opened a couple of folders and labeled one Good Forensics and the other Bad Forensics. She went back to her email and saved the first group of photos in the Bad Forensics folder.

The photos in the first three emails were of no investigative use to Gilles, but in the fourth email he could see clearly into the room where Mickie was sleeping and saw in successive photos a man walk into the room. Other photos showed aspects of the struggle, until Mickie lowered the slats. This series of photos was placed in the Good Forensics folder.

Annie and Gilles spent the next ninety minutes going through the photos, saving them in one or the other of the folders.

"We must have over a hundred photos in all," Gilles commented.

"Are any of them useful?"

"Yes, they are. It's clear that someone came into the room while the patient was sleeping. I can't see everything that happened but I can see that she had a grip on him. I can surmise the rest."

"Doesn't that at least suggest the possibility that the patient was acting in self-defence?"

"Too early to say. And it's my job to collect evidence, not to make final decisions about the investigation at this point."

"Hm. Do you still have to go to New York and arrest your suspect?"

"Yes, of course. But I'm going to send the photographs to Manon Tremblay, the prosecutor. Please send them to me. And two more things: be certain to retain the original emails and the folders we made. It may be the only way we can prove that we didn't do anything to alter the pictures."

Annie sent Gilles the email he requested along with the Good Forensics folder as an attachment. She turned her laptop so Gilles could use it. He signed into his Google account and forwarded the email to Manon Tremblay with an explanatory note.

"Are we done?" Annie asked. "Can I turn this thing off and get back to my show?"

"Absolument, chérie."

Annie and Gilles returned to the sofa to watch another couple of episodes of *The Crown*. Annie was engrossed in the series but it bored Gilles to distraction. Annie turned off the TV and stretched her arms above her head. Gilles understood the sign. He put his arms around her; she lowered her arms and returned the hug. They kissed. Annie and Gilles got up from the sofa and went to Annie's bedroom. They called good night to Pamela and closed the door. Pamela turned up her music.

CHAPTER 12

Saturday – Gilles in New York

The following morning Gilles was careful not to wake Annie up when he got out of bed, dressed and drove to the airport for his flight to New York.

On his arrival he took a taxi to the 114th Precinct. He presented himself to the desk sergeant and asked for Detective Chris Palmer. The desk sergeant took Gilles's name and called up to the squad room, indicating a bench bolted to the wall opposite, where Gilles could wait. He looked at the sorry collection of humanity already seated, sad-looking people probably searching for friends and relatives who had been arrested overnight, and chose to stand.

After a couple of minutes Palmer came down the stairs and walked directly to Gilles and introduced himself. "Let's go upstairs." They entered a large open squad room that could just as easily have been in Montreal as in Queens.

Palmer led the way to his desk. "Is my prisoner ready to go?" Gilles asked.

"Yeah, I kept her in a holding cell overnight. She's with her lawyer at the moment. He's been here for about an hour."

"Berg's here?" Gilles asked incredulously. "How on earth did he get here so fast? He wasn't on my flight."

"He showed up bright and early and demanded to see her. Kind of surprised me, but she has a right to counsel," Detective Palmer explained. "I'll go and get them."

Gilles got to his feet when he heard them approaching Chris's desk.

Jay Berg smiled and said, "Detective Bellechasse, right?" and extended his hand.

"Yes, exactly." Gilles shook the lawyer's offered hand. They had met a couple of years earlier during the trial of a doctor Gilles had arrested for murder. Berg had arranged for a reduced sentence for his client in exchange for a guilty plea. Gilles would have preferred a trial and a longer sentence.

Berg introduced his client to Gilles. "My client will not fight extradition. I'll be on the same flight. And to be perfectly clear: I have instructed my client not to answer any questions. To be on the safe side I'll be between you and my client at all times until we get back to Montreal."

"And then?" Gilles asked.

"And then we'll see."

"I'll be booking your client on suspicion of murder," Gilles told Berg.

"As I said," Berg responded, "we'll see."

While Gilles and the lawyer debated their next steps, Chris Palmer went to a bank of small lockers that covered one wall of the squad room, unlocked one, and brought Mickie her purse and briefcase. Mickie opened the purse and rifled through its contents. She pulled out her inhaler, gave herself a couple of puffs, and inhaled deeply.

Jay Berg watched her and then asked Detective Palmer, "Was my client denied the use of her inhaler while she was in your custody?"

"She didn't ask for it," Palmer replied.

"Is that true?" Berg asked his client.

"Yeah," Mickie said, "sort of. I used it before I was locked up, but there was no one to ask if I needed it."

Berg turned to Gilles. "My client is not to be denied the use of her life-saving inhaler at any point from this moment forward. Get it?"

"I'm not going to take her purse away from her, if that's what you mean," Gilles told the lawyer.

"We're ready to go," Berg stated. He turned to Mickie and asked, "Is there anything else of yours here?" He waved his arm to take in the squad room.

"My suitcase," Mickie told him.

"Detective?" Berg said to Palmer, who went in search of Mickie's possession.

While they waited for Palmer to return, Berg took out his cellphone, scrolled to the Uber app and ordered a car to pick them up.

The three Montrealers were silent on the drive to the airport. Gilles flashed his badge in order to jump the line at the Air Canada counter. He asked for three seats together. The agent gave them the bulkhead seats.

When the plane landed at the Trudeau airport, Gilles once again used his badge to jump the line in the immigration hall. Gilles wasn't certain of the protocol of offering a suspect's lawyer a lift, but thought it was probably easier to do so then get in a pointless argument with Berg over transportation to the Major Crimes Division offices.

Once they were on Gilles's home turf, he took complete charge. He informed Mickie of her rights and had one of the officers take over. "You know the score," Gilles said to Berg. "Your client will be booked and arraigned on Monday."

"Not so fast," Berg said. "I don't want my client to spend a weekend in jail for nothing. She's innocent."

Gilles sat down at his desk and indicated that Berg should take the visitor's chair. Gilles was not the most experienced cop on the squad but he knew that every defense attorney made the claim that their client was innocent. Gilles also knew that there was exculpatory evidence in this case. He didn't have the authority to share it with Jay Berg, but the crown prosecutor did. She could strike a deal.

Gilles had to decide whether or not to tip Berg to the fact that he should call Manon Tremblay. Gilles thought about the morality of the situation. After a couple of minutes, he looked Berg straight in the eye. "I can't make that decision. Cops book suspects. You know that. If you want to take your client home, I suggest that you call Manon Tremblay and see if you can work something out."

Gilles spoke slowly and calmly so that Berg would know that he was not negotiating, but strongly suggesting a course of action. He slid his desk phone towards the lawyer. Berg ignored Gilles's offer of the use of his phone and made the call using his cellphone.

He called Manon Tremblay on her cellphone, assuming that she would not be in the office on a Saturday. All the lawyers of the criminal bar, defense lawyers and prosecutors alike, knew how to get in touch with one another.

"It's Saturday," Manon said when she answered Jay's call. "To what do I owe the pleasure, mon confrère?"

Berg explained the situation to the prosecutor and promised to have his client available for arraignment on Monday if she was not obliged to spend the weekend in jail.

Manon asked to speak to Gilles. Jay handed him the phone.

"Peut-il m'entendre?" she asked when Gilles came on the line. When he responded in the negative, she continued, "Does he know about the photographs?"

"No," Gilles replied without going into details. He knew that if he elaborated Berg would be likely to know that he and Tremblay had important information they hadn't shared with him.

"OK, not a word," Tremblay instructed. "I'll let him take his client. We'll worry about sharing later. I want to review the photographs very carefully first."

Gilles grunted his agreement and handed the phone back to Jay Berg.

Berg and Tremblay discussed procedure for a couple of minutes, the upshot being that Berg promised to get in touch with the prosecutor on Monday morning to make arrangements for an interrogation. He hung up the phone.

"At some point I'm going to have to interview your client. You can't put it off forever. Her information is critical to our investigation," Gilles told the lawyer, hoping he'd allow Mickie to be questioned. There was only the faintest possibility of success but Gilles might not have access to both Mickie and her lawyer for quite some time.

"Yeah, we'll see about that," Berg replied. "I can tell you that if—and it's a big if—if my client had anything to do with the death at the hospital, it was self-defence. And that's the only comment I have. I'll take my client now." Gilles called the cop who had taken charge of Mickie and had her brought back. Jay Berg led the way out of the Major Crimes Division squad room, pulling his client's suitcase behind him.

Once in the Uber and on their way back to Mickie's condo, she said, "Thank you. I was afraid that I would have to spend the weekend in jail. My experience in New York was bad enough."

Jay Berg was staring out of the window of the car, lost in thought. Mickie wasn't certain that he had heard her. He turned. "That was too easy. They know something. We'll find out what it is on Monday."

CHAPTER 13

Saturday – Gilles Back in Montreal

Gilles wrote up his notes regarding his trip to New York and his attempts to question Mickie. He placed a copy of his report on his boss's desk and before he left for the weekend, he called the crown prosecutor, Manon Tremblay. He wanted to know why she released his suspect so quickly. Manon was in no mood for a long conversation. All Gilles got was the most perfunctory of answers: "The photos. They appear to be exculpatory. Have a nice weekend."

Gilles drove straight over to Annie's to get his nice weekend off to a good start. Their plan was to have dinner at one of the restaurants that were opening almost weekly on Notre-Dame West. Their choice for this Saturday was Venice.

Over drinks Gilles told Annie about his very short trip to New York. Annie was more interested in Mickie than the city. As far as she was concerned Mickie was a patient and she had not finished caring for her. Annie pumped Gilles for information about her health. "She had a serious, possibly life-threatening, asthma attack. And an attack of this nature can be brought on by stress. Clearly, I'd really like some details about her health," Annie told her boyfriend.

"She seemed fine. She only used her inhaler once or twice while she was in my custody," Gilles said.

"Well, I intend to call her on Monday, when I'm back at work, and make certain that she's OK."

There was a pause in the conversation while their meals were served. The silence continued as Gilles and Annie took a few mouthfuls. Gilles broke the silence when he said, "Yeah, I get it. But please, be careful not to say anything to her about the investigation."

"What's that supposed to mean?" Annie asked. She rested her knife and fork on her bowl, interrupting her enjoyment of her tuna poke.

Gilles stifled a sigh. He didn't want anything to ruin the evening, but he had to be certain that Annie didn't say anything that might harm his investigation. In his opinion, Mickie was still a suspect in a murder. "I mean, sure, her health is important. But telling her about the photographs you saw is off limits."

"Really? How do you figure?" Annie's questions were really statements. "They're my photos, actually my friends' photos, and I'll talk about them if I want." Having made herself clear, Annie picked up her utensils and returned to eating. Gilles was about to say something but Annie pointed her fork at him. "Tell me again what the crown prosecutor told you?"

"Well, that the photos are probably exculpatory."

"Exactly. Sooner or later she has to know about them. So there's no harm in mentioning them if I want to."

"Chérie," Gilles implored. He looked at his bowl of salmon poke for a moment. "I'm not trying to censor you. But I want to conduct a clean investigation. It's the crown's job to tell Bédard's lawyer about the photos, not mine and not yours. That's all I'm saying."

Annie smiled at Gilles. "I'm sure you'll be fair to my patient. Don't you have other elements to explore?" Gilles realized that Annie knew she couldn't say anything about the investigation and didn't need to be told. He wished he had had this realization before he opened his big mouth.

"Well, yeah, now that you mention it. I plan to find out a lot more about the victim. The American, Simon Connors. He's..." Gilles changed the subject to the possibility of a long weekend in New York with Annie.

After dinner they drove to Gilles's condo where they had a couple of brandies as a nightcap and went to bed. They woke late on Sunday morning and made love again. Gilles prepared brunch and they spent a lazy day together.

They both had work the next day so there was no hope of extending their weekend. Gilles was home in time to watch his favourite TV show, *Tout le monde en parle.*

CHAPTER 14

Monday –
Gilles and Manon Hatch a Plan

Gilles got to the office early Monday morning and reviewed his notes. His intention to spend time trying to get information on Simon Connors did not, on reflection, seem to be the best way to proceed. Gilles planned to call Chris Palmer in New York to see if he had uncovered any additional information on the murder victim. He had to consider the fact that Jay Berg was right, that Michaela Bédard had killed Simon Connors in self-defence. The photographs that Annie had collected from her friends showed Michaela sleeping and a man coming into her room. Even if the fellow had some reason for being there, Michaela could not be faulted for defending herself. Gilles wondered where she developed the skills to dispatch her assailant, and made a note to get the answer to that question.

Gilles pulled his desk phone to him and called the crown prosecutor. After a perfunctory exchange of pleasantries Gilles got to the point. "I need to question Bédard but her lawyer won't let her speak to me. She's as silent as a giraffe. Can we offer her anything? Will you be prosecuting?"

"Écoute-moi, Gilles," Manon told him. "I've been over the photos you had your girlfriend send and it appears that Bédard was the intended victim. I'm going to tell Berg that if she tells her story and convinces us that she was only defending herself then I'll drop the charges."

"And if we don't believe her story?" Gilles asked.

"Then we won't use anything she tells us. It's win-win for her."

"Cela semble plus que juste," Gilles agreed. "What's the best way to proceed?"

"Berg promised to call this morning, and when he does, we'll set up an interview for the four of us. We'll hold it at my office, not yours," Manon explained. "I'll call you when we have time."

Not knowing where Detective Chris Palmer would be first thing on Monday morning, Gilles called him on his cellphone. The two men had a pleasant conversation but Palmer did not have any information that he had not previously shared with Gilles. They agreed to keep in touch and share anything that their investigations turned up. Gilles explained that there was a very good possibility that Michaela Bédard had been attacked and they would very likely be able to get her story on the record.

"Great," Palmer said. "Let me know what you come up with."

Gilles agreed to keep his New York colleague in the investigative loop and rang off.

He next called Daniel Yablon at DiplomRMY and arranged to meet him later that morning at his office on St. Ambroise in the Saint-Henri section of the city.

On his way out, Gilles stopped at his boss's office and reported on his discussions with Tremblay and his plans for the day. Captain Lacroix was pleased that Manon Tremblay had agreed to offer Bédard a deal in order to close the case of Simon Connors's murder. Lacroix liked quick solutions to murders. He was less pleased that Gilles was continuing his investigation. "If Bédard killed Connors, why question Yablon, or anyone else for that matter?" he asked.

"Because I have the strongest feeling that there is more to this case than meets the eye," Gilles explained. "I still have no idea why Connors tried to attack Bédard, if that's indeed what happened. All of this is somehow tied to the business deal she was working on. I want to make certain that there are no loose threads."

"D'accord, Gilles," Lacroix said. "But you don't have a lot of time to waste on this, so wrap it up quickly.

"Oui, boss."

Yablon's office was located in the old Dominion Textile building, a large red brick structure built in 1882. The building was renovated and transformed into its present condition starting in 1999 when new owners renovated and converted it into office space and gave it the name Chateau St. Ambroise. The building was four city blocks long and one deep, and had four entrances, each with a different address. Gilles located the correct entrance and parked in a restricted zone. He ensured that his police ID card was displayed on the dashboard and went in search of the DiplomRMY offices. Gilles made a couple of wrong turns in the labyrinth of corridors in the building. It gave him a chance to appreciate the quality of the renovations. The wooden floors were polished to a mirror-like finish and creaked with age, having been trod on for almost 150 years.

The door to the offices that Gilles sought was marked with small white letters on the frosted glass window. The door was locked and Gilles pressed the bell on the door frame.

"Good morning," a male voice announced. "How can I help you?"

Gilles gave his name and explained that he was from the Montreal Police, looking for Daniel Yablon.

The voice asked to see some identification, which Gilles pointed at the camera he noticed on the wall above the door. The door clicked open and Gilles entered. He found himself in a small vestibule area furnished with a couple of chairs and a small table with copies of the foreign edition of the *Financial Times* neatly placed on it. Beyond the vestibule was a large work room with long tables with men and women sitting at workstations. Some were working on laptops while others were holding quiet discussions in groups of two or three people. Gilles was struck by the difference between how work was conducted in this office and in the games division. The workers in this office gave the impression of concentrated efficiency rather than the creative chaos of the other office. Gilles was about to clear his throat to announce himself when a young man approached him.

"You're looking for Danny," he said. "He's in his office. Come with me." He led Gilles to the back of the work room and stood at the door to Yablon's office. Daniel Yablon got up from his desk and greeted Gilles. Yablon was the same height as Gilles, a shade over six feet. He had straight brown hair which he wore unfashionably long. He was dressed in clean blue jeans and a Croatian soccer shirt. Gilles noticed that, unlike the people in the gaming office, Daniel was tattoo-free. In this office the art was on the walls, not the people. Daniel invited Gilles to sit at a small table next to a large window that overlooked the Lachine Canal. There was a window almost as large in the front wall of the office that looked into the work room. "Can I offer you a coffee?" Daniel asked.

"Thank you, yes," Gilles replied.

Daniel smiled. "Two of your finest," he said to the young man who had shown Gilles to the office.

"You got it. Anything else? There are still some muffins left."

"Coffee's fine," Daniel answered. He turned to Gilles. "How can I help you?"

"Your partners told me that you handled the banking for your upcoming IPO. I have some questions about Michaela Bédard. To start: how well did you know her?"

"I didn't know her at all until François insisted that she handle the banking for our stock offering. I got to know her by working with her. I can't say that I know her well. Why do you ask?"

Gilles ignored the question and asked one of his own, "You weren't in favour of using Bédard's firm to handle your banking?"

"I had never heard of her or her firm until François brought her into the deal. I had nothing against her, or for her, for that matter, but I did want to examine other possibilities before deciding who would handle the IPO."

The young man who had been sent for coffee arrived and placed cups in front of Daniel and Gilles.

"Did you meet with other bankers?" Gilles inquired.

"François was pretty adamant that we use Stevens, Bédard, so no, I didn't look for other bankers. But word must have got out because I received a few calls and a visit from other firms. At least one of them was an American bank."

"Do you remember which one?"

Daniel went to his desk and retrieved some business cards held together with an elastic band. He returned to the table and shuffled through the cards. "Here it is." Daniel handed a business card to Gilles. It was from the Richman, Taylor Investment Bank with a Wall Street address. There was no other information on the front of the business card. Gilles flipped it over and saw the name Simon Connors printed in a neat handwriting along with a phone number.

"Did you meet with Connors? His name is on the back of the card."

"I did," Yablon answered. "It wasn't a long meeting, I can tell you that. I told him that we had selected our bankers, thanked him for his interest and that was that."

"Nothing else?"

"Not really. We talked a bit about New York and he asked if he could get in touch with me a few weeks hence to see if things were still going well with Stevens, Bédard. I told him he was free to call me but I didn't see any point to it. We were committed to Stevens, Bédard."

"He mentioned Stevens, Bédard by name?" Gilles asked.

"Yeah."

"You didn't think it odd that a guy you didn't know knew who your banker was?"

"Now I do," Daniel said. "But at the time, no. I just assumed that this guy knew who his competitor was. We all know that kind of thing in business. Is it important?"

"He was murdered and Michaela Bédard was involved in some way," Gilles explained. "Didn't your partners tell you what I was investigating?"

"They told me it was a murder investigation and that Michaela was involved. But not much more than that."

"Do you know if she knew about Simon Connors?"

"I told her that I had been approached by other banks," Daniel said, "but I don't think I gave her the names of the people I talked to."

Gilles was silent for a moment while he considered what he had learned. Simon Connors knew about Stevens, Bédard, which might explain his presence in Michaela's hospital room. It opened up the possibility that he intended to harm her in order to steal her client.

"I'm curious," Gilles said. "Why did you form a separate company with the security software? Why not just put the entire company on the market?"

"Good question. The short answer is that the companies separately are worth more than the one company with both products. The security software has wide market possibilities and I'm betting that we can make a ton of money with it. If all goes well, we'll list the gaming company in a year or so."

Gilles didn't know much about business or computers, but he did know that there were all kinds of security software on the market. "What makes your product better than the rest?" he asked.

"Let me show you, or at least show you as much as I can without getting into our intellectual property."

There were two laptops on Daniel's desk. He had been working on one of them when Gilles came into his office. Daniel got one of the laptops from his desk placed it on the table and tilted it so Gilles could see the screen. Daniel tapped the computer to live and said, "I use this computer for demos. It's programmed not to retain anything."

Gilles nodded to indicate he was ready for the demonstration.

Daniel pushed the laptop a little closer to Gilles and said, "You're on the Fibonaclé home page. Scroll down to the "create an account" field and enter your name and then a numeric password when prompted. It can be as long as you like but I recommend keeping it to between four and eight digits that are easy to remember. But don't hit the enter key until I tell you."

Gilles did as he was told and entered eight digits, the month and date of his birth, along with his street address.

"OK, now hit the enter key and watch the screen."

Gilles did as he was told and watched as a series of numbers flashed by in a spiral pattern.

"I developed an algorithm that converts the user's password into a long digital string, kind of based on the Fibonacci sequence, which is why I named the software Fibonaclé."

At the mention of Fibonacci, Gilles's mind was cast back to the one math course he took at university. He remembered that the Fibonacci sequence had something to do with numbers that described a spiral. The graphic now made sense to him.

"It changes, but always works with the user's numeric password. It's embedded in the computer they use so even if someone gets a user's password, they can't use it on another computer. Users need a different password, always expressed numerically, for each machine they log in from. It's an uncrackable code. Think of it this way, once the user, whether an individual or a team, enters the world of DiplomRMY, they are in a locked room and no one can see what they are doing. All their communications are totally private. Impenetrable."

"All of them? Even emails and things they might do from other sites?"

"Absolutely everything for those using the software."

Gilles thought for a minute and said, "I used to have a bank account and to use the bank's website I had to have a fob that generated numbers every minute or so. I needed one of those numbers along with my password to gain access to my accounts. How is your software different?"

"Similar idea," Daniel replied, "but a gazillion times more secure. The fob-generated numbers give the user and the bank, I guess, a sense of security, but it's too easy to crack the code. And with Fibonaclé you don't need the number-generating fob. The software does it and the string is so long that it can't be copied or remembered."

"Or even seen. The numbers flash by so fast," Gilles said with a smile. "What happens if someone gets their hands on the password and the computer it attaches to?"

"Good question. You didn't realize it and I didn't tell you but while you were creating your account the Fibonaclé software was taking your photograph. Think about the elements to the security system. A passcode has to match a user and a computer and generate a long number in the Fibonacci system. And it has to do all of this in less than five seconds."

Gilles only had a superficial idea of how the coding worked but he grasped that if it was applied to criminal endeavours, plans could be hatched and money could be laundered and transferred without surveillance. The criminal possibilities were frightening.

"What happens if the person forgets their number?" he asked.

"They're fucked. They're locked out of DiplomRMY or whatever else they're using the password software for, never to regain access. There are no back doors and I couldn't gain access even if I wanted to."

Gilles had no additional questions for Daniel Yablon. He got to his feet and thanked his host for answering his questions.

Daniel walked Gilles through to the front door of the office. The two men shook hands. Just before he left, Gilles said, "Thanks again. I'll call you if I have any additional questions."

"Sure thing," Yablon agreed.

Gilles found his way out of the building, only making one wrong turn this time.

He knew that there were a number of cafés in the neighbourhood and he left his car parked and walked up Notre-Dame to Café Farina. He ordered a double allongé and considered his options. He felt that his investigation was stymied by the fact that he had been unable to question Michaela Bédard. He needed to talk to her in order to determine his next steps and probably close the case.

He sipped at his coffee and decided to take the investigative bull by the horns. He called Manon Tremblay. The prosecutor answered the phone with her typical brusqueness, "Oui, Gilles, je suis au telephone avec Berg. Restez en ligne."

Gilles only had to wait for a couple of minutes before Manon came back on the line. "It's set for two today. Be at my office thirty minutes before that to talk strategy."

"Got it."

"Remember," Manon went on, "if she convinces us that it was indeed self-defence, and between the two of us that's the way it looks from the photos you sent, then we'll drop charges. If we want to proceed against her then the meeting will be off the record."

"Seems risky to me, but yeah, I understand." Manon ended the call before Gilles could say goodbye.

CHAPTER 15

Sunday/Monday –
Chris Palmer Investigates

Chris Palmer had the weekend off and spent Saturday morning taking care of personal chores such as food shopping and cleaning his apartment. By two in the afternoon he was ready for some R & R before he went out with his girlfriend and friends for dinner. He got a beer from the refrigerator and found a college football game on TV. While he watched, his mind drifted to his meeting with Julia. She seemed blissfully unconcerned that her boss had been the victim of an attack and that a cop was looking for him. Chris wasn't certain what he expected but certainly more than casual indifference—unless, of course, she was used to cops searching for Simon Connors—and perhaps knew what had occurred in Montreal.

Chris decided that he would pay her another visit the next day. He knew that it would be very unlikely that his boss would allow him to investigate a crime that had not occurred in Queens, but loose ends bugged him. He decided to give up part of his Sunday to see what he could unearth. He was certain that the dog would need walking and so she would still be at Connors's condo. If nothing came of it then he would not report the interrogation. If something came up then he would look good for showing initiative and investigating a crime on his day off. All in all, win-win, Chris believed, and returned his attention to the game.

Chris and his girlfriend, Sonia, slept in on Sunday morning and it was just after eleven that Chris set out from her apartment in Manhattan to Simon's condo in Queens. Traffic was light and he pulled up in front of the building before noon. There was no answer to his ring and he went in search of a superintendent. It took several tries at neighbouring buildings to find the fellow who took care of the building where Simon Connors had his condo.

A police badge, twenty dollars, and Chris's promise to keep things to himself motivated the super to allow Chris access to Simon's condo.

As they walked to the building Chris asked, "Do you think the dog-sitter took the dog home with her? I didn't hear any barking when I rang."

"What dog?" the super asked.

"Duke, Simon Connors's dog," Chris explained, wondering how it was that the super was unaware of such a large dog.

"Connors doesn't have a dog," the super said. "Believe me, I would know if he had. No dog and no dog-sitter."

"Really?" Chris said, but he didn't ask any additional questions. His suspicion that something was not right about the so-called dog walker appeared to be accurate.

Once the super had unlocked the door to Connors's condo Chris asked him to wait outside. The super complied and Chris pulled on a pair of latex gloves and entered. He searched each room and found no evidence that a dog was ever in permanent residence. He turned on the computer but other than a flashing cursor nothing came on to the screen. "Odd," he muttered. "And odder," he said when he noticed the empty file drawer. Chris thought this warranted getting a forensics team in there as soon as possible. When Chris opened the door to leave, the scrap of paper that Julia had dropped floated up and dropped back to the floor. Chris picked it up and saw that it said YUL and a logo he recognized as that of Delta Airlines. He put the slip of paper into an evidence bag and left.

Chris found the super on the sidewalk in front of the building chatting with a denizen of the neighbourhood. He interrupted and told the super that he could lock up. Chris handed the super his card and told him, "Do not, under any circumstances, allow anyone else into the Connors condo, not even—especially not—the so-called dog-sitter. If anyone shows up call me."

The super grunted his agreement.

"There will be a forensics team from the NYPD coming by today or tomorrow. I'll tell them to look for you to get in," Chris continued.

The super grunted again and walked off to ensure that all the doors were locked.

Chris realized that there was nothing more he could do on a Sunday so he called Sonia to see if she was free to resume their weekend together. She was a professor at Columbia and used Sunday afternoons to prepare her lecture notes for the coming week. She had about an hour's work to do and expected to be finished by the time Chris got to her apartment.

Before heading back to Manhattan Chris called a friend of his in the forensics division. He asked him to get a team to Connors's condo. It took some convincing as there was no open file for a crime committed at the address. Every cop in the world understands that their department works on the exchange of favours. Chris would be in his debt—a favour to be collected at some point in the future.

On Monday morning Chris got to the precinct station early in order to write a report of his work helping the Montreal police. He confirmed that the YUL printed on the scrap of paper he found was the designation for the Montreal airport. He added his discovery over the weekend that a person of interest had left the jurisdiction and was believed to be heading to Montreal. When the precinct captain arrived, Chris went into his office in order to make his report before the captain got busy with other things. "From what you've told me," the captain said, "we've got no skin in this game. The person of interest, as you call her, may or may not have something to do with a murder in another jurisdiction. She's committed no crime here as far as we know. Right?"

"Other than lying to me, yeah," Chris said.

"If we arrested everyone who lied to the cops, the streets of the five boroughs would be empty," the captain said drily. "You've wasted enough time on this. Kick it."

Chris had not been invited to sit down in the captain's cramped and messy office, and just before he turned to leave, he said, "Got it. But I'll call the Montreal cop and tell him that Julia Sutton is on her way to Montreal. He can do what he likes with the information."

"We're done here," the captain said—his way of showing he agreed. Chris failed to mention that he had engineered a forensics toss of the Connors condo.

He returned to his desk and checked Delta flights to Montreal. He was about to call Gilles when a senior detective handed him a sheaf of arrest reports from the weekend and asked him to check the information against the NYPD database and add anything referring to previous arrests. Chris was the junior man on the squad and had no choice but to do the work that each of the officers who made the arrests should have done.

It was mid-morning by the time he completed the task and called Gilles.

Gilles's cellphone rang about ten minutes after he had spoken to Manon Tremblay. He was surprised to hear Chris Palmer's voice when he answered.

"Julia the dog-sitter is not what she appeared to be," Chris explained. "We have every reason to believe that she was on a flight to Montreal, probably Delta 5104, which left LaGuardia last night. She's probably in your city now."

Gilles recorded the flight information. Palmer went on to tell Gilles what he had found when he paid a second visit to Simon Connors's dwelling. "I'm waiting for a report from our forensics team but I'm not hopeful. It looks to me like she disabled Connors's computer. I'll keep you posted."

Gilles thanked his American colleague and promised to keep him informed if he learned anything about Julia Sutton.

Gilles had a couple of hours before his scheduled meeting with Manon Tremblay, so he returned to the office and called the Canada Border Services Agency to see if they had a record of Julia Sutton entering the country. He found himself in voice mail hell, pressing various options in his attempt to reach an actual person. After fifteen frustrating minutes he spoke to an agent who gave him a phone number to a direct line at the airport. It took another fifteen minutes to get confirmation that Julia Sutton had indeed entered Canada at the Pierre Elliott Trudeau Airport the previous evening. She gave a Montreal address on Sherbrooke West. Gilles checked the address on Google Maps and discovered that it did not exist.

The agent sent Gilles a copy of Julia Sutton's passport. He downloaded the photograph of Sutton to his cellphone.

The likely conclusion was that Julia Sutton was in Montreal for the same reason as Simon Connors had been, which had something to do with Stevens, Bédard and the financing of the Fibonaclé IPO. And this meant he had to make another call on Denis Stevens and Daniel Yablon.

CHAPTER 16

Monday –
Julia Sutton is in Montreal

Julia Sutton arrived in Montreal and quite easily cleared Customs and Immigration at the airport. She had a reservation at a hotel, Le Crystal, on boulevard René-Lévesque, several blocks west and south of the fake address she gave on her customs form. She checked into her room and after a quick shower went to the lobby restaurant for a late dinner. While she ate, she reviewed the notes that she had made from Connors's computer and from his reports to her. Julia assumed that Michaela had returned to Montreal. To be certain she decided that she would make it her first order of business on Monday morning to find out where her quarry was.

On Monday morning, Julia went out for a run along René-Lévesque Boulevard. She found running in a new city was a good way to get the lay of the land. As she ran, she took special note of the mountain that dominated the city skyline and guessed that it had paths for joggers. If time allowed, she would treat herself to a run on the mountain. Back at the hotel she showered and dressed, in black slacks, a white DKNY shirt, and a John Varvatos jacket, also black. She found a copy of the *New York Times* and read it while having breakfast in the hotel.

Julia believed that the simplest solution to a problem was the best. In order to determine if Michaela Bédard had returned to Montreal she waited until nine o'clock and called the Stevens, Bédard office. She asked to speak to Michaela Bédard and the receptionist told her that Ms. Bédard was not in.

"Do you expect her soon?" Julia asked.

"Not until sometime this afternoon. May I take a message?" the receptionist inquired.

"Thank you, no. I'll call back later," Julia said and ended the call, certain that Michaela was back in Montreal. Now it was necessary to locate her and finish the job Simon Connors had started.

CHAPTER 17

Monday – Gilles Interrogates Mickie Bédard

Gilles arrived at Manon's office, located in the courthouse on rue St-Jacques. The prosecutors' offices were a lot nicer than those of the detectives. Manon's desk was large and made of wood, not one of the grey metal things that the cops of Major Crimes had. There was a bookcase against one of the walls of her office, a cabinet behind the desk, and the windows, which looked out on the street, had been washed this year. A small table, where four people could sit comfortably for meetings, was placed next to one of the windows. A large abstract painting hung on one of the walls and the office was large enough so as not to feel cramped; it was almost twice the size of Captain Lacroix's office.

Manon was on the phone when Gilles arrived and she motioned him to one of the chairs at the table next to the window. Gilles sat down and opened the file folder he had brought with him. The folder contained notes on the investigation and the questions he planned to ask Michaela Bédard.

Manon, petite and blond and, as usual, fashionably dressed in business attire, sat down in the chair next to Gilles. "I have a plan for our meeting," she said. "I want you to start the questioning after I explain the rules for the interrogation. I've asked our tech people to prepare a slide show using the photographs you sent me. They only used photos that had an accurate time stamp and they are in chronological order, so it's easy to see what transpired in the suspect's room."

"Got it," Gilles agreed. He was pleased that he would be the one to initiate the interrogation. Manon usually liked to handle things herself, and on the other occasions that Gilles had worked with her he was often forced to keep silent during suspect interviews. "I've prepared questions I—we—need answers to." Gilles slid the folder to Manon so she could review his questions. She opened the folder, scanned the questions and slid the folder back to Gilles. "These are fine, Gilles, but not where I want to start," Manon explained. "I want Bédard to explain the photos, the action in the photos. Then we can get into more detail about the victim, banking, and that kind of stuff."

"Okay," Gilles said, and was about to add something when Manon's intercom buzzed. She walked to her desk and answered the call. She hung up following a short exchange with her secretary and told Gilles, "They're here. They're being shown to the meeting room. We'll let them get settled and join them in a moment or two."

Gilles picked up his folder and got to his feet. Manon busied herself with a file of her own and Gilles gazed out the window while he waited for the crown to be ready.

"Okay, let's go," Manon said.

"The photos?" Gilles queried as he fell in behind her.

"On a laptop already in the meeting room," Manon told him.

Gilles and Manon walked down a hall and just before it came to an end in a T-junction Manon opened a door to a room on her right and walked in. Jay Berg and his client were seated at the far end of the table, Jay at its head. He got to his feet and greeted Manon and Gilles. Berg was a couple of inches under six feet tall but his dynamism gave him a presence that made him seem taller. He was dressed as usual in an expensive bespoke suit, a red power tie and matching pocket square. Manon shook Berg's offered hand and told him, "It would be best if you sat next to your client. I have something to show the two of you." She had not released Berg's hand and she gently moved him towards the chair next to Mickie. Berg smiled, shook Gilles's hand and sat down next to his client. Gilles left an empty chair between himself and Mickie and sat down.

Manon pulled the laptop toward her and said, "We have some photographs that we'd like your client to look at."

Jay Berg extended his arm, palm out, and said, "I want it clearly understood that my client is here of her own volition and that this interview is off the record. Nothing said here can be used in court without her express permission."

Manon sighed, "Yes, Jay. We've already agreed to that in writing."

"Just dotting i's and crossing t's," Jay said. "It's show-and-tell time."

Manon opened the laptop and tapped a few keys, bringing the computer to life. She turned it so that Gilles, Michaela and Berg could see the screen, and tapped the enter key. A photo of Michaela sleeping in her room in the ER at the Gursky filled the screen.

"Hey, what is this?" Jay Berg exclaimed, half rising out of his chair. "They film the patients?"

"Calme-toi, Jay," Manon said. She explained that the photos were taken by staff who were celebrating the engagement of one of the nurses and were not part of a hospital surveillance system.

Mollified, Jay said, "Okay, but I want copies."

"Not a problem," Manon agreed. "Now can we get on with things? Gilles?"

Gilles cleared his throat and asked Michaela to explain the action in the photos as they went through them.

"Well, I'm asleep," she stated. Another photo appeared and Michaela said, "I'm still asleep." By the fourth photo the four of them saw Simon enter Michaela's room. Michaela gasped and put her hand to her mouth. "He just walked into my room while I was asleep? I can't believe it." As the photos clicked by, they watched as Simon checked on Michaela.

"What happened next?" Manon asked. She clicked through a couple of photos. Even though they were stills they indicated that a struggle of some sort was taking place.

"He attacked me and I defended myself," Michaela explained. "Just as I've said all along."

"That's not quite what the photos show," Gilles said. "We see the man—we know his name is Simon Connors now—come into your room and check on you but he didn't touch you. At least not as far as we can see."

Berg gave Gilles and Manon a hard stare and said, "It's clear that the presence of a strange man in her room made my client feel unsafe but if you want a blow-by-blow description of what happened we're happy to provide it."

Michaela cleared her throat and looked at her lawyer who nodded his encouragement. "It's like Jay, Mr. Berg, said. I woke when the man hovered over me. At first I thought it was a doctor or a nurse checking on me and I moved a bit and opened my eyes just enough to see it was some guy, not a nurse, in my room."

"And you didn't scream for help?" Gilles asked.

"I was about to but for a moment I was too frightened, panicked, I couldn't make myself scream. It was like the feeling when you're having a nightmare and you can't make a sound although you want to."

"Like being paralyzed with fear," Berg said helpfully. "Continue."

"He moved away...to the chair where my things were, his back was to me so I shifted my position to see what he was going to do. I had regained my senses, I guess you would say. I saw him poke around at my clothes and pick up my satchel. By that time, even though only a few seconds had passed, my training kicked in. I had the advantage because, as I said, his back was to me. That's when I attacked—as much to scare him as to hurt him. He had some fight training. He pushed back at me and I stumbled. I was near enough to the bed to grab the mattress for support and I went at him again, this time in full Krav Maga fight mode. I wasn't thinking, I was reacting to a threat. He came at me again but this time I was too fast for him. I struck him and he went down on the bed."

"That's exactly what the photographs show," Berg said. "As we've contended all along."

"Where did you learn to fight?" Gilles asked.

"I take martial arts courses at the Y."

"If it was self-defence why did you run?"

"I was terrified. Some guy I'd never seen tried to kill me, so yes, I got dressed and took off. I didn't feel safe in the hospital. I couldn't lock the door. I was a pigeon. I figured out where he was from and decided to try to find out who he was and why he was trying to harm me."

"Why didn't you cry for help? Use the call button to get a nurse?"

"I could see the nurses and doctors through the window and they seemed more interested in each other than anything else."

"They didn't react to the sounds of the struggle?" Gilles asked.

"We didn't make all that much noise. What little noise we did make was drowned out by the conversations the staff was having anyway."

"Then why not yell for someone to call the cops? Didn't that occur to you?"

"Yeah, for about a second. I very quickly realized that if I had called for help, raised an alarm in any way, I would be stuck for hours answering questions and not finding out who this guy was."

"The proof of that is," Jay said, "that we're here doing just that."

"I decided to get out of the hospital, get to New York and find out what I could. Of course I knew that sooner or later I would have to answer questions but I thought later would be better than sooner—especially if I could arm myself with information."

"Look," Jay put in. "My client had every right to defend herself in whatever way she thought best. It was hardly her fault she was attacked. If she hadn't cleared out we might be having a very different conversation." He placed a comforting avuncular hand on his client's forearm and repeated, "A very different conversation."

Gilles was about to ask a question but Jay Berg continued speaking. "Before we continue, I want it made clear that you accept my client's story that she acted in self-defence and that she will not be charged with anything."

"What about leaving the scene of a crime?" Manon asked.

"Forget it. No charges," Jay Berg asserted.

"Speaking of which," Gilles said, "how did you manage to get out of the hospital without attracting attention?"

"It's hardly a challenge." Mickie smiled for the first time since the start of the interview. "I got dressed and calmly walked out. The security guard probably thought I was a late-night visitor."

Manon smiled and agreed. "As things stand now there will be no charges against your client, for the record, Michaela

Bédard. We do expect her co-operation in our investigation, though."

"Not a problem," Berg stated.

Michaela and her lawyer relaxed, and the interview carried on more as a conversation than an interrogation. In response to questions posed by Gilles and Manon, Mickie explained that she had had the feeling that she was being followed but could not explain exactly why she felt the way she did at the time. She hadn't seen anyone, just a general feeling.

"You didn't act on those feelings? Did you report your suspicions to anyone?" Gilles asked.

"I'm not a paranoid person. Probably a mistake on my part. But as I said, I didn't see anyone who could have been following me. I chalked it up to overwork."

"I have some questions about your activities in New York, but before I get to them, I'd like to know how you managed to overpower your assailant."

"I already told you I take Krav Maga courses at the Y. I had never used my training in a real life or death situation until ..."

Mickie didn't finish her sentence. Jay Berg completed it for her, "As I said, if she hadn't known how to defend herself, things might have turned out very differently."

"Okay," Gilles said. "You said you ran because you were terrified and didn't feel safe at the hospital. But you had the presence of mind to search the victim and take his wallet."

"Yes, I did. Yeah, I was frightened but not dumbfounded. I wanted to know who was trying to kill me."

"Had you ever heard of Simon Connors?"

"No, he was a complete stranger to me."

"I can almost understand why you fled to safety," Gilles said.

"Almost?" Berg put in. "To repeat. This guy, Connors, tried to kill my client and she ended up killing him in self-defence. Getting out of the hospital was the only smart play. What if Connors had an accomplice, someone who would finish the job?"

"Yeah, almost. Where did you go?"

"I went home, to my condo."

"But you didn't stay there. Didn't you feel safe at your condo? Instead of calling the cops and reporting the attack you took off for New York. How do you explain that?"

Mickie leaned forward and looked Gilles directly in the eyes. "Maybe you have a more sanguine reaction to being attacked, but to me it was fight *and* flight. I was certain that my attack had something to do with the deal I was working on. I saw Connors poking around my briefcase. I wanted— no, needed—to know who was ready to kill me to take a business deal away from me. I had no way of knowing, and still don't know, if there was anyone else after me. Flight was my best option. If there was someone else on my trail, they were very likely in Montreal. I wanted to get to the source of the threat, and that was in New York."

Mickie leaned back in her chair. Manon was about to say something but Jay Berg interrupted. "Makes perfect sense to me. Are we almost done?"

"Jay," Manon said. "We've been more than co-operative. We're done when Detective Bellechasse finishes his questions. Gilles."

"Merci, Manon," Gilles said and returned his attention to Mickie. "You made it to New York and found Connors's apartment. You spoke to the woman you found there," Gilles shuffled through his notes, "Julia Sutton, correct?"

"Julia. Yeah. The dog walker."

"And what did you learn from her?"

"Nothing, other than the fact that Connors was in Montreal. I already knew that…and had the emotional scars to prove it, so to speak."

"What did you do after you talked to Sutton?"

"Nothing. I checked into my hotel and was arrested."

"I think we're up to date," Jay Berg said. "My client has had a rough couple of days and it's time for us to leave."

"Almost finished," Gilles said. "Just to wrap things up, could you please tell us about the business deal that you thought was worth your life and cost Simon Connors his?"

Mickie told them about her business and the importance of working on the IPO of Fibonaclé. "That one deal," she concluded, "would put the firm on a whole new level of banking. We'd be working in a much more lucrative business."

"But riskier, no?" Gilles asked.

"Of course," Mickie explained as if to a child. "That's why the rewards are greater."

Jay Berg got to his feet. "I think we're done here. If you want to speak to my client again give me a call and we'll set something up." He held the back of Michaela's chair and she too got to her feet. He picked up his briefcase, which had been on the floor beside his chair, and headed to the door. He stopped to say goodbye to Manon.

"Before you go," she said, as she reached into her file folder and pulled out a CD in a jewel case. She handed it to Berg. "Your copy of the photographs." He thanked her, shook Gilles's hand and left the meeting room with his client.

Gilles was about to leave as well when Manon put a restraining hand on his forearm. "Just a minute, Gilles. As far as I'm concerned, the investigation is closed. There is no one to charge with anything."

"Don't you want to know more about why Connors was trying to harm Bédard?" he asked.

"In the abstract, sure. But even if you can find that out, what good would it do us? Connors is dead and there is no one to charge with anything. There's no point in wasting money investigating something that won't produce results. Tu comprends?"

"Oui, Manon. But I hate loose ends."

Manon's smile told Gilles that he would have to get used to the idea. She preceded him out of the room and walked him to the elevator.

Gilles drove to the Major Crimes Division offices and in the shopping concourse of the building stopped to buy two coffees: a regular for himself and a cappuccino for his boss. He was going to take a shot at convincing Captain Lacroix to let him devote another couple of days to see if he could find a link between the activities of Simon Connors and someone connected with either Stevens, Bédard or the guys at DiplomRMY. Someone had paid Connors to attack Michaela Bédard and Gilles wanted to know who that was.

Captain Lacroix was alone in his office when Gilles got to the squad room. He tapped on the door and did not wait for an invitation before he entered and placed the cappuccino on his boss's desk.

"Un pot-de-vin, Gilles?" Lacroix said with a smile. "You would have done better with a bottle of wine than a coffee, even a cappuccino."

Gilles took the Captain's smile as an invitation to sit down. "I take it you've already spoken to Manon," he said.

"Yes. And, of course, I agree with her."

"In spite of the fact that someone hired Connors to commit a crime in our jurisdiction?" Gilles asked.

"I can only repeat what Manon told you. You're probably right, but we can't charge Connors, he's dead. And for the same reason we don't have testimony from him. Finally, there is a strong possibility that he was hired in New York and that's their business, not ours."

"Two days," Gilles pleaded. "All I'm asking for is two days and if I can't turn up anything then I'll drop it."

Lacroix rocked back in his chair and gazed at Gilles. He admired his enthusiasm but he could not commit resources to an investigation that was unlikely to yield results.

Gilles had one final argument to make and he made it. "There is a distinct possibility that whoever it was who brought or sent Connors to Montreal sent a replacement. My contact with the NYPD informed me that a person by the name of Julia Sutton is here and she may be up to something. She has a connection to Simon Connors." Gilles did not think it was a good idea to add that she had presented herself as the dog-sitter for Connors.

"Or she may be a tourist," Lacroix said.

Gilles stared glumly at his boss. "Listen," Lacroix continued, "You can have the rest of the day to see if you can develop any leads. If not, you're on regular rotation again tomorrow."

"Oui, patron," Gilles said. "If anything comes up, though, I hope I'll be able to stay on the case."

Lacroix grunted his agreement and motioned for Gilles to leave his office.

Gilles picked up his coffee and left the squad room. He decided that he would interview Denis Stevens one more time to see if he knew anything, and he would make a call to Detective Palmer in New York to tell him that Julia Sutton had not been located and to ask to be informed if he learned anything helpful in New York.

Gilles parked on Crescent Street and mounted the steps to the Stevens, Bédard office. He rang the doorbell and was admitted by the receptionist. If he had bothered to look behind him at the S'Presso Café he would have noticed a young woman wearing dark glasses and a Yankees baseball cap, her blond hair in a ponytail, sitting at a table in the window. Julia Sutton knew from Simon's notes where the office of her quarry was located and the best place to watch it from. She noted the tall handsome man entering the building.

Gilles asked to see Denis Stevens and the receptionist called him to see if he was available. After a brief conversation the receptionist asked Gilles to take a seat in the reception area and told him that Monsieur Stevens would be out to see him in a minute or two.

Gilles waited closer to ten minutes than two and was about to say something when Denis Stevens came down the stairs from the second floor and approached Gilles.

"Comment puis-je vous aider?" he asked.

Gilles got to his feet and said, "Is there somewhere private we can talk?"

"That won't be necessary," Stevens told him. "I spoke to Mickie and I know that she won't be charged with anything and wants to put the whole ordeal behind her. And I intend to help her. As far as we're concerned the investigation is closed and you won't need to waste any additional time on us. Thank you for everything that you've done." He shook Gilles's hand, turned and walked back up the stairs to his office.

Gilles had been coolly and efficiently dismissed. There was nothing he could do to force Denis Stevens to talk to him. He left the building and returned to his car.

He called Chris Palmer in New York and told him that he had so far been unable to locate Julia Sutton, in fact he had been told not to bother trying to find her. He added that his boss had ended any further investigation into the death of Simon Connors and considered it a problem for the NYPD. Chris Palmer commiserated with Gilles and told him that his boss felt the same way with the exception that he considered the death to be a problem for the Montreal police to deal with.

The two cops were bothered by not knowing why Simon Connors had attacked Mickie Bédard, but agreed that their investigations had been stymied, and promised to keep in touch should either of them come up with any additional information.

Frustrated and angered by the fact that his investigation was going nowhere, he did the one thing that was guaranteed to cheer him up. He called Annie. Her shift was almost at an end and they agreed to meet for dinner.

"My turn to cook," Gilles said.

"Actually, I'm on early tomorrow so I'd rather we eat at my place," Annie told him.

"Then I'll pick up some Chinese food on my way over, for the three of us."

"Just for two. Pam is out with friends for dinner."

CHAPTER 18

Monday –
Julia Sutton Has a Coffee

Julia Sutton had left the café by the time Gilles exited the Stevens, Bédard office. It was possible that Mickie would not return. She had earlier checked out the building on Blue Ridge Crescent where Mickie lived and wanted to make the walk from there back to her office in order to get the lay of the urban landscape. She had two problems to solve. The first, the easiest, was to disguise herself. Mickie had had a long conversation with Julia in New York and would be certain to recognize her if she spotted her, and as Julia intended to follow Mickie to work the next day, there was a good chance that she would be seen. Julia was certain the short dark wig she carried with her would go a long way toward making her unrecognizable. Makeup and glasses would do the rest.

Her second problem was more difficult to solve. How was she going to complete the mission that Simon and she had been assigned? She had no desire to spend any more time in Montreal than absolutely necessary. She hoped to complete her assignment the next day, the day after at the latest, so she could return to the safety of New York City.

CHAPTER 19

Monday –
Gilles and Annie Eat Chinese Food

Gilles stopped at the Sun King restaurant on Wellington in Verdun. The restaurant was not located in Montreal's Chinatown but it had the reputation as being one of the best Chinese restaurants in the city and there was usually a line out the door waiting for tables. Takeout service was much faster.

Gilles arrived at Annie's house in the west end of Montreal at about six thirty. Annie had been home for a couple of hours and she had showered and was wearing a pair of old scrubs. Gilles admired the undulations of her breasts under the scrub top as Annie moved about setting the table. Gilles marvelled at his good fortune at meeting a woman who was not only beautiful and sexy but also intelligent and observant. It was Annie's quick mind that had spotted the clue that allowed Gilles to close the case he was working on when they met.

Annie was well aware of the effect she had on Gilles and was amused at his efforts to suppress his politically incorrect ogling.

Over dinner Gilles told Annie about his trip to New York and his interrogation of Mickie Bédard.

"Well then, she'll not be charged with anything, right?" Annie said.

"Yeah, the Crown does not think we could get a conviction," Gilles agreed.

"Because it was clear that she was...?"

"...defending herself."

"And the photos I got for you...?" Annie was enjoying the game.

"...were instrumental in proving that Connors very likely planned to harm her in some way."

"Glad to be of service," Annie concluded.

Gilles smiled and more seriously said, "You're the best. Really you are. Totally." He got up from the table and gathered the dishes and empty takeout boxes and carried them into the kitchen. Annie cleared the rest of the table and brought the cutlery into the kitchen. Gilles was at the sink washing the crockery. After Annie placed the things she was carrying on the counter, Gilles turned and pulled her into his arms. She put her arms around his waist and they kissed.

"Standing in the kitchen with you in my arms is the best," Gilles told her.

Annie smiled and stroked Gilles on his cheek and said, "I couldn't be happier." They kissed again and Annie added, "But romantic babble doesn't get the dishes done, does it?"

Gilles returned to his task and Annie went into the living room to get the TV tuned into Netflix so she and Gilles could watch something before they went to bed.

Gilles joined her and they were watching an episode of *Babylon Berlin* when Pamela came home.

Annie asked, "Did you have fun, dear?" On more than one occasion she told her, "You can only be young and in university once. Enjoy the experience." Pamela usually responded with an exasperated, oh-mom look. Annie was pleased when Pamela took a break from studying and went out with friends.

"Yeah, after labs a bunch of us went out for Thai food," Pamela said.

"Anyone special?" Annie inquired of her beautiful daughter. Annie was at a loss to understand why her daughter didn't have a steady boyfriend, or even an unsteady one.

"Mom," Pamela said, dragging out the syllable indicating that this was not a conversation she was willing to have. "How are you, Gilles?" she added.

"Perfect. Great seeing you. How's school?"

"The usual," Pam replied. "A grind. OK, good night you two, I've got studying to do." Pamela left her mother and Gilles to their TV show and went to her room.

"She works so hard," Annie said. "I hope it's not too much for her."

"She's a great kid," Gilles put in. "I wish some of her ambition would rub off on Émilie."

Gilles's daughter was a couple of years younger than Pamela and in CEGEP, Quebec's system of junior colleges. Émilie had no long-range plans for her life. She was more interested in the social scene at her school than the academics. Gilles's ex-wife, Yvonne, had trouble controlling Émilie and it was only Gilles's constant combination of nagging and cajoling that kept her in school with grades just high enough for her to look forward to going to university.

Gilles had introduced Émilie to Pamela in the hope that she would be a big-sister type of role model. But the two girls had very little in common.

"You know what?" Gilles asked suddenly.

"What?"

"I told you about the cop I met in New York, Chris Palmer. Anyway, he seems like a really good guy. And we talk about going to the city. So why don't we plan to go there with the two girls and we'll try to meet up with Chris as well?"

"Really?" Annie was skeptical. "Two days with Pamela and Émilie? We may need another cop." Émilie had a tendency to find bars and clubs that were not suitable for an eighteen-year-old.

"It'll be fun. We can drive down," Gilles said.

Trapped in a car for eight hours with two teenage girls didn't sound like fun to Annie but she didn't say anything. They turned their focus back to *Babylon Berlin*. At the conclusion of the episode they turned their attention to one another and, doing their best not to trip or to disturb Pamela, headed for the bedroom.

CHAPTER 20

Tuesday – Julia's Plan

Julia knew from the intelligence Simon had provided that Mickie left early and walked to her office. The entrance of Mickie's apartment building on Blue Ridge Crescent was easy to survey. The street cut into the base of Mount Royal and the area behind the building was part of the system of parks that made up the mountain. Julia dressed like one of the joggers that populated the mountain from early morning to late at night. A woman dressed in Lululemon workout gear would hardly be noticed. Julia found a bench that afforded her a clear view of the entrance to Mickie's building and the garage in case Mickie decided to drive to work.

At seven-thirty Mickie walked out of her building and continued on to Côte-des-Neiges. Julia threw on the windbreaker she had with her and followed Mickie down Côte-des-Neiges to Sherbrooke and then east along Sherbrooke and down Crescent to her office. Had Mickie been carrying her attaché case, Julia would have grabbed it and run off with it, completing her mission in Montreal. But Mickie was not carrying it. Again, based on the information she had from Connors, this was unusual. Mickie kept her important documents with her and it was those documents that Connors, and now Julia, were charged with acquiring.

When Mickie entered her office building, Julia adjourned to S'Presso to consider her options. Mickie had been in New

York over the weekend and for whatever reason had not been in the office on Monday, the previous day. The briefcase was very likely at Mickie's condo. Julia decided to return to Mickie's home, gain entry to the building, pick the lock on the door to the condo, locate and steal the documents she was after. Julia figured it would be at least eight hours before Mickie noticed the theft and she would be safely back in New York at that time. If Julia was wrong and Mickie for some reason had brought her files to her office on Sunday then she would reactivate plan A and rob Mickie when she left the office with them. She paid for her coffee, left the café and walked to de Maisonneuve Boulevard where she hailed a cab and was back at the corner of Blueridge Crescent and Côte-des-Neiges before eight-thirty.

Getting into the building proved to be a simple matter; she followed a Filipino maid through the front door and onto the elevator. Julia and the Filipino woman got off the elevator at the same floor and when the woman turned one direction, Julia headed down the corridor in the opposite direction, away from Mickie's condo, pretending to be looking for an apartment number. Julia had the number of Mickie's condo from Simon Connors's files and turned to see if the coast was clear in time to see the woman from the elevator use a key to enter Mickie's. The woman was obviously Mickie's housekeeper and Julia had to abort her plan.

Back on Blueridge Crescent Julia again walked south and continued on to her hotel. She reconciled herself to the fact that she would have to spend another day in Montreal.

If she couldn't gain access to Mickie's condo that evening, she planned to return the next morning and, if Mickie had her briefcase with her, steal it. If she again didn't have it, Julia would break into the condo and steal it from there and head home.

◉

Mickie used her code on the number pad of the front door of the office and the door clicked open. "Mickie!" the receptionist exclaimed. "You're back. How are you? How are you feeling?"

"Better now that I'm back home," Mickie told her.

"Was it awful?" the receptionist asked.

"A night in a cell in a New York police station and then being questioned by the cops here. You have no idea. Awful barely begins to describe it."

"But it's over and you're back with us now, right?"

"Yeah, it's over and it's back to work. Is Denis in yet?"

"Yes."

"Great. Give me a couple of minutes to get settled and ask him to join me if he is not too busy," Mickie instructed the receptionist.

"Will do," the receptionist replied. "Would you like a coffee?"

"Absolutely. Thank you." Mickie walked up the stairs to her office.

Mickie's secretary was working on her computer in her small office when Mickie stopped by. She tapped on the window and her secretary looked up, startled. "Oh, Mickie. It's so good to see you back at work. I was so worried." A virtual repeat of Mickie's conversation with the receptionist followed. Once she allayed her secretary's concern, Mickie turned to head to her office.

"Can I get you anything?" the secretary asked. "Do you need me?"

"No thank you and not at the moment," Mickie replied. "I'll buzz you when I need you."

Mickie crossed the hall and opened her office door. She breathed a sigh of relief when she entered. The office was decorated in a combination of traditional and modern. Mickie's desk was a refurbished pine dining table that had been rescued from a barn in the Eastern Townships. Colourful, abstract modern art graced the walls. The carpet was also an abstract design, in soft blue and beige. Two windows looked out onto Crescent, and a sofa and chair were placed facing the windows. A bookshelf covered the far wall to the right of the entrance and opposite Mickie's desk. The two remaining walls were painted a pastel blue almost the same shade as the blue in the carpet. Mickie felt as at home and relaxed in her office as she did in her condo. And she spent as much time in one as she did in the other.

She went to her desk, made herself comfortable, and went through the stack of pink phone messages that her secretary had left.

The receptionist buzzed Denis Stevens on the intercom line and asked if he was free to meet with Mickie in, say, fifteen minutes. He agreed. The receptionist then went to the lunchroom where the coffee maker the staff used was kept. She was making a coffee for Mickie when Denis came in.

"Is that for Mickie?" he asked, pouring one for himself. "I'll bring it to her." Denis took the coffee from the receptionist with his free hand and mounted the stairs to his office. He placed both coffees on his desk and retrieved the files he thought he would need for his meeting with Mickie. With the files under his arm and one coffee in each hand he made his way to Mickie's office, walking slowly so as not to spill any coffee on the hallway carpet.

Mickie looked up when Denis came in and got to her feet. "Let me help you," she said. She went to Denis, took her coffee from him and said, "Let's sit here." Mickie sat down on the sofa and Denis made himself comfortable in the armchair at the far end.

For the third time that morning, and it was just getting to nine o'clock, Mickie had to recount her experience with the New York police and the police and the crown prosecutor in Montreal.

"That was awful but not as bad as being attacked," Mickie said. Remembering the assault caused Mickie to shudder involuntarily.

Denis reached for her hand and gave it a sympathetic squeeze. Mickie inhaled a couple of deep breaths to help her regain her composure. "It must have been terrible. I can't imagine how terrified you must have been," he said.

"I've never felt fear like that," Mickie agreed. "I had no choice but to react in the way that I did. I could have been killed."

"Unquestionably. You did the right thing. I hate to think what would have happened if you hadn't."

Denis told Mickie about his visit with Detective Gilles Bellechasse. "But that's behind us now," he concluded. "Are you certain that you're able to get back to work?"

"Absolutely," Mickie stated.

"Okay," Denis said and rifled through his files until he found the one he wanted. "Based on the questions I was asked," he said, "I believe that attack on your person had something to do with the Fibonaclé file. Do you agree?"

"Yeah, of course. But I can't see why. It's a pretty straightforward IPO," Mickie said.

"So, the question is: do we want to continue?" Denis asked.

"Of course we do. This is the kind of deal that moves us up in the banking world to where the big money is. I don't know what the point of the attack was, probably to intimidate me so a competing bank could get in on the deal. But I'm not going to be intimidated," Mickie stated firmly.

"You mean *we're* not going to be intimidated," Denis said.

"Exactly," Mickie agreed.

The partners spent the next hour talking about the IPO and other clients that required attention. By the time their meeting was over their coffee mugs were empty.

Mickie beavered through all the work and returned all the phone calls that had piled up in her absence. She had turned her attention to things that had to be done now that she was caught up when her cellphone rang. François wanted to meet with her and they arranged to have coffee at the Pikolo on Park Avenue, midway between their offices, at four in the afternoon. She called Danny Yablon and arranged to meet with him at six. "At my office, or shall we go out for dinner and talk?" he asked.

"It's work and it's private. Your office will be best," Mickie replied.

"Fine with me," Danny agreed. "I'll order something in. Sandwiches okay?"

"That'll be fine," Mickie told him.

CHAPTER 21

Wednesday –
Julia Makes a Second Attempt

Julia wanted to get her job done and get out of Montreal. She decided not to waste another day trying to follow and then rob Mickie if and when the opportunity presented itself. She would beard the lion in its den, so to speak. She made her way back to Mickie's building and politely held the door open for the two people, a well-dressed man and a woman with a Labrador Retriever, leaving the building. She nodded a greeting and heard a snippet of their conversation.

"Taking Roxy out for a walk, Fenna?" the man asked.

"Yes, Mr. Huang. I like to tire him out before I start to clean."

"Well, have a nice day, Fenna."

"Thank you. You too."

Julia waited until the two had walked off before she went up to Mickie's condo. Julia was about to knock on the door but noticed that it was not completely closed. She decided to try the handle. If she could get in and out without being seen then so much the better. She was pleasantly surprised when she tried the door and found it unlocked. Julia slipped into the apartment and almost tripped over Mickie's body. Julia took a moment to feel for a pulse, realized that Mickie was dead. There were no obvious signs of a struggle. She decided to take advantage of her good fortune and search the condo for Mickie's laptop and files. She had no idea if the door was unlocked because Mickie had tried to open it to call for help or if another intruder had entered the condo. Julia listened for the sound of another person and heard nothing. She noticed Mickie's Michael Kors leather satchel lying on a table at the far end of the entryway. She opened it and flipped through the files it contained. They were exactly what she, and Connors before her, were looking for. She paused at the door before leaving to again listen for the sounds of anyone else. Silence. Although she did her best not to make any noise when she entered and grabbed Mickie's satchel, she knew that she had not been completely silent and if there were someone else in the condo they'd have been alerted and likely shown themselves. She waited for a couple of seconds and decided to risk an extra couple of minutes and look for Mickie's laptop. She walked to the hallway at the back of the foyer and saw doors on both the left and right. She tried the one on the left and saw that it was a linen closet. She opened the door on the right, walked into Mickie's home office, and made a beeline for Mickie's laptop on the desk. She only got a couple of paces into the room when a brass lamp fashioned from the footrest of a shoe-shine stand came down on her head, the toe of the brass footrest embedding itself in her skull. Julia was dead before she hit the floor, blood spurting everywhere, splattering onto the chest and abdomen of the murderer.

The murderer picked up the briefcase Julia had dropped and left the condo, unaware of the bloody footprint left at the scene. Thirty minutes later the murderer was home and in the shower. It was only necessary to get rid of the bloody clothing to have successfully committed the perfect crime of murder – double murder.

The murderer put the bloody clothing in a garbage bag and drove around the many construction sites in Griffintown looking for one where cement was being poured. It didn't take long to find, and when the person pouring the cement from the truck to the foundation turned his attention away for a moment, the murderer tossed the bloody clothing into the foundation wall. The murderer did not dispose of the shoes along with the clothing.

The murderer did not know that all construction sites are protected by CCTV in order to prevent the theft of expensive construction materials, especially copper wire.

Not long after the murderer had successfully left the building, Fenna and Roxy returned from their walk. She and the other women who worked as housekeepers in the area took the opportunity of the morning dog walking routine to get together before getting to work.

As she and the dog walked past Mickie's unit the dog stopped and barked at the door. The more the housekeeper tried to pull the dog away from the door the more hysterical it became, barking loudly and tugging at the leash. Roxy gave a hard pull on the leash and nudged the door open with its snout. Fenna shrieked when she saw Mickie's body lying on the floor. She dropped the leash and the dog rushed in. A couple of other residents opened their doors to see what the commotion was about. The first person to get to the door of Mickie's condo tried to get the housekeeper to tell him why she was screaming. She was unable to speak coherently and just pointed to the body on the floor, the dog sitting beside it.

By that time a small crowd had gathered and the man who had arrived first regained enough of his composure to say, "There's been an accident. Everyone please stand back. In fact, if anyone has a cellphone please call an ambulance and the cops." He entered the apartment and knelt beside the body to see if he could offer first aid. He found no pulse, then checked for breath and realized that he was dealing with a corpse. He got to his feet and said, "I think she's dead. Everyone stay out." He joined the crowd of people who stood by waiting for Urgences Santé to arrive. No one left the crime scene, and competing whispered conversations speculated on the events that led to the death of their neighbour.

Fenna did her best to get the dog away from the body, but when she turned to talk to one of the other cleaning women who worked in the building the dog slipped away from her and charged past Mickie and into the study, where he discovered Julia's corpse. Fenna and the man who had taken charge of ensuring the police were called, followed the dog to the study. The housekeeper's shriek was almost drowned out by the man screaming, "Holy fuck!" The woman grabbed the dog by the collar and yanked him out of the room with her. The man followed close behind. Someone in the growing crowd at the door asked, "What the hell?"

The man answered, "Another body and lots of blood. I'll have nightmares for weeks."

The call to 911 was channeled to the Major Crimes Division and Captain Lacroix assigned it to the two detectives who were next in the rotation. But when Gilles heard the address of the crime, he told the captain that he was in the process of an investigation that included a resident of the building on Blueridge Crescent. "Okay," Lacroix said, "it's all yours. Giroux, you're with him. Identité judiciaire will meet you there." Stéphanie Giroux was another of the detectives on the squad. She had joined a year or so after Gilles and the two were often paired. On the drive to Blueridge Crescent,

Gilles filled his partner in on the results of his investigation of Michaela Bédard.

Gilles knew from the apartment number that the murder had occurred in Mickie's condo, so he was not surprised to find her body lying on the floor of the foyer. The uniformed cops who had arrived at the scene before Gilles and Stéphanie had moved the crowd away from the door. Gilles carefully inspected the scene. The body showed no signs of a struggle, there was no blood on or around the victim. The murderer had accomplished the crime without the usual mess that accompanies most acts of violence. Mickie looked peaceful, as if she had died from natural causes, and Gilles had to accept the possibility that she had died from something related to her asthma.

One of the uniformed cops called Gilles to the door of the study. He was shocked and surprised to find a second woman dead in a pool of blood, a lamp, also bloody, lying beside her. "C'est quoi ce bordel?" he exclaimed loudly.

Stéphanie joined him at the door and saw what her partner was looking at. "Merde, Gilles, who's she?"

Very carefully, so as not to disturb any of the physical evidence, Gilles moved around the body in order to get a close look at her face. "Câlice," he said. He pulled out his cellphone to confirm his conclusion.

"What?" Stéphanie asked.

They stepped away from the body. Gilles showed Stéphanie his cellphone and explained, "The vic is Julia Sutton. She's from New York and I'm certain that she was sent to Montreal to harm Bédard in some way. As far as I can determine she was sent to replace Simon Connors, the guy Bédard killed." He paused to let his partner process the information and added, "The guy Bédard killed in self-defence."

Gilles and Stéphanie made their way to the corridor outside the condo while they waited for the forensics crew to arrive. They were quiet for a couple of moments while Gilles gathered his thoughts.

"First impressions?" Giroux asked.

"I missed something in my original investigation. Lacroix thought the case was over when Berg got Manon not to press charges. I knew that was too neat, that there was something else going on. I only asked him for two days," Gilles answered.

"Don't be hard on yourself. You did the best you could with what you had," Stéphanie said.

"Yeah. Maybe. I don't know."

"What do you think happened here?" Stéphanie asked.

"It could be that Bédard killed the Sutton woman and then dropped dead for some reason as she was taking off. She suffered from asthma, but I can't really imagine a scenario where she would be able to kill someone and then suffer an attack serious enough to kill her. There must have been a third person involved. There's no point in jumping to conclusions. We'll know more when the medical examiner gets here and forensics finishes."

Stéphanie Giroux agreed with Gilles's assessment. "Oui, Gilles, there is nothing obvious about this one. There are two bodies, one of which has no outward signs of violence. Curieux, non?"

"Curieux, oui," Gilles replied.

The forensics team arrived and Gilles gave them a brief rundown on what the crime scenes held.

While they waited for the arrival of the medical examiner and for the forensics squad to finish their work, Gilles and Stéphanie took down the names of all the witnesses who were still clustered in the corridor outside Mickie's condo. They devoted some time to interviewing Fenna whose dog discovered the bodies, and the man who had taken charge of calling the police. Every one of the people Gilles and Stéphanie spoke to lived or worked in the building, and with only one exception, none of them had heard anything.

Gilles and Stéphanie discovered that the building did not have CCTV, but learned that one of the cleaning women had come in with someone who had not used a key fob to open the lobby door. This person rode up in the elevator with the woman but she could not give much of a description other than that the person was a man, wearing a beige raincoat or jacket, and that he was taller than her. Because the woman was five feet tall, if that, the description was not all that helpful.

The other witnesses were equally unhelpful. The woman who lived in the condo next to Michaela's claimed to have heard a loud thud from Michaela's unit early in the morning. The woman did not think much about the sound because, as she put it, "It sounded like something falling, maybe a heavy box or something. Nothing suspicious in that. It happens."

Just as Gilles finished talking to the witness, Dr. Charles Lapointe, the medical examiner, arrived. Dr. Lapointe was a tall slim man who always dressed in a three-piece suit and a bow tie. He had an old-fashioned courtly manner that made him a pleasure to work with. In addition to his job as a medical examiner he taught in the medical faculty at the Université de Montréal. He had worked with Gilles on one or two previous cases. "Un autre, Gilles?"

"Oui, docteur. Deux en fait," Gilles replied. The two men shook hands and Gilles was about to introduce him to his partner when Dr. Lapointe greeted her with a warm smile and a handshake.

"How nice to see you again, Detective Giroux," he said. "I hope you are well. And the children, how are they?"

Stéphanie Giroux had a daughter and a son, both in university, one of whom was taking a course Dr. Lapointe gave on medico-legal issues in the law faculty. "Both well," she told the doctor. "Working hard at their studies."

"Excellent," Dr. Lapointe said. "Now down to business. What have we got here?"

Gilles indicated the body on the floor of the entryway and said, "The deceased is Michaela Bédard. She..."

"Wait a minute," Dr. Lapointe interrupted. "How did you come to identify the body so quickly? You haven't moved it, have you?"

"No, of course not," Gilles said. "She was a person of interest in a prior investigation."

"Really?" asked Dr. Lapointe, his curiosity distracting him from the case at hand.

"Oui, she killed the person at the Gursky. It turned out that it was a case of self-defence."

"Right. You solved that one and now she herself is the victim," Dr. Lapointe said. He crouched next to the corpse and gave it as much of an examination as he could without touching the body or in any way disturbing it. He got to his feet and told the two cops, "I don't see any signs of violence. And there's no weapon. Curious. It looks like she dropped dead, literally." Dr. Lapointe gave a short laugh at his joke. "We'll know more after an autopsy. Is there anything else you can tell me about the vic?"

"Only that she suffered from asthma and that she was a helluva fighter," Gilles reported.

"Asthma can be fatal. Not often, but it happens. Make certain that the forensics people look for her inhaler. It may be important," Dr. Lapointe said. "I'll let you know what I uncover once I get her on the table. And there's another one?"

"Please come with me," Gilles said and led Dr. Lapointe to the study. Gilles stood to the left of the doorway giving Dr. Lapointe an unobstructed view of the room. He crouched down to examine the body, which lay face-down on the floor in a pool of blood with a brass table lamp embedded in the skull.

"Mon dieu," Dr. Lapointe said softly. "I'm not easily shocked, but that is a helluva way to die." He looked around the room and added, "A crime of opportunity. Clearly the murderer did not bring the lamp."

There was nothing to indicate a struggle had taken place. The trio standing at the door to the study examined the room without entering it, taking in the built-in bookshelves full of books, the desk on the far wall next to a window that looked out onto the mountain, and a comfortable leather chair and footstool. There was an end table next to the chair with a dust-free circle where the table lamp had sat.

Gilles grunted his agreement with the obvious. He crouched down to examine the footprint in the blood, which he had not noticed previously. He took a photo of it with his cellphone. The impression did not have the characteristics of trainers. There did not seem to be an ergonomic point to the pattern on the shoe. Thin lines angled upwards on the sole and angled downward on the heel. It also appeared that the sole of the shoe was flat; there was no space between it and the heel.

"Do you know anything about the victim?" Dr. Lapointe asked.

"Yes. Her name is Julia Sutton. She's from New York. She has a connection of some kind to the Gursky vic, Connors. I knew she was in Montreal and I wanted to talk to her. I only have a very vague notion about her connection to Bédard. Something to do with a business deal she was working on."

"Good luck with that," Lapointe said. "There's no mystery as to the cause of death, though. I can tell you that the murderer is covered in blood."

Gilles had come to the same conclusion and he decided that a forensic examination of the condo alone was not sufficient. He looked around to see if he could spot the leader of the forensics team. Gilles went in search of him and found him in Michaela's bedroom. Without entering the room, Gilles signalled with a cough to the cop in charge, who looked up. "After you've finished with the apartment, thoroughly examine the corridor of the building, the elevator, stairwell, everything. The perp was covered with the vic's blood and there will likely be a trail in the building and even on the sidewalk outside. There are bloody footprints in the condo." While they talked, Gilles and the forensics tech made their way to the study. Gilles pointed to the footprints that led from the bloody victim to the door of the apartment.

"D'accord," the forensics cop agreed.

Gilles and the forensics cop followed the prints to the corridor and discovered that they had been obscured by the many people who had walked over them before the cops arrived.

The forensics cop used his walkie-talkie to tell one of his team to check the sidewalk for blood and to secure any evidence she found as quickly as possible.

Gilles returned to the study, where Stéphanie and Dr. Lapointe were chatting at the doorway. "There's not much more I can do here. As I told you, I'll know more when I get the bodies on the table." Dr. Lapointe turned and walked to the living room with Gilles and Stéphanie close behind him. "I'll tell the guys from the morgue that there are two bodies for delivery. They'll call for another wagon. Let them know when they can pick them up." Dr. Lapointe said his goodbyes to Gilles and Stéphanie and left.

"There's not much we can do until the forensics team is done," Gilles said. He called to the cop working in the far corner of the living room and asked if he was finished. When the cop said yes, Gilles said, "Great. We can wait here." He walked over to a sofa that had the same view as the study. He and Stéphanie made themselves comfortable. The room they were in was large, with a sofa and three easy chairs arranged in a large circle around a coffee table. There was a shelving unit on the back wall which contained large books arranged neatly by size, mostly on art and architecture. There was a large painting on the wall opposite and smaller paintings arranged in orderly rows, three across and three down, on the wall opposite the sofa where Gilles and Stéphanie were sitting.

"What do you think happened?" Stéphanie asked.

"It's too soon to know the sequence of events, but for me it's obvious that a third person was involved. Was he or she here when Bédard got home? Who knows? I surmise that Sutton was here to get whatever Connors was after. To finish his mission. How did she get in? Did she break in while Bédard was out? The blood is dry. That means that the murders took place last night. Did Bédard find and kill her and then die? Or did Sutton get in this morning? That tells me that they were both killed by the same person. A person unknown."

"Or did she come with the person who killed her?" Stéphanie added. "There are lots of unknowns."

"I'm going to get in touch with the cop I met in New York and see what he can dig up on Sutton."

Gilles and Stéphanie chatted for another thirty minutes while the forensics team finished up their work. When they were done with the apartment they moved to the common areas of the building, working first in the elevator and the corridors so that the people from the morgue could remove the bodies.

Gilles and Stéphanie watched the first crew from the morgue remove Mickie Bédard's body and followed the second crew into the study where the second body lay. The morgue men lifted the body onto a stretcher. Once the bodies had been removed, Gilles and Stéphanie slipped on fresh latex gloves and conducted a secondary search. "Are we looking for anything special?" Stéphanie asked.

"Anything relating to her business," Gilles said. "Until I find out otherwise, I'm assuming the obvious, that there is a connection between the first attempt on Bédard's life, her death, and the death of Julia Sutton."

After an hour Gilles and Stéphanie had bagged Mickie's laptop along with a collection of notebooks and other miscellaneous items that would give them a sense of Michaela Bédard's life.

The two cops gathered up their evidence bags and left the apartment, making certain the door was locked when they left. They taped a police notice to the door advising people not to enter, and sealed the scene with police tape on the door frame and door.

Once on the sidewalk in front of the building, Gilles called to the leader of the forensics team. The leader left his crew to the job of loading their van and joined Gilles and Stéphanie. "Before you ask," Sergeant Paul Lessard said, "there's nothing I can tell you until we get back to the lab and run our tests." Lessard was used to investigators expecting to get a report at the scene of the crime, even though they knew this was impossible.

Gilles smiled and responded, "Oui, oui, je sais, Paul. I have a question about the murder weapon, the lamp."

Lessard sighed and asked, "What is it you want to know?"

"Two things," Gilles replied. "How heavy is it, and would it take much effort to use the thing as a weapon? Would it take any special strength?"

"That's three things," Lessard said, "but I get your point. Unofficially, I would guess the thing weighed about ten pounds, maybe a little more. I'll know for certain when we weigh it. And no, it wouldn't take much in the way of strength to wield it. Anyone who could lift it over their heads could bring it down on the victim with enough force to kill her. Once that brass toe penetrated the skull, I would say that death was instantaneous. Docteur Charles will give you complete details, I'm sure."

"Yeah, that's pretty much what he said. I just wanted to know if we were looking for a man, or could a woman have done the deed?"

Lessard smiled. "Murder is not gender-specific. I would guess that the perp had to be the same height or taller than the victim in order to land the blow they did."

"Well, that narrows the search down to most of the population of Montreal, I guess."

One of the forensics crew called out to Lessard to say that the van was loaded and they were ready to leave. As Sergeant Lessard walked away he looked over his shoulder at Gilles and Stéphanie and added, "Don't forget the suburbs." He got into the van on the passenger's side and it drove off.

Gilles and Stéphanie walked to their car and headed back to the division office. On their way, Stéphanie, who was driving, asked, "Other than the obvious, do you have anything to suggest?"

"Oui. I'm going to talk to everyone I've already talked to and see if I can piece together Michaela's last day or day and a half. And check alibis while I'm at it. As I said I'm also going to put a call in to the cop I met in New York to see if he can dig up any information on Julia."

CHAPTER 22:

Wednesday –
Gilles Reports and Chris Palmer
Investigates

Once back at the office Gilles and Stéphanie made their report to Captain Lacroix. "I knew there was more to this," Gilles said. Captain Lacroix frowned at him. He didn't like so much as a hint of insubordination, especially when he was in the wrong. Gilles wanted to say more but, with effort, held his tongue. He shifted the emphasis of his report to make special mention of the fact that he was about to contact Chris Palmer, the cop he met in New York, to ask him to investigate Julia Sutton.

"It may mean that you'll have to talk to his commander," Gilles pointed out to his captain.

"That won't be a problem," Captain Lacroix said, "but don't think you're going to get another trip to New York out of this."

"Never crossed my mind," Gilles said. He had thought that just such a thing might be necessary.

Stéphanie had some work to finish on a case that was coming to trial, so she left Gilles to call New York and to arrange to see the people in Montreal who knew Michaela Bédard.

It took several tries to reach Chris Palmer but Gilles eventually got him on his cellphone. After a few pleasantries during which Palmer expressed no surprise at hearing from Gilles, he asked, "Did you find the woman, Julia Sutton?"

"That's why I'm calling," Gilles said. "We did indeed find her. She's been murdered."

Chris heard perfectly what Gilles had said, but his reaction was automatic: "She's been what? Murdered?"

Gilles explained that the double murder had been discovered that morning. "I'm guessing that Sutton killed Bédard for some reason and someone killed Sutton, again motive is not clear. Revenge for the killing of Bédard, maybe? Doesn't make sense, not so far at any rate."

"So, what can I do to help?" Palmer asked.

"As much as you can find out about Julia Sutton. And her next of kin will have to be notified. Sooner or later we'll want to ship the body back to the States."

"Got it," Chris responded. "I'll call you as soon as I have some information for you."

Chris checked the time and set about getting information on Julia Sutton. He reviewed his notes from when he'd questioned her, and discovered that she claimed to live on George Street, a short drive from the precinct. Chris decided to get the worst part of his job over with first—notifying next of kin of a death. He knew that even the most senior members of the department hated this task.

Chris pulled up in front of the house, a semi-detached with a small neat lawn barely the size of a double mattress, at 704 George Street. He climbed the three steps to the uncluttered porch and rang the doorbell. He could hear barking from within. While he waited for someone to answer the door, he compared the porch of this house to the others on the block. The others, the ones he could see at any rate, all had toys or other discarded household items on them. This one was bare, not even a chair on it. A short woman with dyed yellow hair showing grey at the roots, wearing a cardigan over a grey T-shirt, answered the door. The woman was braless and wore glasses in a style that had been popular in the nineteen-fifties. She held a cigarette in her left hand and kept her right hand on the inner door. She spoke to Chris through the aluminum screen door. "What?" she asked in a smoker's voice, phlegm gurgling in her throat.

The dog, a German shepherd, barked and lunged at the screen door. The woman removed her hand from the door and held the dog's collar. Chris recognized Duke and did not back away. "Enough, Duke," the woman said.

Chris showed the woman his badge and replied, "My name is Detective Chris Palmer and I understand that Julia Sutton lives here."

"Yeah, what of it?" the woman asked.

Before Chris could begin the standard cop speech, the one that started with, "I'm afraid I have some bad news, is there somewhere we can talk privately..." he heard a man's voice ask, "Who is it, Francie?" The woman turned and spoke to a man Chris could see slowly emerging out of the darkness of a corridor of the house. "It's a cop. He says it's about Julia."

The man, not much taller than his wife, was wearing a faded maroon cardigan over a stained white shirt. Brown trousers and well-worn slippers completed the outfit. He, too, had a cigarette in his hand. "Julia?" he spoke to Chris. "She's not here." He turned to his wife and said, "Shut the door, Francie, it's cold." He was about to turn and walk back to whichever room he'd come from when Chris pulled the screen door open and put his foot on the threshold.

"I have to talk to you. We can do it here so your neighbours can see what's going on or we can talk inside. Your choice," he said forcefully. Duke sniffed at Chris and he scratched the dog between his ears. Chris nodded his head in the direction of the houses across the street so Francie and her husband could see the curtains in the houses parting.

The husband made an unintelligible sound and walked down the hall. Francie took this as acquiescence and stood aside to let Chris in. She continued to hold the dog's collar. She closed the door and Chris followed her down the hall. Chris found himself in a small, over-furnished living room containing a sofa, three chairs, a coffee table and a cabinet that held some glassware and tchotchkes. The man eased himself into one of the chairs and Francie sat on the sofa. "Have a seat," she said to Chris. He took one of the chairs and turned it so he could see both Francie and her husband. "As I said, I'm a detective. My name is Chris Palmer." He pulled a notepad and pen from an inner pocket of his sports coat and asked, "May I have your names?"

"I'm Francie. Frances. And that's my husband, Melvin. Hauser."

"What's your relation to Ms. Sutton?"

"There is none," Francie said. "She rents a room from us."

"What about Julia?" Melvin Hauser asked. He reached toward the ashtray on the coffee table and tapped some ash from his cigarette into it.

Francie had let go of Duke and he wandered over to Chris for another sniff. Chris patted the dog and again scratched him between the ears. The dog placed its head in Chris's lap and Chris continued to scratch him while he spoke with the Hausers.

"I'm afraid I have some bad news," Chris said. "Julia was in Montreal and she's come to some harm. She was murdered. I'm very sorry for your loss." Chris paused to allow the bad news to sink in before he continued. Francie and Melvin

Hauser stared at him but said nothing and did not appear to Chris to be much affected. For a moment or two no one said anything.

Chris cleared his throat and was about to speak again when Melvin Hauser said, "It's not our loss."

"What? What do you mean?" Chris asked. Perhaps the Hausers didn't fully grasp what they had been told. It was not unusual for people hearing very bad news to be slow to process it.

"I told you," Francie explained, as if talking to someone with limited comprehension abilities, "Julia is—was—not kin. Not related to us. But we're sorry about it, I'm sure."

"She did live here, though?" Chris said.

"Yes, as Francie said, she rented a room from us," Melvin said.

"I see," Chris said, "she lived here."

"I wouldn't say that," Francie told him.

Trying not to show his exasperation, he asked, "Then what would you say? You rented her a room but she didn't live in it?"

Francie sighed. "Julia grew up down the street. When her parents passed away, she sold the house but wanted an address in the neighbourhood for mail and that kind of thing, and a place to leave some stuff, personal things from when she lived in the neighbourhood. I doubt that we saw her more than once a month. And she never slept here. We had a room and she paid us a hundred dollars a week. End of story."

"Is this her dog?" Chris asked.

"No, ours." Melvin said. "But she would take him out with her if she was around. He liked her. He likes you too." Chris didn't explain that he had met Duke recently in completely different circumstances.

"I see," Chris said. "I'd like to see the room, if I may?"

"Don't you need a warrant or something to poke around in people's houses?" Melvin asked.

"I don't want to poke around in your house. I just want to see her room. She's been the victim of a crime, not a suspect," Chris explained. He did not add, "at the moment" because he wasn't sure what Julia had been up to. For all he knew she was murdered while committing a crime of some sort in Montreal. "But I can get a warrant if you insist. I'll have a patrol car park in front of your house to be certain that you don't remove anything that might have belonged to Julia."

Melvin Hauser made the same unintelligible sound he had made when talking to Chris at the door and got out of his chair. He stubbed his cigarette out in the ashtray and Francie did the same and then she got to her feet. Chris wasn't certain whether he was about to be shown the door or Julia's room, and he too got to his feet. Melvin led the way to a flight of stairs opposite the front door and slowly led Chris up, with Francie bringing up the rear. Duke followed.

On the landing at the top of the stairs, Melvin opened a door to the right, stood back and said, "Help yourself." Francie again held Duke by the collar.

Chris entered Julia's room. The Hausers stood in the doorway watching him. The room was furnished with a bed and chair along with a dresser. The walls were green and looked like they hadn't been painted at any time in this century. The bed was made, with a coverlet decorated with flowers. The windows were covered with room-darkening curtains that had been white at one time. There was a closet to the right of the dresser and Chris opened it. There was some clothing on hangers but Chris doubted that any of it belonged to Julia.

He closed the door and turned his attention to the dresser. He opened the top drawer and found a bunch of mail. He tapped it into a pile and in so doing he felt a key. He fussed

136

with the envelopes so he could get a look at the key without the Hausers seeing what he was doing. The key was attached to a tag for a storage locker at the UR Storage on Roosevelt Avenue. Chris knew the location. It was near College Point Boulevard just in from the Flushing Creek. He tapped the mail into a neat pile with the key at the bottom of it. He showed the envelopes to the Hausers, the key covered by his hand. "I'll take these envelopes if you don't mind. They're all addressed to Julia Sutton. I can give you a receipt for them if you like."

"Not interested," Melvin stated.

Chris left the room and walked down the stairs. When he got to the living room, he remained standing and said, "For the moment, I only have one more question: How did Julia pay for the room? Cash or cheque?" Duke looked from person to person to person.

"Neither," Francie said. "Direct deposit to our bank. I suppose that will stop now."

"I would think," Chris said. "I'll be on my way now. If I have any more questions, I'll give you a call or drop by. Please give me your phone number." Francie Hauser complied with his request and, along with Duke, accompanied Chris to the front door. Melvin returned to his chair. At the door, just before leaving, Chris turned to Francie and said, "Again, I'm sorry for your loss." Chris gave Duke a farewell pat.

"Yeah, I guess," Francie said and closed the door.

Chris got into his car, tossed the envelopes on the passenger seat, slipped the key to the storage locker into his shirt pocket and headed to the UR Storage location. While he drove, he called Gilles to bring him up to date.

Gilles decided that he would re-interview Denis Stevens first and then the three owners of DiplomRMY. He drove to the building on Crescent Street that housed Stevens, Bédard. He rang the bell, identified himself, and was admitted. Gilles wondered why all this security was necessary as the firm did not keep any money on the premises. The receptionist recognized Gilles from his previous visit and smiled a welcome that made showing his badge unnecessary. Before Gilles could explain the reason for his visit, the receptionist said, "I'm sorry, Mickie is not in. It's odd though, she's not usually this late. Not without calling at any rate."

"I'm afraid that's why I'm here," Gilles said. "Is Monsieur Stevens in?"

The colour drained from the receptionist's face and Gilles noticed a slight tremor in her hand as she tapped Denis Stevens's phone extension into her console. "The policeman is here and wants to see you. He has some news about Mickie." She listened to Denis Stevens for a moment and turned to Gilles and said, "You can go up." The receptionist slid out from behind the reception counter and led Gilles up the stairs to Denis Stevens's office. She knocked once, opened the door, and stood aside to allow Gilles to enter the office. As Gilles was about to cross the threshold, she put a hand on his forearm and asked, "May I join you? If it's about Mickie, I mean."

Gilles shrugged and answered, "Yes, of course."

Gilles and the receptionist walked into the office. Gilles sat down in one of the visitors' chairs without being invited. The receptionist stood.

Denis Stevens looked up from what he was doing and said, "What about Mickie? She's not in yet."

"I'm afraid the news is bad." He turned to the receptionist and said, "Please sit down." He turned his attention back to

Denis Stevens and continued, "Miss Bédard is dead. We're treating her death as homicide."

"No," the receptionist cried out, covered her face with both her hands and began to cry. Denis Stevens had rocked back in his chair when Gilles began to speak and his chair snapped forward. Denis got to his feet and placed both hands on his desk. He gasped for breath and tried to speak, but no words came out. He went white and stared helplessly at Gilles for some seconds as he caught his breath. "It's not possible. What happened?" he sputtered. "The man who was trying to attack her was dead. I don't understand." He flopped into his chair. He reached for a box of Kleenex and blew his nose loudly. He passed the box to the receptionist who dabbed at the corners of her eyes and also blew her nose.

Gilles gave the two a moment to regain some of their composure and told them about the discovery of Mickie's body and the second victim earlier that day. "Are—are you," Denis stammered, "are you saying that someone again tried to kill Mickie, she killed that person and then died?"

"That's not what we think at the moment," Gilles said. "We think a woman—we know who she is but that remains confidential for the moment—murdered Mickie somehow and someone else killed her. Or someone murdered Mickie and then killed the second person who happened on the scene. We're investigating."

Denis Stevens did not look well. The receptionist, although she was upset herself, went to him and put a sympathetic hand on his shoulder. "Are you okay?" she asked. "Should I call somebody? Would you like to go to the hospital?" She looked at Gilles. "He has heart problems. They've been worse since his wife died. And now this."

Denis covered the receptionist's hand with his own. "Thank you, you're very kind, but no, it's just the shock. I'll be fine." He took a couple of deep breaths but did not look any better.

"I'm very sorry for your loss," Gilles told him, "and I know you would rather I left you alone, but I would like to ask you a couple of questions if you don't mind."

The receptionist returned to the chair she had previously occupied. Denis Stevens sighed and replied, "I do mind, but I don't suppose I have a choice. Let's get it over with."

Gilles pulled out his notepad, flipped it open to a fresh page, and said, "I know I've asked this before, but can you think of any reason why anyone connected with DiplomRMY would want to harm Mickie? Please think about my question very carefully. It's more important now than the last time I asked."

Gilles sat silently and waited for Denis Stevens to say something. After a moment he responded, "It's like I told you before, we were taking on a big project but not a dangerous one, for God's sake. I can't think of a reason why anyone would want to harm Mickie...or any of us, for that matter."

Gilles made note of Denis Stevens's opinion. "Surely there were other bankers who wanted to handle the IPO," Gilles prompted.

"I'm sure there were," Denis Stevens replied. "But bankers are not murderers."

Gilles saw that this was, for the moment anyway, a fruitless line of inquiry. He tried a different tack. "How about a personal problem Miss Bédard was having? Is there anything that comes to mind? Someone who might want to harm her?" He turned his attention from Denis Stevens to the receptionist. He knew from experience that women talked to each other about relationship issues and the receptionist might know something that her boss did not.

"Oh," she replied when she realized that Gilles had directed the question to her as well as to Denis Stevens. "No, no one. I think she was seeing someone but she was a very private person and she kept her personal life out of the office."

"Nothing I can think of," Denis Stevens replied. "I'm sure she would have told me if she was having trouble like that. We were very close. More like father and daughter than business partners."

"Okay." Gilles closed his notepad and tapped it with his pen. "There's something else I'd like to know. Have either of you ever been to her home?"

Denis Stevens and the receptionist said "Yes," almost in unison.

The receptionist continued, "We had an office Christmas party there last year. Because of that, yes. But that's it."

"I've been there many times," Denis Stevens explained. "How can that possibly be important?"

Gilles chose to ignore the question and said, "We'll probably want to take a set of fingerprints from you to eliminate them from the ones we find in Mickie's apartment. And while we're on the subject: did either of you have a key to her apartment or know the code?"

"No," the receptionist said.

"Of course not," Denis replied.

Gilles got to his feet. "That's it for now. But if I need any more information I'll drop by again."

Denis Stevens got to his feet and asked, "There is one more thing. When will they release the body? I'd like to arrange for a funeral for Mickie."

Gilles gave him the contact information and suggested that the funeral home Denis Stevens chose would be the best people to get in touch with the authorities.

The receptionist accompanied Gilles out of Denis Stevens's office and downstairs to the front door. As Gilles was walking down the front steps his phone rang. It was

Chris Palmer from New York, who brought him up to date on his visit with the Hausers and told him that he was on his way to Julia Sutton's storage locker.

CHAPTER 23

Wednesday –
Gilles Has Coffee with His Daughter

Gilles made a few notes based on Chris Palmer's information and was about to call François Royer and then Daniel Yablon to arrange to question them further about their knowledge of Michaela Bédard and any associates or competitors they might know. Before he could make a call, his phone rang. It was his daughter Émilie. "Bonjour, Lapin," he answered. "Quoi de neuf?"

"Pas beaucoup. Je dois te parler," she said. "It's important. Can we meet for coffee, like, now?"

Gilles sighed inwardly and agreed to meet his daughter in a café on St. Denis, not far from where she attended CEGEP. The murder investigation would have to wait until he solved whatever problem his daughter was about to lay at his feet.

Gilles and his ex-wife Yvonne did their best to keep the channels of communication open with their daughter. In spite of the divorce, or perhaps because of it, Émilie found that she could talk to her father about the things that bothered her, things that she found difficult to discuss with her mother. As much as Émilie loved her mother, she found her to be more judgemental than her father.

Émilie had some rough and rebellious years in high school but in her final year she worked hard and graduated with marks good enough to get into the Theatre Arts program at the CEGEP du Vieux Montréal, which was located near rue St-Denis, the hip epicentre of Montreal.

Gilles knew his daughter tended to dramatize things and hoped the current crisis could be quickly resolved with some fatherly listening and advice. His commitment to his daughter always came first for Gilles, but he could only take so much time away from a murder investigation.

He found Émilie at a table at the rear of the café, reading a novel, a large cappuccino in front of her. Gilles ordered and joined his daughter. "What's the problem, Lapin? How can I help?"

Émilie was a little surprised by her father's unexpected impatience. She took a second to gather her thoughts and decided to meet his bluntness with bluntness of her own. "I want to live with you, Pa. You live closer to school than Mum."

Gilles stared at his daughter. "Have you spoken about this to your mother?"

"Endlessly. She's totally opposed to the idea. She thinks I'll end up une paresseuse or worse."

"What could be worse?" Gilles asked with a smile.

"Pa," Émilie exclaimed. "Don't change the subject. Can I move in with you? You have the space."

This was true. Gilles's condo had two bedrooms.

"Écoute, Lapin, I'll have to talk to your mother. You know I can't make a unilateral decision. But let's assume for the moment that she agrees. I don't want you to think that you're escaping rules. You have to put your school work first, no screwing around there. You'll need good marks to get into university. Also, there will be the normal rules..."

"Pa," Émilie interrupted, dragging out the "ah" sound.

"...within reason," Gilles continued.

"Yeah," Émilie replied, showing a flash of anger. "You expect me to be a grind like your precious Pamela."

"No, I expect you to work towards your own goals. You've worked hard for the last couple of years and I expect that to continue. Get it?"

"Oui, Pa, I get it."

"Then we understand one another. But there's more," Gilles said. Émilie gave Gilles the same kind of long-suffering look that he used to give his dad when he got the speech. Gilles was able to supress his laughter but not his smile. "You have to take responsibility for your life, and if you don't, there will be consequences. There are some rules you have to follow. Non-negotiable. I work long hours and odd hours. Sometimes I'm away from home until quite late. I have to know that you are at home and safe. So we have to keep in touch by telephone and you have to be at home every night."

"You mean, I'll have a curfew?" Émilie asked.

"Not as such, no. As I said, you have to be responsible for your life. You can't do well in school if you don't keep up with your assignments and get a good night's sleep. If I see you are out late on school nights there will be a discussion." Gilles paused to emphasize his point. "Also, no parties or boys over when I'm not home."

"And you can bet there won't be any when you are at home," Émilie added.

"Glad to hear it," Gilles said. "I think you get the idea as to what I expect. Two more things. I'll make some alterations to my lifestyle in order to be home as much as possible, but there will be nights when I stay at Annie's. The rules apply whether I'm home or not. And finally, you absolutely have to keep in touch with your mother. She loves you as much as I do and I don't want her to think, to even suspect, that your moving is a rejection of her."

"Well, in a way, it is a rejection of the way she hovers over me, interferes in everything I do, has a million questions about things that are none of her business," Émilie explained.

"Your mother and I want the same thing for you. We may differ a little in our approach but that's it. I'll talk to her about the move and I expect you to do the same...and I expect you to visit her at least once a week. A real visit, not a flyby. And frequent phone calls. As I said, non-negotiable," Gilles said.

"I get it," she said, "Work hard and see Maman."

"One more thing," Gilles said. "There will be times when Annie sleeps over at my—well, our—place. I expect you to behave nicely when she's there. D'accord?"

"Absolument. I like Annie. She's great."

Gilles got to his feet and said, "Now give your dad a hug. I have to call your mother and get back to work." Émilie gave her father a hug, holding him tight. He held his daughter just as tightly, her head resting against his cheek. When they broke the hug Émilie brushed her hair out of her eyes and noticed a wet spot where her head had come into contact with her father's cheek. "So, you have to call Maman and catch a murderer, right?" she said.

"Oui, Lapin. And guess which one I would rather do," Gilles said with a smile.

Gilles called his ex-wife as he walked to his car. Yvonne made a few remarks about Gilles's tendency to spoil their daughter but she accepted Émilie's decision and made a surprising confession. "You know, Gilles, this kind of works out for me. I'm...well, I'm seeing someone and this means that we can spend more time together and even go away from time to time." Yvonne ended her conversation with a nervous laugh.

"Anyone I know?" Gilles teased.

"Not a cop, that's for sure," Yvonne replied coolly. "But yes, Michel Genest."

"Our—I mean, your neighbour? The dentist?"

"Exactly. He's recently divorced, so yes, him."

"I'm happy for you, Yvonne," Gilles said, "And for Michel as well." That ended the conversation with his ex-wife. Now it was time to get back to work and solve a double homicide.

CHAPTER 24

Wednesday –
Chris Palmer Investigates

Chris pulled into the parking lot of the UR Storage. The facility was massive, the size of two airplane hangars. Chris had to drive around for almost ten minutes before he found the entrance, which was hidden off to the side of the building. He went in and found his way to a service counter. A young man was sitting on a high stool leaning against the counter, his back to anyone who might happen in. He was wearing a headset and playing a video game on his cellphone. The volume was turned up so loud that Chris could hear the sounds of fake gunfire coming from the game. Chris watched the screen of the cellphone for a moment or two, the action involving a couple of cops shooting at a small group of street thugs—black, of course.

Chris rapped on the counter a couple of times and took an unprofessional pleasure in seeing the kid jump so suddenly that he toppled off his perch and had to grab the counter to prevent himself from falling to the floor. The kid, tall, very thin, and with a bad case of acne, must have held some residual fear from his game because his eyes were wide when he righted himself and looked at Chris.

"Fuck, man, you scared the shit out of me," he said. The kid had an Eastern-European accent so it sounded more like "Fook, man, you scart da shit oudda me."

Chris flashed his badge at the kid and told him that he wanted to see a locker. He gave the number of Julia's storage unit.

"Not without a warrant," the kid said.

"What's your name?" Chris asked.

"Ilya," the kid responded.

"Listen to me, Ilya. I'm not asking you to open the unit. I have a key and permission to look at the contents. I just want you to tell me where it is."

Ilya asked for the unit number again and consulted a map of the building, showing Chris where Julia's unit was in relationship to the office. Chris was surprised to see that it was one of the large units on the ground floor with a gate that opened onto the parking lot.

Chris left the office, letting the door slam behind him.

He drove to Julia's locker, parked in front, opened the heavy-duty padlock that kept the gate down, and pushed the garage-type door up. The space was big enough for a car and was furnished like an office. There were a desk and chair, metal shelving, and two filing cabinets. Chris opened file drawers at random and saw that each folder had a four-digit number plus two digits to the right of a decimal point. The numbering looked a little like the old Dewey Decimal system that libraries used to use. Chris flipped through a couple of files and saw that they contained documents from a bank, the Richman, Taylor Investment Bank. Chris replaced the folders and looked around the office for something that would help him make sense of the numbering system.

There was a large Rolodex on the desk and Chris made himself comfortable and flipped through the cards. Each card had a few words and then a number which must have corresponded to a file number. Chris wondered why Julia had gone to the trouble of creating a numeric file system. Anyone

149

who got into the storage unit would find the cards that gave the key to the system, after all.

Chris rolled the Rolodex to the M section and flipped through the cards looking for Montreal. He found a three-word heading, "Mtl. Stevens, Bédard," and a number. He went back to the file cabinet and found the file, and it, like the others he examined, contained documents from the Richman, Taylor Investment Bank. Chris had never heard of the bank and noticed that it was located at 14 Wall Street, suite 900. From the address he imagined it to be one of the banks that dealt with the one percent.

He kept the file with him and went back to the desk, called his boss and reported what he had found. The captain told Chris to "seal the fucking thing" and asked why Chris was "so fucking determined to create bullshit work?"

"Gotcha, Cap," Chris replied and ended the call before the captain could order him back to the precinct for a more complete report. Chris pulled the garage door closed, relocked it with the padlock and placed a NYPD sticker over the key slot, stating that the locker was sealed and could only be opened by the police. He got into his car and headed home. As he drove, he gave Gilles Bellechasse another call and brought him up to date on his discovery.

"Intéressant," Gilles commented. "We knew there was a connection between her and Bédard. Now we'll have to figure out the nature of the connection."

"More later, dude. I'm going to pay the bankers a visit tomorrow morning," Chris said and ended the call.

Julia Sutton was turning out to be a very interesting murder victim.

CHAPTER 25

Wednesday –
Gilles Investigates DiplomRMY

Gilles was about to call François and arrange to meet him and Éloi but decided against it. He decided to just show up at their office and see if a surprise visit had any effect on the two men. He left the café, got into his car and drove north on St. Denis to Avenue des Pins and then north on Saint Laurent and west to the DiplomRMY offices.

Gilles walked into the DiplomRMY offices and approached the same young woman, Beth, as on his previous visit. He asked to see François and Éloi. Beth did not get up but turned to the young man sitting next to her and told him to call François and tell him that the cop was back. That done she turned back to her computer and ignored Gilles.

Gilles pretended to check something important on his cellphone while he waited for François to come and meet him. It only took a minute for François to appear and he invited Gilles back to the meeting room where they had last talked. Éloi was there waiting for them.

Gilles was about to inform François and Éloi of the death of their friend, but the solemn looks on their faces told Gilles that the young men were aware of the tragedy. "I'm very sorry for your loss. I need your help to find the person or people who did this, this terrible thing," Gilles said.

François inhaled and exhaled a couple of times and replied, "Anything I can do to help. You can count on me."

"Thank you," Gilles said.

Gilles told Éloi and François that he wanted to question each of them separately. François and Éloi looked at one another and shrugged, but neither moved to leave the room. Gilles sighed and said, "Alphabetical. I'll start with Éloi."

François picked up the coffee he'd been nursing and left the room. Gilles placed his pad, open to a fresh page, and his pen in front of him.

"Comment puis-je vous aider?" Éloi asked.

"How did you learn of the tragic death of Mickie Bédard?"

"Her partner, Denis Stevens, called," Éloi responded. "It's awful. Neither of us can wrap our minds around it. François is really broken up."

"Yes, I can see that." Gilles took a sip of his coffee and continued, "What was their relationship? Was it just business? Or was it something more?"

Éloi was silent for a moment or two. He drank some coffee and then said, "I think I'll let François answer that question."

"Fair enough, but I understand from what you haven't said that the relationship was more than just business…or friendship."

Éloi shrugged but said nothing.

"Okay," Gilles continued, "when was the last time you saw Mickie?"

Éloi relaxed into his chair and thought for a moment. "I guess it would be a couple of weeks ago. She met with the three of us to let us know how things were proceeding with the IPO."

"How were things going? Did she report any problems?"

"No, everything seemed fine. Danny asked most of the questions. François and I deferred to him on this stuff."

"I'll talk to Daniel," Gilles said. "Did she say anything about another bank trying to muscle in on the project? Does the name Julia Sutton mean anything to you?

"No, and never heard of her."

"To be clear, Mickie never mentioned her or the Richman, Taylor Investment Bank?"

Éloi paused and thought for a moment before continuing, "Yeah, I think she asked if anyone from that bank had contacted us. The name sounds familiar."

"Well," Gilles prompted, "had you been contacted by the Richman, Taylor Investment Bank?"

"Me, no. And I think I can say the same for François. I'm not certain about Danny. You'll have to ask him."

Gilles drank some coffee and asked, "Have you ever been to Mickie's apartment?"

"Yes, of course. While we were in the early stages of putting together the deal we would meet at her place."

"Did you ever have reason to learn the passcode to the door to her condo?"

"Never needed it. Either we arrived with her or she was home and let us in."

"That's not quite what I asked," Gilles leaned forward and looked straight into Éloi's eyes. "Did you know the passcode? At those times when you all arrived together did you happen to notice the numbers that she punched into the keypad? That's the kind of thing a coder would notice, non?"

Éloi stared back at Gilles and responded, "Oui et non. It is something I would notice. But that does not mean I would retain the information. I'd be more interested in the nature of the numbers, the relation between them or their type, not the numbers themselves."

"What does that mean?"

"Well, were the numbers all primes, were they sequential, were they Fibonacci numbers, that kind of thing."

Gilles made a few notes in his note pad. After he finished, he looked up and said, "Thank you. Those are all the questions I have for you at the moment. Please send François in when you leave."

Éloi got up, picked up his coffee cup, and left the meeting room. A moment later François came into the room and took the chair that Éloi had vacated and placed his coffee in front of him.

Gilles flipped to a fresh page in his notepad, looked at François and asked, "How well did you know Mickie Bédard?"

François sighed and said, "I take it you want more than a one-word answer."

"Exactly. I want to know where and when you met, your relationship, everything. I'd rather not have to pull the information out of you syllable by syllable."

"D'accord. It's not like I have something to hide. I think I already told you that I met Mickie when we were both in university."

"HEC, yeah," Gilles prompted.

"Anyway," François continued, "we were in the same study group. We made all our case studies and presentations together, with the rest of the group of course. But Mick and I worked better together than we did with the rest of the group and we carried more of the load than the others. The profs must have realised it because we consistently got better marks than the others in our group. We didn't mind because we enjoyed working together." François shifted in his chair and continued, "You're really asking if we had more than a study relationship and the answer is yes. Working on things could get pretty intense and, yeah, we became a couple while we were in school."

"And after?" Gilles asked.

"After we graduated, we kind of drifted apart. Once we didn't have the pressure of course work, I guess you would say, the fire went out a bit."

"The pressure of work didn't do it for you?"

"Different kind of pressure. We weren't together for long periods. As I said, she went into the family business and I did this and that until Danny and Éloi and I formed this company."

"And when you decided that you wanted to go public you contacted your old friend, Mickie, right?"

"No, that's not the way it happened. We really didn't have a strong desire to take our company public; we were having too much fun doing what we're doing. I never lost touch with Mick. We would talk every once in a while, just to keep up. And then about a year ago she suggested that we have dinner to really get caught up. So we did and things got... we rekindled our relationship. I'm not even sure why. Things just clicked." François shrugged.

"Bon, you were a couple again?" François had paused to take a gulp of coffee.

"Well, not quite. We'd have dinner or something and spend the night together and this would go on for a couple of weeks and then one or the other of us got busy or something and we wouldn't see each other for a while. It was a kind of on-and-off thing. We enjoyed being together but it wasn't the same as when we were students."

"And this continued for how long?"

"Until now, more or less."

"What does that mean?" Gilles asked.

"Well, we work very long hours here. The way our game works is that we are constantly updating it with information from the news. That makes it very current and both harder to play and more addictive. And..."

"And...you ended up in a relationship with someone here, in the same way that you and Mickie first hooked up," Gilles prodded.

"Yeah, exactly."

"And you had to make a choice?"

François looked glum when he answered, "Yeah."

"I gather from the look on your face that Mickie was not your choice?"

François exhaled and looked miserable. "Yes. I had to tell Mickie that it was over. Not the business part, just the... well...the other part."

"When did you get together to break the news?" Gilles asked. He made a few notes in his notepad.

"We had dinner yesterday."

"The night she was murdered? You might have been the last person to see her alive," Gilles pointed out. "Where and when did you last see her?"

"We had burgers at the Burgundy Lion. I wanted a loud noisy place...I'm sure you understand. After dinner we went our separate ways."

"You didn't take her home?"

"That would hardly have been appropriate under the circumstances. She called an Uber from the restaurant and I waited with her until it came. And that was the last time I saw her."

"How did she take it, the breakup?"

"I would hardly call it a breakup. But she took it well. Better than I'd anticipated. Better than me, really. It kind of made me wonder."

Gilles didn't ask what it made François wonder about. "What did you do after she drove off in the Uber?"

François toyed with his empty coffee cup and said, "Someone was waiting for me."

"I see," Gilles commented, "and that would have been...?"

"Beth."

"Beth? The one who brought the coffee the last time I was here?"

"Yeah, she doesn't do that anymore."

"Je vois. A promotion?"

"You could say," François replied sullenly. "What's that got to do with Mickie?"

It was obvious, to Gilles at least, that if Mickie had, say, threatened to retaliate in some financial way, then François would have a motive. And Gilles was there to ask François questions, not the other way around. "I assume that you had been to Mickie's apartment, correct?"

"Yeah, of course, lots of times."

"And you knew the entry code?"

"Wait a minute. If you're trying to pin a double murder on me, forget it. I had no reason to harm Mickie and I didn't know the other person. Yeah, of course I knew the code to her condo. Beyond that, I have nothing to say, at least not without a lawyer present." François got up. "You know the way out," he said.

"Oui, and I'll use it when I leave, but there's one more person I would like to speak to at the moment. Please sit down while I call for Beth to join us."

"I'll get her," François said and moved toward the door of the meeting room.

Gilles got to his feet and got to the door at the same moment as François, placing his hand on the door. "I'll not ask again. Sit down. I'll get Beth."

François flopped into a chair. Gilles opened the door and signalled to Éloi who was hovering near by and said, "Is Beth nearby? I want to talk to her."

Éloi pointed to a work area about ten metres from where they were standing. Beth must have sensed that they were talking about her because she looked up from her computer. "S'il vous plaît," Gilles said and motioned Beth to come to the meeting room. Beth pointed at herself and mouthed "Me?" Gilles nodded. Beth strolled over to where he and Éloi were standing.

"What?" she asked looking from Éloi to Gilles.

Gilles replied. "I'd like to ask you a question or two." He preceded her into the meeting room and told François he could leave.

"Sit down," Gilles invited.

"I'd rather stand," Beth replied and leaned against the table. She gazed at Gilles.

Gilles shrugged and asked, "Where were you yesterday evening?"

"Christ, you're serious, aren't you? Well, I met François at a bar in Griffintown, the William."

"What time did he arrive?"

"I don't know. Half past seven, I guess. Maybe just before eight."

Gilles made a note in his note pad and asked, "And at what time did you last see him?"

Beth smiled and answered, "Well, we came into work together this morning so I would say a couple of seconds ago when he left this room. Will that be all?"

"For the moment, yes."

Beth walked out of the meeting room and back to her workspace. Gilles noticed that she did not stop to talk to either François or Éloi, who were both standing a couple feet from the door to the meeting room.

Gilles put his notepad back in his pocket, walked out of the meeting room and headed toward the exit. As he passed François and Éloi he said, "I'll see myself out. I may want to talk to one or both of you later." He planned to see the third DiplomRMY partner first thing the next morning.

CHAPTER 26

Thursday –
Chris Palmer Meets Bankers

Chris had to put his plan to visit the offices of Richman, Taylor on hold. His boss had other work for him. He was kept busy writing reports for the other investigations he was working on. It wasn't until late afternoon that he got out of the squad room in Queens and headed to Manhattan.

Chris drove to the Wall Street address he had for the Richman, Taylor Bank. He made slow progress and had to use his siren a couple of times to get around the traffic as he drove through Brooklyn and across the Brooklyn Bridge. The building was one of the older ones in the area, originally built in 1910, with an art deco addition built twenty years later. Chris checked the lobby directory and saw that the Richman, Taylor Bank was located on the ninth floor along with a number of other businesses, everything from real estate agents to designers to psychologists to holistic health managers— whatever they were. Clearly, the Richman, Taylor Bank was not one of the major players of American capitalism.

He took the elevator to the ninth floor—and discovered that he was on a floor leased by a shared office space company, Regal Offices. The space was divided into smaller offices and rented to people who wanted a classy address without having to pay classy rates. There were two young women at the reception desk. The space behind the desk was furnished in typical bland office style. There were plenty of places to sit, either chairs or three-seat sofas, and a half a dozen cubicles, for those who couldn't afford to rent offices, Chris assumed.

He asked to see someone at the Richman, Taylor Investment Bank and one of the receptionists asked if he had an appointment. Without waiting for an answer, she consulted a large appointment book and said, "I don't see anything here."

Chris showed the young woman his badge and replied, "Well, that's a good thing, isn't it? It means that someone is available to see me."

The receptionist got to her feet and gave Chris a warm smile. "Why don't you have a seat, and I'll call and see if anyone is in at the moment." She led Chris to the waiting area and indicated the one easy chair in the room. "Can I get you something while you wait?" she asked.

Chris returned the receptionist's warm smile and said, "I'm fine."

"Yes, you are," she said and touched Chris on his forearm. She walked back to her desk and Chris could hear her on the phone explaining that a cop was looking for someone at the Richman, Taylor Investment Bank.

Chris decided not to sit down but wandered over to the window that looked south.

The receptionist returned to where Chris was standing looking out the window, admiring the new World Trade Center. Standing close to him, she said, "Mr. Taylor will be with you in a minute."

After a short wait, a middle-aged man approached Chris with his arm outstretched. "Are you looking for me?" he asked. "I'm Ben Taylor." Chris shook the offered hand and took Ben Taylor's measure. He was a couple of inches shorter than Chris with grey hair that was thin on top and curly on the sides. He was pudgy and wore glasses that had slid down his nose. The man looked like a cartoon version of an absent-minded professor. Chris flashed his badge.

"I'm Detective Chris Palmer. I'd like your help with an investigation. Is there some place we can talk?"

"Oh dear," Ben Taylor replied, "a police investigation. We can talk in my office." He pushed his glasses up to the bridge of his nose, turned and led Chris down a hallway. He stood back from an open door and invited Chris to enter. Chris found himself in an office furnished with a desk and chair, two filing cabinets, and two visitors' chairs. The desk itself was clear but a computer terminal and printer were on the desk return that ran along the wall. The office was devoid of any form of decoration, neither a plant nor a print nor a photograph.

Ben Taylor indicated one of the visitor's chairs and squeezed past the filing cabinet to occupy the desk chair. Chris sat down and crossed his legs.

Ben Taylor didn't say anything but moved his chair backward and forward in a slight rocking motion. Chris asked, "Do you know Julia Sutton?"

"Julia Sutton," Ben Taylor said as if hearing the name for the first time. "Do you have reason to think I know such a person?" he asked.

"Yeah, I do. Or I wouldn't be here."

"Well, why don't you tell me why you think I know such a person?"

"Why?" Chris asked, losing patience with the man. "Why? Because I found a large number of files with your name on them in filing cabinets of hers."

"I see," Ben Taylor said. He stopped rocking and half rose out of his chair and called out, "Murray, could you come in here for a moment?"

Chris turned to see who Ben Taylor was addressing. A moment later another middle-aged man, taller, slimmer and with more grey hair than Ben Taylor, appeared in the doorway. "This is my partner, Murray Richman," Ben Taylor explained. Chris rose from his chair to shake the man's hand. Richman sat in the chair next to Chris. "He's a policeman, investigating something, and wants to know if I know someone by the name of Julia Sutton. Do we?" Taylor asked.

Murray Richman moved his chair a few feet backward, bumping into the filing cabinet, so he could look at both Chris and his partner. "Perhaps you could offer us some context," Murray Richman suggested.

The partners were a test of Chris's patience. "Context? I'll give you a bit of context. Julia Sutton was murdered in Montreal and we, me and the police in Montreal, think she was working for you. Is that context enough for you?"

The partners were silent for a moment or two. Finally, Ben Taylor spoke. "Murdered. How awful. But what's that got to do with us?"

Chris got to his feet and said, "You know what? You guys are jerking me around. I think we should continue this down at the police station. It's in Queens. Please come with me."

Neither of the partners made a move but Ben Taylor spoke. "I don't think that will be necessary. Yes, we knew Julia. We're shocked to hear that she's been murdered."

"We are," Murray Richman agreed. "Yes, we are. This is horrible news. How did it happen?"

Chris sat back down. "We'll get to that. First, I want to know what her connection was to you. I should add that the Richman, Taylor Bank is unlike any bank I've ever seen or heard of. But we'll get to that later as well. Tell me about Julia Sutton. How did you know her?"

Without speaking the partners somehow decided that Murray Richman would act as spokesperson. "She worked on negotiations, I guess you could say."

Exasperated, Chris motioned for him to get to the point. Richman continued, "If we hear of a deal, a potential deal I guess you could say, we send someone like Julia out to evaluate it and then, if it looks like a winner, bring it to us. We then meet with the principals and move ahead."

"Oh, Christ," Chris said, "what the fuck does all that mean?"

"There's no need for that kind of attitude," Ben Taylor lectured. "Murray means finance, we arrange financing for companies about to take the leap into the market."

"Really," Chris said, "I thought that was the kind of thing that banks like Morgan Stanley did. Big banks."

"Well, yes, you're right. But there's room for little guys like us as well," Ben Taylor continued. "We don't get the Apples and Amazons of this world. We deal with smaller companies that will be big one day. Companies that can't get in the door of the big players."

"And that's why you had Julia Sutton in Montreal? She was investigating a deal?"

"Absolutely," both men answered, not quite in unison.

"And...?" Chris prompted. "What was the deal she was working on?"

Murray Richman sighed. "There's a gaming company there that developed some amazing security software. They want to go public and we wanted to see if we could be of assistance in some way. Banking, financing. It's what we do."

"Well, she was murdered as she was trying to further your business interests. Seems like she was more than investigating a deal. Did you know that Julia Sutton was found on the scene of another murder? That of Mickie Bédard. Did you know her?"

"Dear God," Richman exclaimed. "We never met her but I know that she was handling the IPO of the company. This is tragic."

"Yes. And it does seem suspicious, no, that two deaths are connected to you and your deal?"

Chris was silent for a minute. He wanted to see if either man reacted to his statement before he asked his next question. Both men sputtered something noncommittal, small ragged red blotches appearing on their cheeks. "And while we're on the subject, do you know Simon Connors? He was also murdered in Montreal. Was he another one of your people?"

The partners got to their feet and Ben Taylor said, "I think our business here is concluded. We're in New York, not Montreal, so we don't have to answer your questions. We've tried to be co-operative but you're implicating us in two murders. We're done for the moment. We'll be happy to give you the name of our lawyer. You can get in touch with him to arrange any future meetings with us." Ben Taylor opened a desk drawer and pulled out a small stack of cards held together with an elastic band. He slipped off the elastic, shuffled through the cards and handed one to Chris. "Here's his card."

Chris stood up, accepted the offered business card and slipped it into his shirt pocket.

"Would you like one of us to show you out?" Murray Richman asked.

"I'll be okay," Chris told the man, and with only a few wrong turns found the corridor that led to the reception area and the elevators.

Murray and Ben were silent for a couple of minutes. Ben closed the office door and said, "Shit. What the fuck is going on up there? Two murders of our people? Even if the bank up there was on to us it's a bit extreme. Jesus."

"Way more than a bit," Murray responded. "We have to call Felix." Murray pulled the phone towards him and dialled.

"How we doin'?" Felix asked.

"Not good. We've just had a visit from the police. It turns out the second person we sent to Montreal was also murdered. That's two for two. I thought you guys were peace-loving. No guns. That kind of thing."

Felix was silent for a long time while he absorbed the news. Murray worried that the call had been disconnected. "Are you still there?"

"Yeah, I'm here. What kind of people do you use? They're supposed to come up here, not attract attention to themselves, get the information we need and go home. They're not supposed to get themselves killed. You guys are supposed to provide cover so I stay in the background, out of sight. Get it?"

There was another pause before Felix continued. "You know what? This is what you're going to do. You're going to get your asses up here. Apply some pressure on Stevens and get me what I want. And don't get yourselves murdered while you do it."

Felix hung up, not waiting for an answer.

Murray told his partner that they would be going to Montreal.

As he walked past the receptionist to take the elevator Chris had an idea. He turned back and spoke to the receptionist who had been friendly when he arrived. "Would you have time to talk to me after work? I need some information."

The receptionist gave Chris a warm smile that faded when he added, "About the two guys I just saw."

"I get off soon, at five thirty. Meet me in the lobby bar of the Moxy Hotel. It's on Anne Street. Believe me, neither Taylor nor Richman has ever seen the inside of the Moxy."

"Got it," Chris said and smiled. The receptionist returned the smile and got up to walk Chris to the elevator. She pushed the down button for him and gave his bicep a friendly squeeze as the elevator doors opened. "My name is Tiffany, by the way," she said as the doors slid closed.

Chris left his car where it was, checked the Citymapper app on his cellphone to find the hotel, and walked the few short blocks to Anne Street. The Moxy Hotel was not the kind of place he would stay at if he was travelling somewhere. The hotel was too modern and certainly very expensive. He found the lobby bar and made himself comfortable at a table within sight of the entrance. A waitress came to his table and placed a coaster on it from the supply she had on her tray. She asked what she could bring him. He ordered whichever IPA they had on tap without specifying the brand.

While he waited for Tiffany to show up Chris sipped at his beer and made some notes about his meeting with Taylor and Richman. Other than having the impression that Taylor and Richman were up to something that was very likely unethical and possibly criminal, he did not have much in the way of information.

Tiffany walked into the bar about thirty minutes later, spotted Chris and walked to his table. Every head in the room turned to follow Tiffany. She was no longer wearing the cardigan she had had on at the office and the dress was sleeveless. Her black hair brushed her shoulders. She had refreshed her makeup and Chris could not help the ego boost that came with the lucky-dude glances the other men in the room sent his way. He held the chair as Tiffany slid into it.

She ordered an old-fashioned and Chris ordered another beer. They clinked glasses once the drinks arrived. Before Chris could ask his questions about Taylor and Richman, Tiffany peppered him with questions about himself. When Tiffany paused to take a sip of her second old fashioned, Chris asked, "What can you tell me about Taylor and Richman? What kind of bank is it that operates out of two rooms in a group office?"

Tiffany smiled broadly. "Not much of one. The term 'bank' only applies very loosely to what those guys do."

"Which is?" Chris prompted.

"Other than it being sketchy, it's hard to say. My guess is that they are really in the business of blackmailing successful businesses. Not blackmail, that's the wrong word. From what I gather they find out when a business is about to make some kind of deal and they get in the middle of it and get paid to leave well enough alone."

"And how do you know this?" Chris couldn't imagine that either Taylor or Richman would talk about their business dealings with Tiffany. And he certainly could not imagine Tiffany associating with either of them outside of office hours.

"You may have noticed that there is a coffee bar against one wall in the waiting room, where there's a TV." Chris nodded. "Well at lunch time a lot of the tenants hang out there, having a coffee or eating, you know?" Chris nodded again so that Tiffany would continue. "Well, when I'm not busy I hang out there as well and listen to the conversations. Some of our tenants have serious little businesses and I hope to pick up a market tip...or maybe something about real estate. You never know."

"I get it," Chris said. "What did you hear from Taylor and Richman?"

"Nothing I can use, but I do hear them brag about their scores. One time they talked about a company that was about to close a deal to sell the software it had designed to a chain of health-food stores. Somehow, they found out about the nuts and bolts of the deal and made a bogus proposal on behalf of a fictitious client and the software company paid them a healthy fee to back off. Greenmail, that's the word I'm looking for," Tiffany concluded.

"But couldn't the real company just have waited the fake company out?"

Tiffany gave Chris a slightly condescending smile. "I guess they don't teach much about business on the police force. In business you want to close fast. Any delay could cost you a deal. Maybe the Richman, Taylor client was a fake but there are always others that aren't, just waiting for a deal to fall apart so they can jump in. The software company had competitors it beat out for the contract and one or more of them would have jumped back in if the deal didn't close."

Chris may not have had much of a business background but he was quick to understand underhanded activity, even if it was legal—sort of. Tiffany was describing a version of the protection racket that made millions for the Mafia and other criminal organizations. "Do you know if these guys had any dealings in Canada?" Chris described Julia Sutton and Simon Connors and asked if Tiffany had seen either of them at the Richman, Taylor office.

"I don't know about Canada, but the woman you describe sounds like someone who came to see those guys from time to time. Hard to say about the guy. He could have been any one of a number of people that came to the office."

"Do you remember the last time you saw her?" Chris asked.

"Not for several weeks. Why, what happened to her?" Cops didn't ask questions for no reason.

"She was murdered in Montreal. They both were," Chris told her.

"Oh dear God, that's awful. And you think Taylor and Richman had something to do with it?"

Chris mimed zipping his lips.

"I get it," Tiffany said, "but I can tell you that those guys were at the office every day, so..."

"Got it," Chris replied. Tiffany could only have been referring to weekdays and only those on which she saw the two men.

"What about phone calls?" Chris asked. "Do you know if they made any calls to Montreal...or received any, for that matter?"

"We get a lot of calls for our tenants. It's all I can do to answer the ones that come through the main line with the company's name. I have no idea if they made or received any calls from Montreal...or anywhere."

"Can you check?" Chris gave Tiffany what he hoped was a thousand-megawatt smile.

"Yeah," Tiffany replied. After a pause, she added, "If I'm careful or if you have a warrant."

"I don't have a warrant." He took one of his cards from his shirt pocket and slid it across the table to Tiffany. "My contact information. Just in case." Tiffany palmed the card and then flicked it a couple of times with a manicured fingernail before she put it in her purse.

"Well then, I'm going to have to be very careful. And it's going to cost you."

"Cost me?" Chris said, smiling again. He covered Tiffany's hand with his. "How much?"

"To be determined," she replied. She didn't pull her hand out from under his.

There wasn't much more information that he could get from Tiffany, even though it was clear that she would have been happy to spend the rest of the evening with him. He had no desire to cheat on his girlfriend. He drank the last of his beer and said, "I have an early day tomorrow. Can I offer you a lift home?"

Tiffany made a moue of dissatisfaction and said, "Are you certain?"

"Yes," Chris was about to say something else but thought better of it.

Tiffany took a pen out of her purse and wrote something on the napkin. "My phone number," she said, "In case you change your mind later." She folded the napkin in half and placed it between her lips, leaving an imprint of her lipstick. She folded it again and slipped it into Chris's shirt pocket.

"I live in Hoboken. I take the train. Thanks anyway."

They left the hotel together and Chris walked her to the nearest subway station.

On his way back to his car, Chris called Gilles and reported the new information he had uncovered. It was clear to both cops that Taylor and Richman had something to do with Julia Sutton being in Montreal and thus with her death. It was unclear what the connection was, though. Gilles opined that the two so-called bankers had something to do with Simon Connors as well. In all likelihood, the cops concluded, Connors, Sutton, and Taylor and Richman were trying to extort something from DiplomRMY or Stevens, Bédard—or both.

He gave his Montreal colleague a blow-by-blow description of his conversation with Tiffany, including the price of the drinks.

Gilles chuckled as he listened to Chris's description of events and said, "It sounds like you missed a chance de t'envoyer en l'air."

Chris did not speak a word of French and only caught the word air. "What?" he asked, "What does any of this have to do with air?"

"Je m'excuse, I'm sorry," Gilles said. "I meant a friendly benefit."

"Yeah, no kidding. But I chose to be a good boy and I'm on my way to my girlfriend's place. I'll let you know if I get a phone number from Tiffany."

"And the cost of getting it," Gilles teased as Chris ended the call.

Chris got into his car, called Sonia and arranged to meet her for dinner.

CHAPTER 27

Thursday –
Gilles Talks with Chris Palmer, Again

Gilles spent Thursday morning working on his reports on the double homicide. The case was one of the more complicated that the Major Crimes Division had handled, as it was unclear if it was in fact a double homicide. It was possible that Mickie Bédard had died from natural causes. On the other hand, it could just as easily be a triple homicide investigation. There was a connection, when all three were alive, between Simon Connors, Mickie Bédard, and Julia Sutton. Gilles's written report ran to twenty typed pages as he laid out all the possibilities he had to explore.

He had just finished his oral report to Captain Lacroix when Chris called from New York. It was well after the end of normal office hours when Gilles got off the phone with Chris, but he figured that people in the tech business worked different hours than the rest of the world, and he called Daniel Yablon to see if he would be available for a short visit to clear up a few points. "No problem," Yablon told Gilles. "I rarely leave the office until nine or later."

There was no traffic and it only took Gilles about twenty minutes to get to Yablon's office in the Chateau St. Ambroise. Gilles pressed the buzzer at the front door to the DiplomRMY space, identified himself and was admitted. Daniel was deep in conversation with a couple of the coders when Gilles arrived. Gilles could overhear the conversation Daniel was having and understood not a word of it. It had something to do with a way of making the software more reactive—whatever that meant. Daniel and the coders came to some kind of conclusion and he turned his attention to Gilles. "How can I help you?" he asked.

"Is there some place we can talk?" Gilles asked.

"Sure, let's find an empty office." Daniel led Gilles to an office at the back of the space. There were a desk and chair along with a round table with three chairs. The two men sat at the table. The office had a window that looked out on the work area occupied by a dozen men and women focused on their computer screens. Gilles wondered what it was like to spend one's working life tethered to a machine. He thought of the scene from *Modern Times* with Charlie Chaplin caught in the gears of a machine, except the coders were caught in an endless series of zeros and ones. Daniel cleared his throat.

"I take it that you've heard of the death of Mickie Bédard by now," Gilles said.

Daniel nodded and expressed his sadness at her passing. "I didn't know her well, but in working with her I came to like her. She was very smart and I like working with smart people."

"Had you ever been to her home?"

"Yeah, a couple of times we had meetings there. Why?"

"Did you know her access code?" Gilles asked.

Daniel thought for a minute before he replied. "Well, I knew it when I saw her enter the numbers. That's the kind of mind I have. I retain numbers. But I also forget the ones I don't need. I can't say I know the code now. The last time I was there was a month ago, maybe two."

"Can you think of anything that she said or did or that you observed that would indicate that there was anyone who wanted to harm her?"

"As I said, I didn't know her all that well. François wanted her to do our deal and I went along with him. My only contact with her was work related, so no, I can't imagine why anyone would want to harm her, much less kill her. Are you certain that it had something to do with us?"

"Yeah. I don't know what the problems are but so far three people connected with you and your company have been murdered."

"Well, you won't find a connection to all those deaths here, that's for certain."

"I've been looking at this from the perspective of the IPO and the security software you've been working on. Is there some possibility that there's a connection with the game itself?"

"Can't see it. Mickie didn't know much about the game. I don't even know if she ever played it."

"Well, gaming is a guy thing, isn't it?" Gilles asked.

"Used to be. More girls, women, are playing now. Our game is very popular with women because there's a lot of strategy to it. Women like the shoot-'em-up games less," Daniel explained.

"Really," Gilles said. "Maybe I'll get one for my daughter."

Daniel smiled and said, "You don't buy it like in the old days. It's online; you sign up and pay that way. It's the only way. I thought you understood that from our previous meeting. I'll give your daughter a couple of hours' free access to see if she likes it. Give me a minute." Daniel went to the desk and rooted around in its top drawer and found a thumb drive and loaded the information onto it. "This will keep her amused for up to six hours. Total access for her and as many friends as she wants. Just plug it into an Xbox."

"And after six hours she has to pay, right?" Gilles asked. He was concerned about the ethics of accepting a gift from someone he was investigating. He figured that six hours of game play, which she might not even use, did not represent a conflict of interest. Gilles slipped the thumb drive into his shirt pocket.

Of all the people that Gilles had interviewed on this case thus far, he liked Daniel the best. He exhibited no nervousness and answered the questions in a straightforward fashion with no sign of dissembling. Gilles paid him the compliment of asking for his advice. "Two people associated with Mickie and your IPO plus Mickie herself have been murdered. I'm seeing a connection but not a motive. Can you think of anything I've missed?"

"I see your point, but because there is no motive, I'm not convinced that the murders have anything to do with us. Maybe take a look at other things she was working on."

"That's the problem," Gilles said. "She didn't seem to be working on anything else at the moment."

"I wish I could be more help," Daniel said.

Gilles got to his feet and handed Daniel one of his cards. "If you think of anything or remember something please give me a call."

"Will do." Daniel dropped the card on the table and escorted Gilles out of the office.

Back in his car Gilles called his daughter. Émilie answered, "Oui, Pa." The fact that she answered after only two rings seemed like a small thing but Gilles understood it to be a major change in his relationship with his daughter. Up to now her tendency was not to answer, which meant that Gilles would send a text telling her to call and she would return his call anywhere from thirty minutes to three hours thereafter. He never left messages on her voice mail for the simple reason that she never activated it. Her generation knew who had tried to call them by using the missed-call function of their cellphones.

"It's getting close to dinnertime, Lapin. Where are you? I can pick you up."

Another step in the right direction: Émilie agreed that she and her father would eat together. Without hesitation she said, "I'm at Dawson College." It was one of the English CEGEPs. "We had an exchange class with them. Where are you?"

"Believe it or not, I'm just down the hill, near the Atwater Market. I can pick you up in fifteen minutes," Gilles told his daughter, pleased that things were going this smoothly.

"Okay, I'll be at the de Maisonneuve entrance."

"Perfect," Gilles said and rang off.

As he drove, he called Annie to see how her day had gone. "Tiring. Like all the others," she reported. "How about you? Would you like to come over for dinner? I'm just getting started."

"Love to but I'm on my way to pick up Émilie," Gilles replied. "She's going to live with me for the foreseeable future," he told Annie. "Until she gets tired of my rules."

"I think it's great. You'll now have a better idea of my life. Why don't the two of you come over for dinner? I made a shepherd's pie, there's plenty. I'm off for the next three days so I won't be falling asleep by nine o'clock. It will be nice to see Émilie again."

"Wonderful," Gilles agreed. "This may sound like a stupid question, but do you have a game console?"

"It's not a stupid question but it is a very surprising one, I have to say," Annie commented. "No, I don't have one, but I'm pretty sure that my sister has at least one. Why?"

"Can you borrow it?" Annie's sister lived next door so it would not be difficult for her to get the game console.

"I'll ask. But, again, why?"

"I have a game that I want Émilie and Pamela to play. It's part of my investigation and I'd just like to know what they think of it."

"Curiouser and curiouser," Annie quoted. "There's a reason I don't have one of those things but I'll do my best to borrow it. I expect a fuller explanation of a murder investigation that requires playing a computer game."

"Much appreciated," Gilles said. "I'm picking Émilie up at Dawson. I'll see you in about half an hour."

"I'll call my sister," Annie said. "See you soon."

Gilles turned onto de Maisonneuve and double-parked in front of the entrance to Dawson. Émilie was waiting inside the glass door. "Where do you want to go?" she asked. "Or are you planning to cook something?"

"We're going to Annie's," Gilles told his daughter.

"Oh," she replied. "Why?"

"Well, she invited us and I want you and Pam to help me with something."

"Vraiment?"

"Oui, Lapin, vraiment." Gilles explained that he had a copy of DiplomRMY and asked his daughter if she had heard of it.

"Just about every guy I know plays it."

"But not your girlfriends?"

"I don't know that many gamers," Émilie explained. "But from what little I know about it, if the girls I know are going to play a game that would be it. I can't say why, though."

"Maybe you'll have a better idea once you give it a go. The copy I have is a onetime thing, I don't have the game itself. I got it from the company that makes it."

Émilie shrugged and said, "Cool." She and her father were silent on the rest of the drive to Annie's place. Gilles made a brief stop to pick up a couple of bottles of wine. In the liquor store Émilie broke her silence to advise Gilles on the choice of wine, suggesting a Valpolicella Ripasso. Gilles purchased two bottles and resisted the temptation to ask his daughter when she became a wine connoisseur.

Annie lived on the upper floor of a duplex. She waited at the top of the stairs to greet Gilles and Émilie. Émilie was ahead of Gilles and Annie gave her a warm hug. With both hands on Émilie's shoulders, she stood back and said, "It's so nice to see you again. I think you get more beautiful every time I see you."

Émilie smiled and said, "Bonjour, Annie."

Annie and Gilles also hugged, but it was mutual, and accompanied by a kiss.

"Come on in," Annie said. "Pam is in the kitchen."

"Émilie, hi," Pam said.

"Oui, bonjour," Émilie replied but made no move to approach Pam. The kitchen table was between them.

"Everything's ready. Come and sit down."

Gilles placed the two bottles of wine on the kitchen counter where Pam was tossing a salad, the shepherd's pie cooling in front of her. "You sit," Gilles said to his daughter and Annie. "I'll help Pam serve." He and Pam two-cheek-kissed in greeting. Annie and Émilie sat at the kitchen table. "Perhaps Émilie will open the wine. She made the selection," he added.

Gilles kept the conversation moving while they ate by asking Pam about her studies and getting his daughter to talk about the theatre program she was in at her CEGEP. Émilie was not all that interested in Pam's life as a pre-med student but loved talking about what she and her fellow students were doing in the theatre. All in all, the dinner passed amiably.

"I have a favour to ask," Gilles said at the end of the meal. He reached into his shirt pocket and pulled out the thumb drive with "DiplomRMY" on it and handed it to Émilie. "I'd like you to play the game and tell me what you think of it."

"I borrowed an Xbox from your cousin," Annie explained to Pam. "It's in the living room. All you have to do is hook it up to the TV. Go ahead. Gilles and I will clean up."

The two girls got up from the table and went into the living room.

Gilles and Annie each had a full glass of wine and chose to remain at the table to drink and talk. "So, what kind of case are you investigating that requires two girls to play a computer game?" Annie asked. "I told you on the phone that there's a reason I never bought a game console. As far as I know most of the games are violent, and especially violent against women and black people. I hope the game you have is not one of those."

"No, no, it's quite different. A strategy game, as I understand it," Gilles said.

"It'd better be. I swear, if I hear one use of the N-word or an attack against a woman, that thing is out of here. Investigation or no investigation."

It was rare for Gilles and Annie to have a disagreement that rose to the level of a fight. This was an exception.

"I understand. I didn't know how you felt. If it will help, I met the guys who designed the game and it's not one of the bad ones. Émilie even told me that she knows girls who play it."

Annie stared at Gilles and said, "Yeah, we'll see."

Neither of them said anything for a minute or two.

Gilles cleared his throat and said, "The case I'm investigating is a murder, a double murder, maybe a triple."

"You don't know?" Annie asked. "Wouldn't the body count give you some kind of hint?"

"C'est ça," Gilles agreed. "There are two bodies, three if you count the murder in the ER. I know the deaths are related. But at the moment I don't know how."

"More seriously," Annie said, "why don't you lay out the circumstances for me? Maybe I can triage your murders." Annie had been a big help in a previous murder investigation, Gilles's first. She had a keen diagnostic way of thinking and highly developed observation skills. It's impossible to be an ER nurse without them, especially if you work in triage. In the earlier case, Annie made the observation that led to the arrest and conviction of the murderer. Gilles was glad to have her opinion.

"Okay. First, we have the murder in the ER. Mickie Bédard killed Simon Connors, presumably in self-defence. But things didn't end there. With the help of a detective on the New York police force I discovered that Connors was working for a so-called bank. Really a couple of very sketchy guys who named their company a bank. These two New York 'bankers' sent someone else to do whatever it was that Connors was supposed to do or have done. The person they sent, Julia Sutton, was found murdered in Mickie Bédard's condo. She was clubbed to death with a brass lamp. We discovered the body when we were on the scene after the discovery of Mickie Bédard's body."

"How was Mickie murdered?" Annie asked.

"Not certain. There were no signs of violence. She was found lying on the floor of her condo, just inside the door. I'm waiting for the coroner's report. Did she kill Sutton and then die of something? If she died first then who killed Sutton? Or did the same person kill them both? If that's the case, how was Bédard murdered without leaving any signs of an attack? Nothing. Is it possible to kill someone without leaving a mark on them?"

"I hate to tell you how easy it is," Annie said. "The simplest way would be for the murderer to surprise the victim from behind with a towel with a large knot in it that would go in the victim's mouth. If the murderer was wearing gloves, surgical gloves or cotton gardener's gloves to name two types, he—I'm assuming it was a he—would hold the towel tight with one hand and use the other to cover the victim's nose. There might be a struggle but unless the victim was naked there would not necessarily be any marks. And it wouldn't take all that long."

"Je vois," Gilles said. "Would the killer have to be a man?"

"Not necessarily. It would be helpful if the murderer was bigger than the victim. Strength is not the key factor here. It's mechanics. If the murderer were taller, say, than the victim and had a good stance, as the victim struggled, she would make matters worse. The knotted towel would be forced into her air passage."

"How long would it take?"

"She'd be unconscious in a minute and dead two minutes after that. Make sure the coroner looks for bits of material in her nose, mouth, and throat."

"And strength would not be a factor?" Gilles asked again.

"Size is more important than strength. At the point that the victim loses consciousness she would fall to the floor. A stronger person would be able to control her fall and a weaker one would probably have a bit of trouble keeping their grip as she fell to the floor. There might be some bruising if she fell hard while she was still alive. In any event, she would be unconscious and, as I said, if the murderer could keep her breathing passages closed, she'd be dead in two minutes."

Gilles was silent for a couple of minutes while he considered what Annie had said. With his eyes closed he slowly rotated the stem of his wine glass and pushed his lips in and out. Annie knew the signs that Gilles was deep in thought, whether analyzing the clues in a murder case or contemplating his next move in a board game, and she did not interrupt his thoughts.

He opened his eyes, sipped some wine and said, "From an investigative point of view it's better to be looking for one person who committed two murders than two people who committed a murder each in the same place. Or one murderer who killed a woman who had committed two murders, even if one of them was in self-defence."

"The other possibility is that Mickie was defending herself a second time and killed Sutton and then died or was murdered. Or the reverse. Sutton somehow killed Mickie and then someone else killed Sutton."

"Exactly," Gilles agreed. "You see my problem. I have to work out who killed whom and in which order. Bédard and then Sutton or the other way around?"

"Let me know what you learn from the coroner, maybe I can be more helpful then," Annie said. "Not to change the subject, but what has the game got to do with all of this?"

"The business at the centre of everyone's interest created both the game and a security system that appears to be worth a serious amount of money. I was curious about the game and one of the developers gave me a copy that can be played for a short time. I wonder how the girls are doing with it," Gilles said.

Annie and Gilles listened for sounds coming from the living room.

There would be periodic bursts of shooting emanating from the game that made Annie purse her lips, and then a discussion between the two players. Pamela would analyze the situation and explain the options to Émilie. Émilie would sometimes agree and sometimes disagree and from time to time say something like, "Look, up in the mountains." To which Pam would respond, "Christ, didn't see that." This would be followed by a volley of shooting and the smack of hands as the girls high-fived each other. "Got 'em!" The last comment usually made by Pamela but frequently echoed by Émilie.

"Well," Annie said smiling, "I don't know if the game has anything to do with your investigation but it seems to have given our daughters something to do together."

"Ouais, sans blague."

They listened to the girls playing DiplomRMY for another couple of minutes and then discussed their plans for the weekend. Gilles suggested that Annie come to his place for dinner on Friday.

Gilles and Annie washed the dishes and then went to the living room to interrupt the game. It was time for Gilles and Émilie to leave. Émilie was reluctant to leave before they had exhausted as much of the game as was available for free.

"What did you think of the game?" Gilles asked.

"Fun. Really a lot of fun," Émilie answered.

"I liked it," Pamela added. "It requires analysis. There's a lot of information to absorb. It's not just a shoot-'em-up."

"Although there's plenty of that," Émilie added.

"How'd you do?" Annie asked.

"We got up to level five. We were playing against a bunch of guys, German I think. It was great to show them some Canadian girl power." Pamela replied and raised a hand which Émilie slapped. Another high five.

"Okay Lapin, but we've got to go."

Before they left, Pamela and Émilie exchanged phone numbers and email addresses so they could find a way to play DiplomRMY again. Annie didn't seem happy at the prospect, but only said, "The Xbox is going back to my sister's."

CHAPTER 28

Friday –
Captain Lacroix Gets Impatient

Gilles got up early and made coffee for himself and Émilie. She had no classes on Friday and Gilles did not expect her to be up before he left. He made himself breakfast and wrote a note to his daughter telling her that the coffee was ready and to call him when she got up to let him know her plans for the weekend. He added the suggestion that it would be nice for her to spend some time with her mother.

He got to the office at eight and put in calls to the coroner and the Computer Crimes Division. There was no one in either department to give him the information he desired so he left messages and got busy amending the reports he had written the day before, including the information he received from Chris Palmer in New York. He added a couple of sentences saying that he took a look at the game DiplomRMY to see if anything suggestive was hidden in it, covering his ass. Nothing there, he concluded. He didn't want it coming out at some later date that he took a freebie from the subject of an investigation.

He left the revised reports in a neat pile in the centre of Captain Lacroix's desk.

Gilles was coming back from getting himself a coffee in the food court downstairs when he ran into Captain Lacroix in the elevator. "Qu'est-ce que vous avez pour moi?" Lacroix asked.

Gilles followed his boss into his office and gave him the updated information that was in his report. He added that he was waiting for call-backs from the coroner and Computer Crimes Division.

"Three murders," Captain Lacroix said. "We need a solution." Gilles took this to mean that the meeting was over.

Gilles got to his desk just as the phone rang. It was Constable Suzanne Rigaud from Computer Crimes. "Tell me you have something for me," Gilles said.

"We had almost no problem getting into the vic's computer. It was password-protected, but I have a workaround for that."

"Great. What did you find?"

"About what you would expect. A lot of financial stuff. All kinds of spreadsheets and reports. Pretty boring stuff."

"Anything about DiplomRMY or Fibonaclé?"

"Actually, yes," Suzanne said. "You'll need a forensic accountant to make sense of it. There's a lot of financial information, profit and loss reports, projections, that kind of thing. Dull but probably important."

Gilles was not encouraged by what Suzanne told him. He could have predicted that someone in the business of finance would have financial information on her computer. "What about emails? Anything there?"

Suzanne had a habit of saving the best information for last. "Funny you should ask," she said. "Her emails are a little less boring than the rest of the stuff on her computer."

"Tabernac, Suzanne, do I have to drag it out of you?"

Gilles sensed Suzanne was smiling when she said, "Calme-toi, Gilles, it's not *that* fascinating." Gilles exhaled loudly and Suzanne continued, "There are some emails from a guy, François, kind of wimpy, arranging to meet for coffee. Looks like a breakup email to me. And then there were a bunch of short emails from a guy in New York, Ben Taylor. They were interesting in that they referred to a previous conversation or conversations and the emails said, in a variety of ways, that the time for talk was over and Taylor would let her know how much he expected to receive. In the later emails he kind of changed his tune. He wrote that he was in the final stages of his research and would let her know how he expected to structure their partnership."

"Send me all the emails to and from the New York people," Gilles instructed. "But if I understand you correctly, they claimed that they, the New York people, would soon be in possession of information that would require a payout of some kind. And then moved away from demanding money and insisting on a partnership of some kind, right?"

"Yeah, that's about it. You'll see for yourself when I send you the emails. Do you want the breakup email as well?" Suzanne asked.

"Sure, why not," Gilles said.

"They're online to you," Suzanne said. "Until next time."

Gilles drained the last of his coffee and his computer beeped, indicating the arrival of the files Suzanne Rigaud had sent him. He read them over and it was clear to him that the Richman, Taylor Investment Bank was up to something. It wasn't clear yet that it was illegal. Chris Palmer had told Gilles about his visit with Taylor and Richman and Gilles decided to get his opinion of the emails.

He called Palmer and after exchanging greetings and the necessary talk about the weather that seemed to be the opening of all long-distance calls, he told his American colleague what he had uncovered. "I'm not surprised," Chris said. "I thought these guys were sketchy. Can you send me the emails? I have an idea."

"No problem," Gilles agreed. "What's your plan?"

"I think I'm going to spend some time looking through the files I found in Julia Sutton's storage locker. If these guys were up to something illegal then the information is there."

"I wish I could help you," Gilles said. "Please let me know what you find. The email files are on the way."

His next call was to the medical examiner's office. Dr. Lapointe was not in, but one of the technicians was able to give Gilles the report on the autopsies. Mickie Bédard, he was told, died from unknown causes. There were some external bruises on the body but they could have been caused by the fall. No known poisons were found in her system. Gilles asked specifically about the presence of any materials in her nose or mouth. Nothing. "It was entirely possible that she died of natural causes. In fact, if there had not been another body in the condo, that would have been the assumption, as there was no evidence to the contrary," the technician explained.

"The presence of a murder victim puts all that in doubt," Gilles said.

"Exactly. But as things stand now, we don't have a cause of death."

"What about a time of death?" Gilles asked.

"Based on rigor and livor mortis I would say within a couple hours of the discovery of the body and possibly a little less. The body was still warm," the technician said.

"And the other body? Julia Sutton?" Gilles asked.

"Cause of death was pretty clear. She was clubbed with the bronze lampstand found at the murder scene."

"And the time of death?" Gilles asked.

"More or less the same time as the other death, based on the same indicators: rigor and livor mortis."

"Is there any way of knowing the sequence of the deaths? Who died first?" Gilles queried.

"That's above my pay grade. It's for you to determine, no?"

"Oui, sur la base de preuves médico-légales," Gilles said. "My next call."

"Good luck." The technician agreed to send Gilles the full written report as soon as Dr. Lapointe signed off on it.

Gilles called the forensics people and asked if their report was ready. "Preliminary only," he was told.

"Anything about prints? Especially on the lamp."

Gilles heard the cop on the other end of the line shuffling through some papers. After a half minute or so she said, "Victim one's prints on it. Obviously, it was her lamp." There was more shuffling of paper and the cop came back on the line and added, "One thing is kind of strange, though. It looks like the prints were smudged, as if someone with gloves held it after victim one. There'll be more when we finish."

"Does Victim One mean the first person murdered?" Gilles asked.

"For us it means the first body discovered. We don't have enough evidence yet to form another conclusion."

"When will the final report be ready?" Gilles inquired.

"We're kind of backlogged, but I would say Monday, Tuesday at the latest."

"Okay," Gilles said. "Keep me posted." He'd learned early in his tenure in the Major Crimes Division that there was almost no way to rush the forensics people. They refused to be rushed for the simple reason that they wanted their findings to be able to stand up in court if a case went to trial. Defense attorneys and their experts gave the reports a thorough review and it was a career-ender for a forensics cop that did not have an airtight report for the prosecution. The cops and the prosecutors blamed television shows such as CSI and NCIS for setting unreasonably high expectations—especially since most of the tests in those shows did not actually exist.

The preliminary evidence suggested to Gilles that Mickie died first and that a person or persons unknown killed Julia Sutton. For Gilles that was the explanation for the smudge prints on the lamp. But that was only an assumption at the moment. A firm conclusion would have to await supporting evidence.

◉

Gilles decided that he wanted to interview Denis Stevens again. There were too many details about the work that Mickie was doing on the Fibonaclé IPO that he didn't understand. The one thing that he did understand all too well was that large sums of money and murder were not strangers to each other.

He told the captain where he was headed and left the division offices.

As he mounted the steps to the door of the Stevens, Bédard office one of the two men descending bumped shoulders with Gilles. "Excusez-moi," Gilles apologized.

"Watch it, Bub," said the man who was at fault.

Gilles rang the doorbell and announced himself to the receptionist. He was admitted. She recognized Gilles and correctly assumed that he wanted to see Denis Stevens. While they waited for Denis Stevens to appear, Gilles asked her if the two guys he had seen leaving the office were clients.

"Hardly," the receptionist explained. "They were Americans who showed up without an appointment and insisted on seeing Mr. Stevens."

"Really?" Gilles said. "I'll be back. I want to talk to those guys." He turned and rushed out of the office. The two men were on the sidewalk in front of the greystone looking lost.

One of them was tapping on his cellphone. Gilles approached them, showed his badge and said, "I'd like to talk to you, if you don't mind."

"Actually, we do mind," the man not using his cellphone answered. "We've just called for an Uber."

"Then I'm putting you under arrest as material witnesses in a police investigation." He took Richman by the elbow and began to lead him away. Ben Taylor had pocketed his phone and shouted, "Hey, you can't do that. We're Americans and we don't know anything about your investigation."

Gilles knew perfectly well that he had no legal right to arrest the men or in any way keep them from getting into their Uber when it arrived. But he decided to continue the bluff to see where it got him. "The fact that you're getting ready to leave the country is the reason I'm holding you." Gilles maintained his grip of Richman's arm. "You're attempting to leave the jurisdiction."

"Fucking right," Richman said, attempting to free his arm. "We have a constitutional right to do what we like."

"Not here you don't. You're in Canada. We can do this the easy way or the hard way. Your choice."

Both men looked slightly taken aback. It had apparently never occurred to either man that the American constitution had no force outside of the United States.

"What's the easy way?" Ben Taylor asked.

"We go for a coffee, you answer my questions, and you're on your way," Gilles explained. He indicated the S'presso Café across the street. To emphasize his point Gilles used his free hand to get his cellphone, dialled a number and barked some orders in French, which he hoped sounded to a couple of guys he was certain could not speak French like he was calling for backup. For good measure he repeated, "Oui, backup, pour deux hommes."

Richman and Taylor suspected, strongly suspected, that he had no right to detain them, but they didn't want to push their luck if they could avoid trouble by having a coffee with him and answering a few questions.

"Yeah, OK," Murray Richman agreed. "You can take your hand off me now."

"What about our Uber?" Ben Taylor asked.

"He'll have to wait. I see a coffee and a big tip in his future," Gilles said and led the two men across the street. Once they were settled with coffees in front of them, Gilles asked their names. He properly introduced himself and handed each man a business card. "My first question is: what is the nature of your business with Monsieur Stevens?"

Murray Richman didn't say anything, which meant that Ben Taylor had to be the spokesman for the two of them. He explained that they had a small investment firm in New York.

"And the purpose of your visit to Monsieur Stevens?" Gilles prompted for a second time.

"It's kind of obvious, isn't it?" Ben Taylor responded. "We knew that his partner had died. We were working with her and offered to take over all the heavy lifting, so to speak. We thought Mr. Stevens had other things to worry about."

"I see," Gilles said, seeing only that Taylor was doing his best to avoid providing Gilles with any useable information. "Would that business have anything to do with the company DiplomRMY or Fibonaclé?"

"Yes, absolutely," Murray Richman said.

"Exactly," Taylor agreed.

"I'm investigating homicides. Both of the victims are Americans and have, I believe, a connection to your firm."

"What makes you think that?" Taylor asked. "You haven't mentioned who you are talking about."

"Julia Sutton," Gilles said. "And my source of information is a New York cop, Detective Chris Palmer. I believe you've met."

"Detective Palmer. Yes, we've met," Taylor agreed.

"And the other victim as well, Simon Connors, I believe is an associate of yours."

"Yeah, Connors, right," Murray said. He had no idea how much Detective Palmer knew and how much of that he had shared with the cop questioning them in Montreal.

"Yes, he was murdered while trying to rob Michaela Bédard, Denis Stevens's business partner. And then a week later her dead body was discovered in her condo, where, by the way, the body of Julia Sutton was found."

"I hadn't realized Montreal was such a dangerous city," Ben Taylor commented. "We had better be careful."

"It is my belief that Julia Sutton was sent to replace Simon Connors and that both of them were on assignment from you. The danger, I think, is attached to your business, not my city. I want to know what these people do—did—for you. Stop the dancing and give me the information so you can be on your way. Do I make myself clear?"

Ben Taylor sighed and replied, "Both people worked for us. They were investigating investment possibilities in Canada, in Montreal, and, yes, DiplomRMY and the other company, the one with the funny name, were the companies they were looking at. Nothing illegal in that."

"That's to be determined," Gilles said. "How did Mr. Stevens react to your offer to help?"

Ben and Murray spoke at once, one of them saying, "Well, you know," and the other, "He said he'd think about it."

He was about to ask another question when he was interrupted by the ringing of Murray Richman's cellphone. Richman looked at the phone to see who was calling and showed the phone to his partner so he could see as well. He tapped the red button, disconnecting the call. It rang again. "Answer it," Gilles directed.

"It's probably the Uber driver," Richman said. He tapped the green button and said, "Murray Richman speaking. How can I help you? We'll only be a couple of minutes."

"What the fuck are you talking about?" Felix Nergal demanded, loudly enough for Gilles to hear.

"Oh, it's you," Murray said. "I thought it was the Uber driver. We're in a café being questioned by a foreign cop."

Taylor was busy tapping a text message on his phone to the Uber driver explaining where he was and asking him to wait.

Gilles grabbed Richman by the wrist that held the telephone before he could say another word. "Listen to me," Gilles said, barely able to control his temper. "First of all, you're in my city. And secondly, Taylor is the one that called the Uber so stop fucking around and answer my questions. What are you up to and who are your Canadian contacts?"

Taylor looked at his partner and nodded. Richman pulled his wrist free from Gilles's grasp and told Felix Nergal, "I'll call you back." He said to Gilles, "Okay, yeah, both Connors and Sutton worked for us. We don't know why they were killed. We were in New York at the time and had nothing to do with it. And we certainly don't know anything about the death of Bédard."

"And that was our Canadian contact on the phone," Richman said, "Felix Nergal." Taylor hoped that they could deflect Gilles's interest away from themselves so they could get out of the city.

"Give me his contact information," Gilles commanded.

Ben Taylor provided Gilles with the information he required. "Are we done here? Our Uber is outside."

"Yeah," Gilles agreed. "If I need more from you, I'll ask Detective Palmer to pay you another visit."

The two Americans got up from the table. They wanted to get out of the café before Gilles changed his mind. Without saying another word, they rushed out and got into the waiting Uber.

Gilles watched the Uber drive off and considered his next move. First and foremost, he planned to meet with Felix Nergal.

CHAPTER 29

Friday –
Felix Nergal Takes Matters into Hand

When the New Yorkers had told Felix about the death, murder, of Mickie Bédard, he insisted that they make the trip to Montreal and meet with Denis Stevens to offer to work with him on the Fibonaclé deal. He thought Stevens would have welcomed the proposition. Things apparently didn't work out that way.

The minute Felix Nergal got off the phone with his two American colleagues he knew he had a serious problem. It was clear that he could not rely on the bozos from New York for anything. They had been in Montreal less than a day and managed to be found by the cops. He had heard the last bit of conversation between Richman and the cop before the line went dead. While he was considering his next steps, his phone rang. It was Richman. "Tell me you're not in jail," Felix said.

"We're in an Uber getting the fuck out of here."

"Did you meet with Stevens?"

"Yeah, it's no go. He wants to talk to his clients before he does anything."

"This is totally fucked up," Felix said. "I'm going to have a chat with Stevens and move things along. What did you tell the cop?"

"He knew that Connors and Sutton worked for us, he's working with a cop in New York, and he wanted to know about you."

"And you told him…"

"Where to find you," Richman said.

"Just what I fuckin' needed." Felix ended the call.

Nergal was certain that it wouldn't be long before the cop dropped by for a visit. In order to ensure that that didn't happen until some time in the distant future, he called down to the concierge and told him that as far as anyone was concerned, he was not at home. Nergal made it clear that he didn't care who came looking for him, the concierge was not to call but to state as often as necessary that Mr. Nergal was not at home, period.

"Yes, sir," the concierge said. This was not the first time he had had such a request from one of the owners of a condo in the building. His stubborn discretion was handsomely rewarded.

In his business dealings Nergal preferred to remain far from the action. He financed operations and reaped the benefits anonymously if at all possible. The Fibonaclé IPO had turned out to be the exception to his modus operandi.

His next call was to Denis Stevens. He had to see the man to ensure that he was fully briefed and that things would move ahead in spite of the fact that his partner was dead.

"Meet with me?" Stevens asked, "Why? Work on the IPO is probably on hold for the moment. For obvious and tragic reasons."

"Listen to me," Nergal said. "Shit happens. But business keeps moving. I'll be at your office in less than thirty minutes. I live close by." Nergal hung up on Denis Stevens before the investment counselor could change his mind.

"Shit happens is right," Nergal mumbled to himself as he got ready to walk over to Stevens's office. "And I'm usually the one that has to make it un-happen." Nergal chuckled at his joke.

Nergal changed out of his track suit, his standard attire when relaxing at home, into a blue cashmere Burberry blazer and grey flannel slacks. He wore a red-checked shirt open at the collar. He put on his Burberry trench coat and checked himself in the hall mirror. He silently complimented himself on how good-looking he was. Sure, he could stand to lose some weight, twenty or so pounds if he were to be honest. But he carried it well. He patted his hair, which he wore brushed straight back from his forehead.

Nergal lived in a condo on one of the upper floors of the Ritz-Carlton on the corner of Mountain and Sherbrooke, a walk of about five minutes to the office of Denis Stevens. As he strode through the lobby of the building, he asked the concierge, "Anyone?"

"Not so far."

"Good. As far as you know I left a couple of hours ago and you don't know when I'll be back."

Felix Nergal went through the lobby, out the door, and turned left onto Sherbrooke Street. As he walked south on the west side of Crescent, Gilles Bellechasse was walking north on the east side of the street.

Gilles approached the concierge desk in the condo lobby of the Ritz and showed his badge. The concierge stared at it for a moment then looked up at Gilles and inquired politely, "How can I help you, sir?"

"I'd like to see Felix Nergal," Gilles informed the man.

"I'm afraid that's impossible."

"And why is that?" Gilles asked.

"Mr. Nergal is not in."

"I see. Do you know when he'll be back?"

"No," the concierge replied.

"Then you won't mind if I wait," Gilles said. The lobby was nicely furnished with comfortable-looking sofas upholstered in beige. There were two high-backed chairs upholstered in the same material. Gilles guessed that the furniture cost more than he'd spent to furnish his entire condo.

"Not at all, sir. Would you like a newspaper?"

"Oui, s'il vous plaît," Gilles told the man.

"I'm afraid we only have the *Globe & Mail*," the concierge said, handing Gilles a newspaper. Gilles took it and made himself comfortable in one of the high-backed chairs opposite the concierge desk, as it gave him a view of the concierge along with the entire lobby. Gilles had a strong suspicion that Felix Nergal was indeed at home, and expected the concierge to call him.

After a couple of minutes of watching the concierge doing nothing at all, Gilles gave up and read the newspaper.

As soon as he saw that Gilles was reading the *Globe*, the concierge tapped a text message in his cellphone which was below eye level at his desk. He sent the universal prohibition symbol and the word "lobby" to Felix Nergal.

Felix was buzzed into the anteroom of Stevens, Bédard. He got the message from the concierge just as he approached the reception desk. He smiled and returned his phone to the inner pocket of his blazer.

"Won't you have a seat? I'll tell Mr. Stevens you're here," the receptionist said. Felix chose to pace while he waited for Denis Stevens to appear.

Denis Stevens descended the stairs and approached Felix Nergal, who was pacing and at that moment had his back to him. Denis waited for Nergal to turn and face him. He looked up at the big man and asked, "Are you the person who called me?"

"I am indeed," Nergal said affably. He extended his arm and walked to where Denis Stevens was standing. Denis looked at the outstretched hand for a few seconds and then shook hands with the man he considered an intruder on his afternoon. "Thank you for seeing me on such short notice."

"Well, you hung up on me before I could tell you not to bother. I guess you were in the neighbourhood."

"I live not far from here," Nergal stated bluntly, his previously affable demeanor gone. "Is there some place we can talk?" Felix Nergal managed to make the question sound like a command.

Denis Stevens glared at the man and without a word turned and headed up the stairs to his office. Felix Nergal followed him.

Denis got comfortable behind his desk and waited for Nergal to toss his coat on the sofa and arrange his bulk in a chair. "What can I do for you?" Denis asked.

Nergal crossed his legs and said, "It's more what I can do for you."

"Really?"

"Really. We haven't met," Nergal explained, "so you've had no way of knowing that I'm a principal in the IPO that your late partner was working on. A terrible tragedy. Please accept my condolences."

"I was unaware that you knew her. She never mentioned your name."

"Be that as it may, I work with...ah...intermediaries. I believe you met them. They're from New York." Nergal didn't wait for a confirmation from Denis. "Under the circumstances," he continued, "I thought it best to take matters into my own hands. First off, I want to assure you that things will continue as before. We owe it to Ms. Bédard to see things through, don't we? But my colleagues and I will do all the work. Of course, your firm will get the customary finder's fee."

This was the second time in almost as many hours that a stranger had showed up and offered Denis money. He shifted uncomfortably in his chair. He had no idea who this man was or even if he knew Mickie. Unquestionably he had an interest in the IPO, but Denis could not fathom what that interest was. He was only half listening to the man; he wanted to get him out of his office. He wished that he had never heard of DiplomRMY or Fibonaclé and the bloody IPO. "I know very little about the deal. Mickie, Ms. Bédard, handled all the details. I only met the client once or twice."

"Yes, exactly." Nergal got to his feet while he spoke. He placed his hands palm down on Denis's desk and looked down at his host. "That's exactly why I'm here. It would be a good idea to arrange a meeting with your clients and ourselves as soon as possible. Say, tomorrow morning at ten. That works for me." Nergal sat down and crossed his legs again.

Denis Stevens was about to laugh at the notion of a meeting the next morning, a Saturday, but thought better of it. "I'm afraid that will be impossible. I would have to talk to the clients first."

"I'm sure your secretary can get in touch with them. I can't believe that no one knows how to reach the clients. That doesn't even begin to make sense. I'll wait while you arrange the meeting." Felix Nergal leaned back in his chair, uncrossed his legs, and stretched them out in front of him as far as they would go, his heels on the floor and the tips of his shoes resting on the modesty panel of Denis's desk.

Denis Stevens had never in his life met someone with the effrontery of the man opposite him. He was too large to physically remove from his office even if Denis were younger and more fit. He wondered what would happen if he got up and left his office. He feared that Felix Nergal would block his path. Denis sighed and reached for his phone. He dialled his secretary's extension and said, "Please call the DiplomRMY people and tell them that I would like to see them in my office tomorrow morning at ten."

"À dix heures? Un samedi?" she queried. She could not remember the last time her boss had worked on a weekend.

"Faites comme j'ai demandé," Denis told the woman. "And confirm when it's done." He ended the call. Felix Nergal was examining his fingernails as if there was something written on them.

"Excellent," he mumbled. He got up and strolled to the window and, hands behind his back, stared out at the people walking on Crescent Street.

After fifteen silent minutes, Denis's phone buzzed. Denis pressed the speaker button so Nergal could hear what she had to say. "C'est fait, monsieur," she reported. Denis made a mental note to apologize to his secretary for his abruptness. She was obviously upset by his tone.

"Do we have further business to discuss?" he asked his visitor.

Felix Nergal turned to face Denis, who was now standing behind his desk. "Yes and no. I want to lay out the agenda for tomorrow's meeting. We can talk about it now or I can meet you before the meeting tomorrow morning. At nine thirty."

Denis sat down again and said, "Now."

"Excellent," Nergal agreed. He walked back to the chair he had previously occupied but did not sit down. He placed his hands on the chair back and said, "Do you have something to write on? You might want to take notes."

Denis pulled a pad over and picked up a pen. He couldn't imagine Nergal saying anything worth recording but if this helped to get rid of the man he would accede to his request. "I'll co-chair the meeting with you," Nergal began, and continued to tell Denis Stevens what he expected to discuss and the intended outcome. All in all, Nergal's exposition took about ten minutes. Denis hid his doodling with a cupped hand at the top of the pad while Nergal spoke. "I'll see you tomorrow, a little before ten," Nergal concluded. He walked to the sofa to retrieve his trench coat and left the office.

Denis breathed a sigh of relief and wondered, not for the first time, what kind of business Mickie had got the firm into.

Gilles spent an uneventful and unprofitable half hour hanging around the lobby of the Ritz. From behind his newspaper he kept an eye on the concierge, who did the things that Gilles figured a concierge in an expensive condo would do. He signed for packages, he directed visitors to the elevator after calling the condo owner to ensure that the visitor was expected, he chatted with the maids who passed through the lobby with their bosses' dogs, and so on. As far as Gilles could tell the concierge made no effort to contact Felix Nergal.

Gilles finally decided he had wasted enough time. Before he left, he called Annie to discuss their plans for the evening and for the weekend. He had to consider his daughter's plans as well now that she was living with him.

CHAPTER 30

Saturday –
Felix Nergal Attends a Meeting

Felix Nergal woke early on Saturday morning and spent an hour in the gym and then twenty minutes in the sauna. He had breakfast sent up to his condo from the hotel dining room and, over coffee, read *The New York Times*. He understood that the DiplomRMY people were the kind of young people who wore hoodies and jeans at work and at business meetings. Felix was tempted to dress casually but decided it would be better to impress on the DiplomRMY people, kids really, that he was their superior in every way. He selected a single-breasted charcoal grey Tom Ford suit that, in its understated way, communicated power. He chose a white shirt with a starched collar and a striped red and gold power tie. He'd purchased the suit because he saw Daniel Craig wearing it in a publicity photo, and even though he was a little taller and a lot heavier than Craig, Felix felt every bit as suave and confident as the actor was in his role as James Bond. He brushed his hair back, wishing his forehead was a little broader, to give him a more intelligent look.

He donned his Burberry trench coat and left his condo.

He arrived at the Stevens, Bédard greystone at nine thirty and rang the bell. Denis Stevens opened the door and greeted Felix coolly, ignoring his outstretched hand. Stevens led his guest up to the second-floor meeting room. Felix removed his coat and held it for a moment, expecting Denis Stevens to take it. When that did not happen, he threw it over the back of one of the chairs and took the eleven o'clock position with his back to the windows. Denis sat as far from him as possible.

Felix examined the art on the wall opposite him, Tom Thompson-style landscapes, then turned to Denis and said, "The reason for the meeting is simple. I want the principals to know that, in spite of recent tragedies, this deal has to go ahead as planned."

"What if I disagree? Mickie Bédard was handling the details and I'm not certain that I have her knowledge," Denis said, doing his best to keep the emotion out of his voice. He missed his partner and wanted the comfort of running his business in the way he'd been doing for decades. He had no interest in continuing the new type of investment banking that Mickie wanted to try.

"I'm afraid that's not an option," Felix said. "Things have progressed to the point where you have to continue. Richman, Taylor will take the American part of the deal off your hands. They offered to do the whole thing. You refused. I'm available to you as necessary to make certain that things run smoothly." After a pause Felix added, "And successfully."

"I see," Denis said and was about to add something when the doorbell rang. "That will be the clients," Felix pointed out needlessly. "Perhaps you can see them in."

Following the meeting Felix returned to his condo and, once there, changed into more comfortable clothing, a navy-blue track suit with white piping. He flopped into a recliner in the living room and, using his landline, called his accountant.

It only took a moment or two for Nergal to bring him up to date.

"Are you satisfied with the way things are going?" Scroyle asked.

"Yeah, more or less. But I think we should get together with some of the other guys and talk things over, bring everyone up to date."

"And make a contingency plan should one be necessary," Scroyle added.

"Exactly. Do you mind calling Gio and Aggie?" Felix asked. Giovani Lapenna and Agostinho Bastinhado were Felix's valued associates. "Let's say two tomorrow afternoon at the Greco Café."

"Sunday?" Rob asked.

"Yeah, Sunday. You got a problem with that? You charge time and a half or something?"

"Just checking," Scroyle said. "I'll call the guys."

Scroyle very much minded being treated like Nergal's secretary, but agreed to make the calls. He knew from experience his client liked to delegate tasks that he could easily accomplish himself. Scroyle added an hour of billing for each ten-minute phone call he made in this type of situation.

Nergal hung up the telephone and reached for the TV remote, found a football game on the big screen TV, and settled in to watch it.

CHAPTER 31

Saturday/Sunday –
Gilles and Annie Have a Discussion

Gilles woke up early on Saturday morning. Annie was lying on her side near the edge of the bed, one hand hanging off the edge. Gilles gently tapped her shoulder and she rolled over into his waiting embrace. She didn't wake up but made a happy sleep sound as she got comfortable. Cuddling with Annie early in the morning usually allowed Gilles to fall back to sleep for, at least, an hour. But not this morning. He had a lot on his mind. After fifteen minutes he slid his arm out from under Annie and slipped out of bed without waking her. He pulled on a sweatshirt and pyjama bottoms and padded noiselessly down the hall, heading to the kitchen.

The door to Pamela's bedroom was closed and he wondered where his daughter was sleeping. He checked the living room and found her asleep on the sofa, her head on a pillow and covered with a blanket that Pamela had found for her.

Once in the kitchen, Gilles made himself a cup of coffee and sat at the kitchen table sipping it.

"How long have you been up?" Annie asked, bringing Gilles out of his thoughts. She was barefoot and wearing an old pair of scrubs. She padded over to Gilles and kissed him. Gilles put his hands around his coffee cup and said, "I'm not sure. Long enough for my coffee to get cold. Half an hour, I guess."

"I'm going to make some fresh coffee while you scramble some eggs and then you're going to tell me what you're thinking about."

Between mouthfuls Annie asked, "What's on your mind, detective?"

"I'm trying to solve a murder and I've got one victim too many."

"Unless, of course, the same person killed Mickie and Julia," she pointed out.

"Clearly. But now I have to figure out who had motive to kill two people who did not appear to have a history and barely knew one another."

"It may be true that the victims didn't know one another, but either the killer had some connection to both of them, or maybe only to one of them, which meant..."

Gilles grasped Annie's meaning and completed her sentence, "...which meant that the other one was in the wrong place at the wrong time for some reason."

"The murders took place in Mickie's condo, right?"

"Yes."

"Then that means that for whatever reason the other woman was the one in the wrong place at the wrong time," Annie said.

"Right," Gilles replied. "That moves Felix Nergal up on my list of suspects. He knew both women and may have arranged to get them together for some reason." Gilles thought for a moment. "There's someone we—I—forgot. She may not be important."

"Who is it?"

"Her name is Beth. I don't know her last name. She works at DiplomRMY. She's going out with one of the guys, François, who used to date Mickie. Maybe jealousy played a role in one of the murders."

"You never know," Annie commented.

Émilie came into the kitchen and looked wide-eyed at her father and Annie, not certain what to say. This was the first time she had seen them at breakfast. She bent her head forward as she added milk to her coffee, hiding behind her hair.

"As-tu bien dormi, Lapin?" Gilles repeated Annie's question.

Émilie mumbled something that sounded like "Oui, Pa."

The three of them sat silently, not sure how to start a conversation or what to talk about. Gilles was about to say something when Pamela walked into the kitchen. Like her mother she was dressed in an old set of scrubs. Pam was a morning person. She usually awoke in a cheerful mood. "Coffee," she announced, "Just what the doctor ordered." She poured herself a cup and sat down. "Did everyone sleep OK?" She turned to Émilie and said, "I hope the sofa wasn't too uncomfortable."

"It was fine," Émilie replied. "But I badly need a shower and a change of clothing. I slept in these." She stared at her father, hoping he got the message that she wanted to leave.

Gilles got to his feet and said, "I'm going to get dressed and take my daughter home."

On the drive to Gilles's condo he and Émilie discussed her plans for the weekend. She wanted to go out with her friends on Saturday night but he convinced her to spend the weekend with her mother. "Your moving out is a big change for her," Gilles pointed out. "She loves you, you know that. I think she would very much appreciate knowing that you love her. Giving up one Saturday won't kill you and it will mean a lot to her."

Émilie grudgingly agreed with her father. "But we're going to have to work something out. Saturday nights are mine," she said.

"Whatever you and your mother work out will be fine with me," Gilles said.

"In which case I expect you to drive me," Émilie said. Gilles hadn't planned on driving his daughter to her mother's house on the South Shore, but agreed.

After dropping his daughter off Gilles returned home, stopping on the way to pick up some groceries and a couple of bottles of wine.

CHAPTER 32

Sunday –
Felix Nergal Has Coffee in Little Italy

Felix Nergal, dressed in a Harris Tweed jacket and slacks and a blue shirt open at the collar, got to the Greco Café, located on Dante Street midway between Alma and Henri-Julien in Little Italy, fifteen minutes before two on Sunday afternoon. The owner, Giacomo Greco, had been a friend since their high school days and they enjoyed spending time gossiping about old friends and their current activities.

Rob Scroyle arrived at two sharp. Scroyle joined Nergal at the counter and participated in the conversation to the extent that he could. Fifteen minutes later Bastinhado and Lapenna came through the door at the same time. Once greetings were made and orders given, the four men made themselves comfortable at a table in a back corner of the café. Nergal and Bastinhado sat with their backs to the wall so they could keep an eye on the door. Greco busied himself with the coffee orders and had the one waitress on duty deliver them to the men.

Bastinhado, also a close friend of Giacomo Greco, asked him to join them and offered to let him participate in any deal that grew out of the meeting. Greco preferred to keep his investments in things he understood and that were unlikely to attract the attention of law enforcement.

During his many years in practice as an accountant, Scroyle had developed a skill in turning money from various sources into legitimate capital. It was because of this skill that he had no problem convincing Bastinhado and Lapenna to attend a meeting on a Sunday afternoon. "I asked you here," he said, looking in turn at Bastinhado and Lapenna, "because Felix has a deal he would like to discuss with you. I may be able to fill in some details if Felix can't."

Felix adjusted his chair so that he could make eye contact with the other three men, took a sip of his double allongé, and said, "Rob brought a deal, an IPO, to my attention. It has to do with a piece of software that will allow secrecy in transactions of the kind we make. We have the same kind of problems moving our money around and this will facilitate that. Also, there is a problem acquiring equity in the company. The investment bank is limiting the number of shares any one person, other than the three original shareholders, can buy. They want to keep control. In fact, it is saying that the issue is fully subscribed. But I think we can get them to see the advantage of letting us in."

"In other words," Scroyle said, "Our group will hold as much equity as possible."

Bastinhado, physically the largest of the four men, was also the loudest and least reflective. Lapenna liked to think before he talked. "It's not that I don't trust either of you, Nergal, but I need more in the way of details before I make any investment decisions," he said. "And not to seem ungrateful, but why include us at all? You can handle the financing without us."

"For sure," Nergal said. "I don't want to call attention to myself by being the only person making a move on the IPO. There's safety in numbers—especially if they're numbered companies." He gave his joke a short laugh. "And, as Rob said, collectively we own more than I could as an individual."

For the next hour Nergal and Scroyle did their best to explain how a computer game company developed a security product, how it worked, and the benefits to those in the business of transferring money away from the prying eyes of the taxman. Rob drew a schematic on one of the Greco Café napkins to demonstrate how the software would prevent information about money from being accessible to prying eyes once it moved through a couple of transactions. Once Lapenna and Bastinhado had seen it, Felix stuffed it into his right pants pocket.

When Lapenna and Bastinhado ran out of questions the two men decided to step out for a smoke. They reviewed all that they had been told and agreed that it was worth taking a flyer on the IPO. One of the many advantages they perceived was the ability to know which of their competitors and colleagues were buying and using the software.

They returned to the café and told Nergal and Scroyle that they were in. Neither man was surprised. Bastinhado proposed adjourning the meeting to a bar in the neighbourhood where they could drink a toast to the success of their enterprise.

There was no shortage of bars and restaurants where Lapenna would be welcome along with Nergal and Scroyle. Bastinhado was less popular because he was proud of his Portuguese heritage and tended to become loudly and volubly dismissive of Italian culture when someone made the mistake of thinking he was Italian. He was unaware of this and thought himself a valued patron of whichever bar or restaurant he graced with his presence. On the other hand, waiters loved him. He ordered a lot of food and tipped generously.

The four men bade farewell to Giacomo Greco and walked the short distance to Johnny Deluca's. The restaurant was large, as was the bar area, and was open for business on Sunday afternoon. The bar was frequented by Italian soccer fans from all over Montreal. The four men knew that anything they said would be lost in the din of the football fans; in fact, they would hardly be noticed.

After a couple of hours of drinking and watching the game on the big screen TVs, the men decided to have an early dinner before heading home.

They left the restaurant at dusk, agreed to keep in touch, and headed in their separate directions. Felix refused the offer of a lift and called an Uber to pick him up at Deluca's. Half an hour later he stepped out of the car in front of the Ritz. As he crossed the sidewalk to the front door of the hotel/condo complex a man came up behind him and dug a gun into his lower back, just below his rib cage. Nergal jerked in surprise and was about to turn around. "No," the man with the gun said, "I've got a gun pointed at your guts. Keep your eyes forward and keep walking."

This was not the first time that Nergal had had a gun poked in his ribs—a situation that usually ended badly for the assailant. "A gun?" he asked. "Are you sure it's not a pen, or your finger?"

"You can find out the hard way. Keep walking and turn down Drummond."

Nergal shrugged and did as he was told. The man with the pistol raised it until it was directly behind Nergal's heart. Nergal knew there was an alley that ran behind the hotel coming up on his right. He planned a move to turn the tables on his assailant when they got there. To his thinking, the only unknown was the height of his attacker. This meant that Nergal did not know how high to aim an elbow thrust. When they were level with the alley Nergal quickly moved his right elbow back in an upwards motion. The assailant saw it coming and moved a pace to the left and, without intending to, pulled the trigger. The gun was close to Nergal's body, which muffled the sound somewhat.

Nergal was dead before he hit the ground. The assailant was at first stunned at having killed him; he was paralyzed for a moment or two. But he recovered his senses and realized that he would have to get away quickly. He looked both ways on Drummond and saw that there was neither pedestrian nor automobile traffic. Another glance told him that Nergal's body had fallen so that it was resting against a small dumpster in the alley. The assailant rushed into the alley and moved the dumpster, which was on wheels. Nergal fell behind it. He did his best to pull Nergal's heavy body farther into the alley behind the dumpster.

He didn't think anyone had seen him on Sherbrooke Street but decided to stick to the shadows as he walked south on Drummond. "People just don't listen," he mumbled to himself as he strode away from the murder scene. It didn't take him long to find a place to ditch the murder weapon.

CHAPTER 33

Monday –
Gilles Looks for Felix Nergal

Gilles was up early on Monday morning. He planned to pay Felix Nergal a visit and wanted to get to his condo at an hour, eight in the morning, when Nergal was likely to be home and unable to hide behind the stalling tactics of the concierge. He checked on Émilie and saw that she was fast asleep. He had an impulse to awaken her so she wouldn't be late for class but stopped himself for two reasons. The first was the obvious one: he didn't know if she had a morning class. The second was the more important of the two: he didn't want to be in the position of nagging her to get to school. School was Émilie's responsibility and she would succeed or fail on her own—and enjoy the consequences of her success or failure.

It took Gilles thirty minutes to shower, shave and get dressed and he was in his car listening to a House of Blues compilation disc on his way to the Ritz-Carlton at seven. Traffic was light and he got there at about seven thirty. The concierge, a different one than the man who had been there on Gilles's previous visit, looked about ready to fall asleep. Stifling a yawn, he asked, "Je peux vous aider?"

Gilles flashed his ID and stated, "I'm here to see Felix Nergal. Have you seen him this morning?"

"No. I'll ring him." The concierge picked up the phone and tapped a few numbers into the number pad. He stared at Gilles while he waited for an answer. When none came, he replaced the receiver and told Gilles, "There's no answer. He's probably still sleeping. You'll have to come back later."

Gilles tapped his badge on the counter. "I don't think so. I'll go up and knock on his door. That should wake him up. What is his apartment number?"

The concierge was fully alert now and did not like being pushed around by anyone; he didn't care that Gilles was a cop. "That's not the way it works. I announce and if Monsieur Nergal agrees I give you his unit number and up you go. If not, not."

"I'm a cop."

"Yes, I know. But that doesn't give you special rights." The concierge paused for a second or two and added, "Unless you have a warrant, of course."

Gilles ground his teeth and was about to say something officious but decided there was no reason to get into an argument with a functionary, especially an argument he couldn't win. "I'll wait," he said returning his ID to his jacket pocket. He turned and walked to the hotel waiting area. He pulled out his cellphone and called Manon Tremblay, the crown prosecutor. He left a message on her office voice mail and then called her on her cellphone.

"Gilles," she answered, "Sais-tu quelle heure il est?"

"Oui. I'm sorry, Manon, I hope I didn't wake you."

"Hardly, I was on my way out the door. What do you want?"

"I've got a problem," he explained. "I want to interview a person who is either a suspect or a witness to a couple of murders and I can't get past the concierge of his building. Can I get a warrant?"

"You know better, Gilles. You have to have a reason and the fact that someone doesn't want to see you early in the morning is not a good one."

"I think he's..." Gilles's conversation was interrupted by the beeps that told him he had another call. He checked his phone and saw that it was his boss, Captain Lacroix. "Criss," Gilles mumbled and then said, "I have my boss on the other line. I'll call you back."

"Gilles," Captain Lacroix said. "I need for you to get over to Drummond and Sherbrooke, an alley just south of Sherbrooke. A 911 call reported something about a body. A squad car is on its way."

"That's where I am, Captain. I'm looking for a suspect."

"You're where?"

"At the Ritz-Carlton."

"Well, get over to the alley and check it out."

Gilles slid his phone into the inside pocket of his blazer and strode out of the hotel. Once on the street he jogged around the corner to the alley that ran behind the hotel. A garbage truck was backed a short distance into the alley, and three garbage collectors were standing at the back of the truck. Gilles went to where they were standing and identified himself. The three garbage collectors stood aside and one of them said, "Regarde. He was behind the dumpster." He pointed to a blue dumpster which was on the hoist above the opening at the back of the truck.

"Did you touch anything?" Gilles asked.

The three men shook their heads in unison. Two of them looked as if they were going to puke. "If you're going to be sick," Gilles said, "Do it in the hopper of your truck. I don't want it on the crime scene."

The three men walked away from the body and leaned against the front of the truck, which was blocking traffic on Drummond. Gilles crouched down to take a closer look at the body. There was no need to check for vitals; the pool of blood and pallor of the victim told him that he was looking at a corpse. His instinct told him that he was finally meeting Felix Nergal. He slipped on a pair of surgical gloves and, using a pen, lifted the victim's jacket and extracted his wallet from the inside pocket. He opened the wallet and checked the driver's license.

Gilles got to his feet just as the squad car rolled to a stop and turned off the siren but not the flashing lights. Before the two cops could ask, Gilles identified himself and told them to secure the scene with yellow crime-scene tape, and call forensics and the coroner. One of the garbage collectors approached Gilles and asked when they could leave and get back to collecting garbage. "Leave your names and contact information with the cops. Someone will be in touch if we need more from you." Gilles took the precaution of recording the truck and license plate numbers. "Which of you is the driver?" Gilles asked.

The guy who'd been doing all the talking said, "Moi."

"OK," Gilles said. "Be careful where you drop the dumpster. Pull ahead and place it away from the police tape."

The garbage collectors complied with all of Gilles's orders and drove off to finish their route.

It didn't take long for the people from the Service d'investigation judiciaire to arrive and take photographs and collect evidence, followed soon after by the coroner's van. The coroner's employees stood aside to wait for the forensics team to release the body. Dr. Lapointe approached Gilles, shook his hand in greeting, and said, "You've found another one, have you? You've become quite the Charon."

Gilles didn't get the mythological reference but took it as some kind of joke. "Can you guess at the time of death?"

Dr. Lapointe slipped on a pair of surgical gloves and crouched beside the body. He felt its forehead and took a thermometer from a small case he had clipped to his shirt pocket. He slid the thermometer into the mouth of the victim, waited for a minute or two and looked at it. "Just a guess, an educated guess, but I'd say at least twelve hours from when the body was discovered. Maybe a little less. I'll know more after an exam. Figure ten to twelve hours."

Gilles checked his watch and said, "So around seven thirty or eight last night, maybe as late as nine thirty or ten."

Dr. Lapointe got to his feet and Gilles crouched down and poked around in the victim's pockets, discovering the napkin from the Café Greco. He called one of the forensics people over to photograph the napkin and place it in an evidence Bag. Using his cellphone, Gilles took a photo of the napkin and then looked up the address of the Café Greco.

Dr. Lapointe asked the forensics tech if he had finished photographing the body and signalled to the men from the coroner's office. Once the body was loaded on the gurney, the forensics tech carefully examined the area where the body had been lying, looking for a shell. There was no shell on the ground. The tech reported this fact to Gilles and Dr. Lapointe who were in conversation.

"Either the murderer was very careful or he used a revolver," Gilles said. He walked to where the uniformed cops were standing around chatting. "Écoute, there was no shell casing at the scene. Search every garbage can and dumpster starting in a two-block radius between Sherbrooke and René-Lévesque. Look for the weapon."

Once Gilles was satisfied that there was nothing more he could do at the scene he called Captain Lacroix and made his report. He told the captain that his next step would be to pay a visit to the Café Greco to see if he could unearth any helpful information.

Gilles got to the Café Greco at twelve thirty. It was half filled with people, most of whom worked at the Jean-

Talon Market, which was a couple of blocks away. Gilles approached the man who appeared to be in charge, asked if he was the owner, and showed his badge. "I'm the owner," Giacomo Greco told him. "What can I do for you?"

"I would like to ask you a couple of questions about a guy who I think was here yesterday. Is there somewhere we can talk?"

Giacomo indicated the half empty café and said, "Take your pick?"

Gilles pointed to a table in a corner and said, "How about that one?"

"Have a seat. I'll be there in a second. Would you like a coffee?"

"No, thank you." Gilles walked over to the table and sat down with his back to the wall, affording him a view of the room. He noticed that unlike most cafés, the tables in this one were spaced far enough apart to keep conversations private. He also noticed that no one was working at a computer. People were chatting while they ate. A moment or two later Giacomo Greco appeared at the table with two cappuccinos. He placed them on the table and lowered his six-foot frame into a chair. He had removed his apron with the name of the café in bold letters on it. "What can I do for you?"

"Do you know Felix Nergal?"

"Since high school. Why?"

"I'm afraid I have some bad news for you. Mr. Nergal was murdered yesterday evening."

Giacomo said nothing for a short time as he digested the news. Finally, he said, "Geez, Felix. I just saw him yesterday. What happened?"

"That's what I'm trying to find out. You said you saw him yesterday? Tell me about it."

"He was here with a few of the guys. Nothing unusual."

"Do you know what they were talking about, the reason for meeting here?"

"Business, I guess. I didn't listen to the conversation. Our customers' conversations are private."

Gilles pulled his phone out of his blazer pocket and showed Giacomo the photo of the napkin with the drawing on it. "We found this in Nergal's pocket. Does it mean anything to you?"

"Other than it being a napkin from here, no. Should it? It looks like a schematic of something."

"Yes, it does. Do you know the names of the people Nergal met with?"

Giacomo Greco did not say anything as he considered the question. "You know, people who come here expect us, me, to respect their privacy."

Gilles leaned forward and looked Giacomo in the eyes and said in a calm but firm way, "There is no such thing as barista-client confidentiality. This is a murder investigation and you have no choice but to co-operate. We can have this conversation at my office if you prefer."

"With lawyers present?"

"With as many lawyers as you want. You're not a suspect. You're being interviewed because you might have information that will assist in the investigation of a murder. Frankly, if Nergal was a friend from high school, I would think you would want his murderer caught."

Giacomo Greco exhaled. "Okay, he met with three guys. I knew two of them, Giovanni Lapenna and Agostinho Bastinhado, very well. The third guy I kinda knew. Rob something, I forget his last name."

Gilles wrote the names down in his notepad and smiled to himself. He didn't know Lapenna but Bastinhado was, as they say, known to the police. This would not be the first time his name had come up in a murder investigation. "How long were they here for?"

"I don't know. A couple of hours maybe, maybe less. I don't monitor my customers."

"Do you know where they went when they left here?"

"Yeah, they went to Deluca's for something to eat." Gilles got directions to Deluca's and got up from the table. Giacomo walked Gilles to the door of the café. Just before he left, he handed Giacomo one of his cards and told him, "Call me if you remember anything else." Gilles was about ten paces away from the café when Giacomo called after him.

"Scroyle," he shouted.

Gilles turned around and asked, "What?"

"The fourth guy, his name was Scroyle, I have his card somewhere."

Gilles returned to the café and waited while Giacomo went through some papers in a drawer under the cash register. He handed Gilles Rob Scroyle's business card.

Gilles walked to Johnny Deluca's restaurant and saw that it was closed until five that evening. He called the phone number on the door and left a message, making a reservation for two for seven that evening. On his way back to his car he called Annie and made plans to pick her up for dinner at Deluca's.

In the five minutes it took him to walk back to his car, Gilles decided that the next person to visit would be the accountant, Rob Scroyle. Interviewing the other suspects could wait. He hoped that the accountant would provide him with a fresh lead or two. Owing to construction detours, the thirty-minute drive to Scroyle's office took forty-five minutes.

Gilles presented his identification to the receptionist and asked to see Mr. Scroyle. The receptionist explained in her British accent that Mr. Scroyle was busy and only saw people by appointment. Gilles suppressed a smile and explained, "My badge means I have an automatic appointment when I need one." The receptionist was about to say something but thought better of it, picked up her telephone and called Rob Scroyle to tell him that a cop was looking for him. The receptionist had only been working for the firm for a couple of months but knew from office gossip that this was not the first time cops had come calling.

The receptionist hung up and told Gilles, "His secretary will be out to get you in a minute. Please have a seat."

Gilles looked around the tastefully and comfortably furnished reception area and found a chair near a window with a south-facing view. The wait of a minute turned into fifteen minutes and Gilles was about to tell the receptionist that he was not impressed with Scroyle's effort to play the alpha male. Before he could say anything, a woman came into the reception area and announced, "Mr. Scroyle will see you now."

Scroyle was making notes on a legal pad and, without looking up, held up a finger, indicating that he would be another minute on something that was so important he couldn't look up from it. Gilles hoped that there would be a reason to arrest the arrogant bastard.

After a minute he finished whatever it was that he was doing. He got to his feet, extended his hand and said, "I'm Robert, Rob, Scroyle. It's nice to meet you."

Gilles shook his hand and introduced himself. He noticed that the view from Rob's office was north, up the mountain, which told him that the firm's offices occupied at least a quarter of the floor. That impressed Gilles more than being kept waiting.

Rob sat down and asked, "What can I do for you?"

"I have some questions about a client of yours. Felix Nergal."

Before Gilles could explain why he was interested in Felix Nergal, Rob interrupted, "Yes, he's a client, but there's not much I can tell you. Our relations with our clients are confidential."

"I'm afraid I have some bad news, Mr. Scroyle. Felix Nergal is dead. He was murdered yesterday evening."

The colour drained out of Rob's face. "Dead? Murdered? I was with him yesterday."

The confidence had gone out of Rob's voice. Gilles could see that it was difficult for him to process the information. He waited before continuing. "Yes, I know. That's why I'm here. I'd like to know what you and Nergal talked about and the time you last saw him."

Rob took a deep breath and answered, "Yesterday, as I said. We talked business and then we had dinner. I guess we left the restaurant at seven or seven thirty."

"Yes, I know, you had dinner at Deluca's. I'd like to know what you and he were talking about and if there was anyone else at your meeting."

"I told you, business. I can't see what our discussion had to do with a murder. It must have been a street mugging or something."

"I'm the one who decides what is and isn't germane to a murder investigation. But I'll lay my cards on the table. I've actually been trying to see Mr. Nergal as part of another murder investigation. The victims were associated with a company called DiplomRMY."

"Jesus, fuck," Rob exclaimed. "It's a game company with an IPO. That's what we were discussing. No one would get themselves killed over that."

"You could not be more wrong. Nergal is the fourth person with a connection to that company to be killed."

"Wait, what, four murders?"

"Yeah," Gilles replied. "Now to get back to my question. Who else was with you?"

"There were four of us. Me and Felix, Agostinho Bastinhado and Giovanni Lapenna."

This confirmed what Greco had told him. He knew that Bastinhado was involved in various questionable activities but had never been convicted of anything. His involvement with the DiplomRMY people opened up new possibilities of investigation.

"And you were discussing…?" Gilles prompted.

"The game company. The IPO. Nothing complicated, we wanted to get in early. Like I said, business."

"Most stock purchases don't end in murder. Tell me where I can find the other two people." Gilles took out his notepad and pen and waited for Rob to provide the information he requested.

"Like I said, there's such a thing as client privilege."

"Not unless one of you is a lawyer or a lawyer was present," Gilles countered.

Rob sighed and gave Gilles the information he sought. While Gilles recorded the information, Rob made a note to call Agostinho and Giovanni and warn them that a cop would be calling on them.

Rob got to his feet, but Gilles did not move. "We're not done. I have some more questions. The most important of which is: how did you find out about DiplomRMY?"

Rob sighed and sat down at his desk. He made a tent of his fingers and rested his chin on his thumbs while he considered how best to answer Gilles's questions. "I advise my clients on investments. In order to do that I have to keep my eye on upcoming IPOs. A banker I know told me about DiplomRMY."

"I see. Was that banker Mickie Bédard or someone else at Stevens, Bédard?"

Rob did not want in any way to be connected to Stevens, Bédard. To do so was to be connected to murders. "No. It was someone else."

"Does that someone else have a name?"

"Look. I deal with a lot of people. If you want to know who passed me a piece of information you'll have to wait. I'll go through my notes and files and try to remember. I'll send you the information."

"I'm sure you will," Gilles said. "Why did you think these clients in particular would be interested in a game?"

Rob leaned forward in his chair and looked Gilles straight in the eyes. "The game wasn't part of the IPO. It was the security software that I thought was a worthwhile investment."

"And why was that?"

"Businesses have to have ways of moving money without risk, that's why." Rob got to his feet again. "That's all I can tell you at the moment. I'll be pleased to talk to you again any time you like—as long as my lawyer is present."

Gilles realized that he had gleaned as much information as he could from Rob. He would be more than pleased to interrogate him in the future. It will also be my pleasure, Gilles thought, to wipe that smug look off his face—with as many lawyers present as he wished.

Gilles got to his feet and said, "This will do for the moment, but as I learn more, I'll likely be back to ask follow-up questions."

"I'll have my secretary show you out," Rob said. He called her on the intercom and she appeared in the office a moment later and accompanied Gilles back to the reception area.

While driving to his office, Gilles received a call telling him that a uniformed cop had found what he thought was the murder weapon. The weapon in question was a revolver and it had been sent to the forensics lab for examination.

Once at his office he spent the afternoon doing cop stuff: writing reports and gathering information from one of his colleagues, Detective Sergeant Normand Simard in the Fraud Squad. Simard had a thick file on Agostinho Bastinhado but a good deal less information regarding Giovanni Lapenna. He had heard of Felix Nergal, but unlike the other two men, he was not known to the police.

According to the Fraud Squad, Bastinhado had a colourful history. He started off working as a street dealer for the Mafia. He wasn't part of an existing family so he was given a territory that didn't generate much revenue, just enough to keep him and his crew working. Bastinhado surprised his superiors by turning his territory into a money-maker. He rose about as far as he could in the syndicate. He was proud of his Portuguese origins and never let those around him forget that the Portuguese were building an empire while the rest of Europe were fighting stupid wars with one another. This didn't endear him to his bosses. He served a short term in prison and, according to Fraud Squad and Gang Squad sources, the big players thought that would be the end of his criminal activities. The suspicion was that he had been set up in order to get rid of him.

In a way, the crime lords were correct. Bastinhado realized that he had no future in direct criminal activities. But, and this was his genius, he realized that he could provide a service that all the crime families in Quebec needed and needed badly. Money laundering. Bastinhado, through layers of corporations, opened a number of companies that did most of their business in cash: laundromats, dry cleaners, dollar-type stores, car washes, dépanneurs and the distribution companies that supplied them, and so on. The crime families and syndicates found him to be reliable and his commissions reasonable. Bastinhado handled most of the money laundering in Quebec and was expanding into the rest of Canada.

Gilles's contact in the Fraud Squad explained that because of the layers of corporations that owned the Bastinhado businesses it was proving extremely difficult to charge him with anything.

Lapenna assisted Bastinhado in managing the large number of businesses he had under his control and liaised with the sources of illicit funds. The Fraud Squad knew almost nothing about Nergal. He had only recently come to its attention as an associate of Bastinhado's who provided capital for his operation when necessary. He had his hand in any number of enterprises that were, on the surface, legal. He was seen as an equal of Bastinhado who had somehow escaped police notice—a tribute to Nergal's success and cleverness.

Gilles shared what he knew about the DiplomRMY security software with Detective Simard and they agreed that this was the type of software that would make the tough job of following the money even harder.

"I guess my final question," Gilles said, "is why haven't you arrested Bastinhado? You have a lot of information regarding his activities."

"As you are aware, knowing and proving are vastly different things. If you look up any one of the companies we think are Bastinhado connected, you find so many corporate layers it's very difficult to know who owns what. Plus things are structured so that one company is lending money to another, which means that a lot of the transfers are disguised as debt or repayment of debt. But we have forensic accountants sorting through the information and sooner or later we'll get them."

Following his conversation with Detective Simard, Gilles spent ten minutes in his boss's office reporting on progress and next steps. During the course of the afternoon Gilles received a call from Dr. Lapointe giving him the details regarding the time of death of Felix Nergal. The victim had died somewhere between seven thirty and eight thirty the previous night. This meant that it was likely that he had headed home directly after dinner, no stops along the way.

Just as he was about to leave to pick Annie up for dinner, he received a call from the forensics lab that the recovered revolver was indeed the murder weapon. It did not surprise Gilles to learn that it had been wiped clean of fingerprints and that the serial number had been burned off.

CHAPTER 34

Monday –
Gilles and Annie Dine at Deluca's

Once Gilles and Annie were settled at their table at Johnny Deluca's, Gilles asked their waiter to tell the owner that he wished to talk to him. He showed his badge in as discreet a manner as possible. A minute or two later, Johnny Deluca introduced himself. He was five feet ten with a round head and black curly hair, dressed in a dark sports jacket and a white shirt open at the collar.

"What can I do for you, Officer? Do you mind if I join you?" He pulled a chair over from an adjoining table.

Gilles introduced Annie and explained that he was investigating the murder of Felix Nergal, who had had dinner at the restaurant the previous evening.

"Yes, he was here. I heard that he had been murdered. A terrible, terrible thing. I didn't know him but it's awful just the same. *Punk di strada, probabilmente.*"

"That's to be determined," Gilles said. "Did you know the other men he was with?"

Johnny Deluca held up both hands, palms out, but before he could say anything Gilles interjected, "I don't want to hear anything about client confidentiality. There's no such thing as restaurateur-client confidentiality."

Deluca smiled, placed his hands palm down on the table and said, "I know Giovanni Lapenna, but the other two guys not so much."

"Did you hear what they were talking about?"

"Business. I wasn't sitting with them. It's just what I gathered."

Gilles was suspicious that Deluca was not being totally forthcoming but had no information with which to challenge him. That would have to wait until after he interviewed Lapenna and Bastinhado. "Thank you," Gilles said. "I'll come back if I have additional information to check with you."

Johnny Deluca got to his feet and said, "I would like you to be my guests this evening."

"Thank you," Gilles said, "but that won't be necessary."

Deluca shrugged, signalled to the waiter to come and take their order, and was about to walk away when Annie smiled at him and asked, "Is there something you can recommend this evening?"

Johnny, the waiter, and Annie had a chat about the menu choices and the specials and she and Gilles placed their order for food and wine.

Over dinner Annie asked how the investigation was going. Gilles, speaking softly so as not to be overheard, brought her up to date. He discussed features of his cases with Annie in greater detail than was SPVM policy. He appreciated her insights. Because she was a nurse, she was a brilliant diagnostician.

"I thought that Felix Nergal was a likely candidate for the crimes until he himself became a victim. Now I'm back to square one, more or less, looking for a motive."

Annie swirled the wine in her glass and said, "That's the difference between your job and mine. Your starting point is motive. I'm only concerned with symptoms. Motive doesn't enter into it. Disease has no motive."

"I hadn't thought of it that way," Gilles said. "But of course, you're right."

"Tell me about each of your suspects so far without reference to motive and maybe I can come up with something."

"Well, I have yet to interview Lapenna and Bastinhado, but all the others, including the victims, seemed to be hot on getting in on the action at DiplomRMY." Gilles went on to describe his meeting with Rob Scroyle and recapped what he knew about the others. He ended his overview by saying, "There's another victim, in a way. And that's Denis Stevens. He lost his wife to COPD a while ago and now he's lost his cousin and partner. They were the two women, the two people really, he was closest to. Every time I see him, he seems to be sadder."

Annie perked up at the mention of a disease. "COPD? Is that what his wife died from?"

"Yeah, I didn't think it was a fatal disease."

"It's a bad one. It gets you sooner or later. Was she a young woman?"

"I don't think so. In her fifties probably. Maybe older."

Their salads had been set before them while they talked and they were silent for a moment while they ate. Annie rested her chin on the back of her right hand, her salad fork swinging gently. "Do you know what medication she was on?"

"No," Gilles responded. "Why do you ask?"

"Well, there's a medication that sufferers from COPD take that can be fatal to people with asthma."

"I thought the diseases were related."

"They are," Annie agreed. "But drug companies work in mysterious ways."

"What's it called?"

"There are a number of meds with the same formula. Axnor is the most popular. It's an anticholinergic and long-lasting beta-adrenoceptor agonist with about two dozen or more side effects. It can be fatal with asthma."

"If it's that awful, why would anyone use it? Why would anyone prescribe it?"

"If you can tolerate it, it's effective. It's not a first-choice med."

"Well, I can't see what kind of motive Stevens would have but I'll have to find a way to see what meds his wife took. I don't suppose there's a database of all the prescriptions written, along with the patients and so on, is there?"

Neither of them said anything as the busboy cleared their salad plates and the waiter brought their main courses. Blackened trout for Gilles and a risotto for Annie. With her fork poised over her plate, Annie said, "Actually there is."

"Really?" Gilles replied. "I don't suppose you can run a check for me?"

"You don't suppose correctly. I'm sure you can check it with the proper warrant."

Gilles smiled at his girlfriend. He admired Annie's honesty and sense of professional ethics. He knew she would help where she could but would never cross an ethical line.

"I hope you're not surprised," Annie said. "I'd be very disappointed if you were."

"Pas du tout. I was kidding. It is good to know that such a database exists, just in case. I shall send a note to Dr. Lapointe to look for it in Bédard's blood, though."

Conversation drifted away from crime to life in the ER, parenting, and on the like. In other words, their regular table talk.

CHAPTER 35

Tuesday –
Dr. Lapointe Looks for A Poison

As soon as he got to the office the next morning, Gilles called Dr. Lapointe and told him what he had learned about the meds that Denis Stevens's wife might have been taking.

"I'll redo the blood work and look specifically for Axnor. But it's up to you to discover if Stevens, or anyone else for that matter, had access to it. By the way, did anyone check the vic's medicine cabinet? There is always the possibility that for some reason she took it herself. By mistake. Maybe a doctor prescribed it in error."

"A doctor making a mistake," Gilles commented. "I didn't think such a thing was possible." Dr. Lapointe harrumphed at the other end of the line. "I'll check and let you know if I find anything suspicious."

Gilles opened the murder file and flipped through the paperwork until he found the list of the contents of Mickie's condo. He read the report twice to ensure he didn't miss anything. She had some prescription medications and he made a note of their names so he could check them with the medical examiner, but there was nothing with the trade name Axnor. He marked his place in the file and Googled the drug to see if there was a generic. He discovered that there was none.

Gilles rocked back in his chair and considered his options. To determine whether Denis Stevens had the means to kill his partner he would have to visit the man's home. Gilles was certain he would not find Mrs. Stevens's meds in her husband's office. He was not certain he would find them at their home but the odds favoured that location. It was one thing to pay Denis Stevens a visit at home and quite another to get access to the places where people usually keep their meds: bathrooms, bedrooms, and kitchens. There was no hope of a warrant at this point. He would have to play the situation by ear. There was no point in calling on Stevens at home during the day. The visit would have to wait until the evening.

Gilles was just as suspicious of the guys at DiplomRMY and decided to see them again. He had no desire to chase them from office to office so he called Daniel Yablon and asked him to be at the Van Horne office later that morning.

He left the squad room and drove to the DiplomRMY office on Van Horne, parked and arrived for his meeting just after the agreed-upon time of eleven o'clock. He noticed that Beth was no longer at a workstation close to the door. He scanned the room and saw that she was at a computer in the far corner, away from both the front door and the larger of the meeting rooms.

At the DiplomRMY office Gilles decided to break with protocol and interview all three partners together. He didn't get much information from them when he interviewed them separately and he hoped that if there was any information to uncover perhaps a look from one or the other of the guys would provide the sign he was looking for. For Gilles, motive was the most important element against which to judge physical evidence and he was still looking for a reasonable motive for a triple murder.

Éloi greeted Gilles and they walked to the boardroom at the back of the space, where the other two partners were waiting. Someone had set up a coffee station and Éloi offered to pour a coffee for Gilles.

Gilles started by asking them a general question. "Are you moving ahead with the IPO in light of all the things that happened?" He expected a noncommittal answer of some sort. It was one of the few times that Gilles got an answer he had not anticipated.

"We don't have much of a choice," Daniel replied.

"What do you mean? It's your business, surely you have a choice?"

The three partners looked at one another. Finally, Daniel answered. "It turns out that there are other people involved now and they want to push ahead."

"Do you mean," Gilles flipped through his notes, "Felix Nergal and a couple of Americans?"

"We don't know about the Americans but Nergal, yeah, we met him."

This was the second unexpected piece of information. "When? When did you meet with Nergal?"

"We were called to a meeting at the Stevens office on Saturday," Éloi explained. "Nergal was there and seemed to be in control. He acted as if he knew Mickie and that she'd been working with him. If that were the case, I'm certain Mickie would have told us. We had no idea who he was but he made it clear that he expected us to move ahead with the IPO."

"I see," Gilles said. "And Denis Stevens agreed."

"Reluctantly, I would say," Daniel answered. "I think he would have liked to postpone it for a while. God knows we wouldn't have minded. Losing Mickie was a tragedy for all of us."

"We thought that's why we were called to a meeting on a Saturday. It's not unusual for us to work weekends, but not bankers," François said.

"You agreed?"

"We didn't feel we had a choice at that moment. It was easier to agree and consider our options later. We haven't really had a chance to talk about it in detail but I'm sure that if we want to hold off for a while, we'll be able to find a way to do it," Daniel said.

"Your meeting with Nergal must have made it obvious that his interest in your software was for uses that were perhaps criminal, no?"

The three men were silent. Finally, Daniel spoke. "Our software was created to provide a secure method of making online payments and fund transfers. We can't police the end-user any more than the manufacturer of bullets, or, better, knives, can know if the user is going to carve a turkey or... well, you get my meaning."

"In other words, you knew or suspected what Nergal's intent was."

"What we knew or didn't know didn't help find out who killed Mickie, did it?" Éloi asked.

Gilles sipped at his coffee and thought about what he had been told. He couldn't see how it made much of a difference to his investigation at that moment. He had a triple homicide to solve and the solution might itself prevent the business deal from moving ahead. He asked each of the guys general questions about their whereabouts the previous Sunday afternoon and evening. They all had alibis of a sort but nothing that could withstand an investigation. There was a lot of time unaccounted for.

"Look," Éloi said. "No one plans every second of their day unless they need a cover for a crime. When you think about it, the lack of an airtight alibi is the proof of innocence."

"And," Daniel added, "you haven't told us why you're asking about Sunday evening."

"Another murder," Gilles told them. "This time it was Felix Nergal."

"We didn't like him much but none of us knew him well enough to want to kill him. Given his personality I would guess that there was no shortage of people who didn't like him," François said.

Gilles shrugged and returned to the day that Mickie and Julia were murdered. He pointed out that none of them had airtight alibis for that time either. He reviewed the information they had given him and ended by saying something about François having a witness to some of his time in that he was with Beth.

"Beth?" Daniel asked. "Our Beth, the programmer?"

François went red in the face and mumbled something.

"Dude, we have rules about dating the employees," Daniel said. "You're the boss. You can't do it."

François was about to say something when he started to cough and wheeze and turned a deeper shade of red. He reached into his pocket and pulled out an Axnor inhaler, flipped it open, and gave himself a dose. When he was able to speak, he said, "Yeah. I know. But sometimes things happen."

"Yes, things do happen and they often end up in lawsuits. Don't you watch the news or read stuff on the web?" Daniel exclaimed. "If you're going to keep seeing her, she'll have to get another job. At the very least I'm moving her to my bailiwick. She can't stay here."

François managed to get his breathing under control and said, "Right. I know, you're right. I'll talk to Beth and, yeah, she'll transfer to your division. I think she'll be cool with it, it's an easier commute for her."

Gilles had remained silent during the exchange between Daniel and François. "Are you OK?" he asked.

"Yeah," François replied. "COPD, it happens when I'm stressed."

"You're stressed now?" Gilles asked.

"Yeah, murder investigations, especially when there is an undercurrent of accusation and my partner being pissed. So, yeah, I'm stressed."

Éloi and Daniel did not look happy. Before Gilles could say anything, Daniel turned to Éloi and asked, "Did you know about this?"

"Come on, dude," he replied. "You know these things happen. I'm sure it was a normal boy-girl thing."

Daniel glared at his partners. Gilles looked at François and asked, "Would you like to continue the conversation privately? At my office?"

François remained seated and said, "No, I don't think so. If you're not arresting me, I don't have to go with you."

"Of course not. It was just a suggestion," Gilles said.

"No one's going anywhere and certainly not without a lawyer," Daniel stated. He moved to stand between Gilles, his partners, and the door to the conference room.

Gilles looked straight at Daniel. "I understand and appreciate your defense of your friend. I'm not trying to make anybody's life difficult. But I am investigating a multiple murder and I won't be hindered from achieving that goal. One of the victims, Mickie, was your friend and I'm sure you want me to succeed. I'll need to question François further and perhaps the rest of you as well. But I have another appointment today. We can put that off until tomorrow, tomorrow morning."

Gilles looked around the room and saw three stony faces. He continued, "My office at ten in the morning. I'll give you the address." Gilles removed his notepad from his inner pocket, wrote the address on a blank page, tore it off and slid it across the table to François. François looked at the slip of paper but did not touch it.

"With a lawyer," Daniel added.

"Certainly, if that is what he prefers."

François did not look happy at the prospect at being questioned at the office of the Major Crimes Division. The two others looked equally stressed at the prospect but no one gave Gilles an argument.

Gilles walked back to his car and drove off. He was in search of a café in a part of Montreal with which he was not completely familiar. He drove south on Park Avenue and because he remembered seeing a café on Fairmount, turned right on that street. Sure enough, the café/restaurant La Croissanterie was a long block to the west. He parked and went in, found a table and ordered a sandwich and a coffee. As he ate, he prepared for his next move—a visit to Bastinhado's office.

After lunch he walked to the address he had for Bastinhado, on Fairmount, just east of Park Avenue. The three-storey building had at one time been residential. It was badly in need of a paint job and repair to the brickwork. Gilles feared that he had been given the runaround by Scroyle and that he was looking at a deserted building. But there was a sign in one of the dirty windows that said the building was occupied by a plumbing supply company. Gilles mounted the steps and pushed at the door. It was locked. He rang the bell and after a short wait a large man with his hairline close to his eyebrows answered the door. He opened it a crack and kept his foot against it. Gilles did not wait for the man to speak. He flashed his badge and said, "I'm Gilles Bellechasse of the Major Crimes Division. I want to speak to Agostinho Bastinhado."

"I'll see if he's in."

"How about I accompany you?" Gilles pushed against the door. It didn't move but the man blocking his way shrugged and allowed Gilles to follow him. They went up a flight of stairs and into an office that looked out on Fairmount. "A cop to see you," the man said.

Bastinhado got up from behind his desk and extended his hand. The office was large but cluttered. There were old green filing cabinets, a large sofa, and a table with empty takeout food containers. Bastinhado did not seem the least surprised by Gilles's visit. He stared quizzically at Gilles.

"Do you know why I'm here?" Gilles asked.

"My accountant called and told me the sad news about Felix. We were just talking about it."

"We?" Gilles asked.

"Yeah, me and Gio Lapenna."

"He's here?"

"Yeah, he just went to the can." At that moment Giovani Lapenna walked into the room, drying his hands on a paper towel, which he tossed in a garbage can. Introductions were made and Lapenna, who was slimmer than Bastinhado and shorter than Gilles, sat down on the sofa next to the henchman who had brought Gilles up to the office.

Lapenna and Bastinhado talked for a moment or two about how distressed they were to have learned about the death of their friend.

"The two of you were probably the last people to see Nergal alive," Gilles said.

"No," Bastinhado said. "The murderer was the last person to see him alive. And that's not us."

Gilles shifted in his chair so he could see Lapenna and asked him about his whereabouts on Sunday afternoon and evening. Lapenna gave Gilles pretty much the same information he had learned from Greco, Scroyle, and Deluca. Bastinhado told essentially the same story. Both men claimed to have been home with family overnight. Gilles questioned them for half an hour but could not find a flaw in their stories.

Gilles got up to leave and informed the men that he would very likely want to talk to them again. The henchman accompanied Gilles to the door and locked it behind him.

Gilles drove back to his office and spent a couple of hours catching up on paperwork. He could barely concentrate on what he was doing and knew he would probably have to redo some of it. He was nervously waiting for Dr. Lapointe's phone call. If it turned out that Axnor was not one of the murder weapons Gilles knew he was at a dead end.

Finally, late in the afternoon after the rest of the day squad had left, he received a phone call from Dr. Lapointe. It was worth the wait. Dr. Lapointe said, "I don't know how you knew about the cause of death but you were right."

"Merci, that's terrific. I know who killed Michaela Bédard and Julia Sutton and probably Felix Nergal."

"The trifecta. How did you know to look for Axnor? It's not a chemical we normally test for in autopsies."

"Two words," Gilles replied. "Annie Linton."

"Ah, the clever nurse again?"

"Exactly."

After speaking to Dr. Lapointe, Gilles spent some time thinking about how he planned to handle the next morning's meeting. He decided that he would lay out his evidence and watch François's reaction.

Gilles decided that he would call on Denis Stevens at home in the hope that he could poke around without a warrant. He checked the address and drove to the house in upper Outremont. He rang the doorbell and was about to ring again when a maid opened the door a crack. Gilles identified himself and asked to see Denis Stevens. "Il n'est pas à la maison," the maid told him.

"When do you expect him?"

"Later."

Gilles realized that he was not going to get anywhere with the maid so he tried a cop trick that always worked. "Thank you. May I use your bathroom?"

The maid stared at Gilles for a moment and opened the door wider to admit him. She pointed to a door just off the foyer and said, "Go ahead."

Gilles found himself in a powder room. There was a mirror on the wall but no medicine cabinet. He flushed the toilet and washed his hands. The maid was standing by the door when he came out and ushered him out of the house. Gilles was not pleased by not being able to give the Stevens home a surreptitious search. On the other hand, he was impressed by Stevens's maid. It occurred to him that Denis Stevens was actually at home but there was nothing he could do about it at that moment.

As he drove home, he called his daughter and was pleased to learn that she was there and hoping he would pick up some Thai food. Gilles was pleased to oblige.

CHAPTER 36

Wednesday –
Gilles Interrogates a Suspect

Gilles got to the office early on Wednesday morning. He stopped at the café in the mall and bought two coffees, one for him and the other for Captain Lacroix. The coffee was still hot when the captain came in and got himself comfortable at his desk. Gilles made a full report, finishing with the news that he expected the suspect to come in for an interview, with or without counsel, at ten.

"And if he doesn't show up?" Captain Lacroix asked.

"Then I'll arrest him. I think he's smart enough to come in." Gilles paused for a beat and added, "With his lawyer."

Gilles spent the next couple of hours going over his notes and ensuring that no one else had plans to use the conference room. He didn't want to use one of the interrogation rooms; they were too intimidating, and tended to induce both fear and silence in suspects, especially those not accustomed to being interrogated by the cops. The conference room would give the impression that Gilles and François were continuing their discussion of the previous day.

At ten thirty, just as Gilles was getting ready to go out and arrest François, he appeared with his lawyer, Jay Berg. Each of them was carrying a coffee and Gilles understood that their tardiness was to throw him off his game.

Gilles led the two men into the conference room and set the tape recorder to record. Maître Berg pulled a small recorder from his briefcase, set it to record and placed it on the table. "I'm sure you don't mind," he said.

"There's really no need. This one records in duplicate and you get a copy."

"Yeah, well, better safe than disappointed by an unexplained silence. Shall we begin?"

"I have to say," Gilles said, "I'm a little surprised that you've agreed to act for François. Isn't that a conflict of interest? We're investigating the murder of another of your clients, Michaela Bédard."

"Nice of you to point it out but I'm quite familiar with the canon of ethics. While we're on the subject I can state that my client is pleased to help with the investigation in any way that he can but wants to make it clear that he had nothing to do with the murders of Bédard and Sutton. If that's why we're here, the meeting won't last long. In any event, there's no conflict as my client is innocent. He didn't murder anyone."

"We'll see," Gilles said. "To start: Can your client confirm that he uses a medication called Axnor for his COPD?"

Berg looked at François who nodded. Berg looked back at Gilles and said, "Yes."

"I would like your client to tell me where he was on the evening and the night when we believe the murders took place."

François repeated the information that he had previously provided Gilles. As he spoke Gilles checked what he said against his notes. The two accounts agreed.

"You can see that there are plenty of gaps in his timeline and he could have taken the time to go to Ms. Bédard's condo."

"And why would he do that?" Berg asked.

"To see if the poison he somehow managed to feed her had done its job."

"Poison? I don't remember anything about poison," Berg said.

"Yes, poison. We found out yesterday that Ms. Bédard was poisoned with a drug that your client uses for his COPD."

Jay Berg got to his feet and said, "If that is the direction this conversation is going to take, the meeting is at an end. We're outta here, François."

François was half out of his chair when Gilles said, "Just one more question, if you don't mind. Can you explain where you were on Sunday night, say between five and ten?"

"You already asked me that yesterday," François said.

"What's that got to do with anything?" Berg asked.

"That's when another murder took place. The murder of Felix Nergal," Gilles explained.

François sat back down but his lawyer remained standing with his hand on his client's shoulder. "You don't have to answer that."

"Ça va," François said. "As I already told you, I was at a friend's house all afternoon. We watched the NFL game on TV and then we went to another friend's place for a birthday party. I doubt that I spent ten minutes alone from about one o'clock on, until late that night."

"Where do your friends live?"

François gave him the locations. He watched the football game at a flat in the Plateau. The birthday party was at a condo on Simpson—not all that far from the Ritz.

"I'll need names and phone numbers so I can check," Gilles told him.

"As I said, we're done here," Jay Berg said. "You'll get the information you want as soon as we see some justification for providing it."

François got to his feet, as did Gilles. "The justification for the information is," he said, "that your client is suspected of murdering three people."

"Really?"

"Yes, really. I believe François Royer poisoned Michaela Bédard in order to end a relationship she refused to end. He went to her condo to see if the poison had done its job. He admits he knew the number code for the entry system. While there, Julia Sutton unluckily came by to see Michaela for some reason. She found Royer and the dead body of Michaela Bédard. Royer could not have a witness to his deed so he used some ruse to get her into another room and killed her with the lamp that was the first thing that came to hand."

"And the Nergal person who my client..." Berg paused to have a whispered conversation with François and continued, "...barely knew. Why kill him?"

"That's to be determined. That's why I need the list of the names of the people your client claims he was with." Gilles turned slightly to address François directly and said, "François Royer, I'm arresting you for the murder of Michaela Bédard and Julia Sutton."

The blood drained out of François's face and he fell back into the chair he had just vacated. "Are you out of your mind? I didn't kill anyone."

Berg put a comforting hand on his client's shoulder and said to Gilles, "You don't have enough and you know it."

Gilles stared at the lawyer. He held up three fingers on his left hand and ticked off the three points as he spoke: "Motive, means, and opportunity."

Jay Berg imitated his gestures and said, "*Nada, gornisht,* and nothing. You haven't come close to making a case for opportunity. Means? Even if what you say is true, do you know how many people have access to Axnor? I'll wager that COPD is a common condition. And most importantly, there is no motive. There was no animus between François and Mickie. The relationship was over. Hardly the first time it had happened to either of them. We came here to help and we're still prepared to do that. But if you think you can arrest my client with what you've got, nothing more than a theory that, even if true, applies to more than one person, then go ahead. He'll say nothing, I'll have him out of custody as soon as I can find a judge and our co-operation, and possibly your career, is at an end."

Gilles sat down to consider what the lawyer had said. He wasn't impressed by the threat but he understood that he would have a much stronger case if he could check François's alibi for the Sunday when Nergal was murdered. Gilles reached behind him to a cabinet on which there was a stack of yellow legal pads and ballpoints. He picked up one of each and slid them across the table to François. "Names, phone numbers, and addresses if possible. All the people you were with on Sunday." He turned to the lawyer and said, "I'm nothing if not reasonable. I'll release your client to your custody. I expect you to produce him if and when I require it. And I want it in writing."

"Hand me a pad and pen," Berg instructed. While François made a list of his friends Jay wrote out a simple agreement that guaranteed that his client would walk out of the building on that day and return if and when necessary.

Gilles was not pleased with the turn of events but believed he would close the case with a little more legwork. He was less thrilled about the prospect of reporting the delay to his boss. He gave a full report of the morning's interrogation.

Captain Lacroix was, as anticipated, not pleased. Gilles was able to convince him that he retained his belief that he was on the verge of making an arrest. Lacroix smiled. It was hard for Gilles to determine if it was a smile of encouragement or a smile based on the captain's experience dealing with Jay Berg, which suggested that Gilles had a lot more work to do. Gilles did not ask for an explanation and excused himself from his boss's office and returned to his desk.

He had a long list of people who had spent time with François on the afternoon and evening of the murder of Felix Nergal, and as Gilles was convinced the three murders were committed by the same person, he had to check François's alibi. He sighed and pulled his telephone towards him and made the first of what would turn out to be a great many telephone calls. After three hours of talking to François's friends and associates, Gilles was hoarse but he had enough information to establish a timeline of his suspect's activities.

Gilles brought his notes to a whiteboard and drew a timeline for François's activities of Sunday afternoon and evening. From about one o'clock until six he was watching the football game on TV and all those present claimed he was with them and left the room only to use the bathroom or refresh his beer. He was never out of sight for more than a couple of minutes.

He took an Uber with a couple of friends to the birthday party on Simpson and his alibi at the party was full of holes. Gilles spoke to six people who were at the party with François and all of them gave him partial alibis. When Gilles transferred the timeline from his notes, he saw that it was more than possible for François to have disappeared for as much as thirty minutes. It was a party and his friends could not report on the exact time that they were with François or when they saw him with others. Like all those in attendance he moved around a lot, talking to this group, dancing with that girl, and so on. Notably, Beth was not at the party.

Gilles spent a solid hour examining his handiwork, checking the timeline against his notes, looking for a contradiction to his conclusion that François was still his number one suspect. To be certain, he made follow-up phone calls to some of the people whose names François had given him, people he determined had been at the birthday party but were not part of his close circle of friends. They either did not have a clear idea of who François was or confirmed the information previously provided.

There was nothing to contradict Gilles's conclusion that François had means and opportunity and a motive: Mickie was a problem for his personal life, Julia unluckily appeared at the scene of the crime and thus was collateral damage. Felix was a business problem and François probably felt that murdering a third person would solve a business problem without any additional risk to him. François could easily have slipped out of the party and walked the few blocks to the Ritz. It would have been a simple matter to call Nergal and find a pretext for them to get together. He would have been back at the party less than forty-five minutes later.

Gilles tidied his desk and left a Post-it Note on the whiteboard saying that the information was not to be erased.

Gilles left the office and picked Annie up at her house. Both he and Annie liked Indian food, so he had made a reservation at Rasoï on Notre-Dame Street, about a block west of Atwater. Parking was difficult in that neighbourhood and Annie teased Gilles about leaving his police parking permit on the dashboard of his car when he was out for dinner.

Once settled at the restaurant with their food order placed and beers in front of them, Annie asked Gilles how the investigation was going. Gilles was pleased to explain his progress thanks to Annie's knowledge of COPD medications.

Annie listened to Gilles as she sipped at her beer and when he had finished his explanation she said, "That's great. Good for you. Didn't you tell me that one of the other people involved with the victims had COPD?"

"Yes, the wife of one of them, Denis Stevens, died from complications or something related to COPD," Gilles said.

"He might have had access to Axnor, too," Annie pointed out. "You didn't tell me how it was that you eliminated him."

Their entrees arrived and Gilles nibbled on an onion bhaji before he answered. "Well, he's not eliminated, but his motive is weak. I don't think he had a reason to kill Mickie. She was like a daughter to him, or so I gathered."

Annie swallowed the bite of pakora she was eating and said, "You know, sweetie, as I told you, when we're diagnosing a patient, we evaluate all the information we have. Even if something seems redundant or not important or whatever, we don't eliminate it until we've carefully considered it."

Gilles dipped his naan bread into the sauce of the sag lamb and looked glumly at his girlfriend. He understood all too well what she meant. "There's no question that Stevens is still a suspect. My problem is that in my interview with him he was very careful in what he said and I had no way of getting into his house. I tried but didn't get past the foyer. But I see another possibility. I'll speak to the Crown about a warrant even if it's only on the excuse that I need it to eliminate him."

"Not only are you a great cop but you're becoming a great diagnostician as well, looking at all the evidence in all its possible contexts." Annie smiled.

Gilles returned her smile and said, "Yeah, thanks, one day I hope to be as smart as you. At one point I thought I had one too many bodies and now, assuming that Denis Stevens had access to Axnor, I may have one too many suspects."

Gilles realized that he would have to find supporting evidence to know which of the two candidates was, in fact, a murderer. Gilles had two additional thoughts, one following on the heels of the other. He knew what to look for and how to look for it. The report from the Identité judiciaire was not all that helpful in that it added little to what Gilles had observed at the crime scene on Blueridge Crescent. The blood was that of the victim, Julia Sutton, and the murderer would have had blood splattered all over his or her clothing. Thus far, the forensics people had been unable to identify the make of the shoe that left the footprint but did determine that it was a size eleven.

For the rest of their dinner they talked about all kinds of things that had nothing to do with murder or patient care.

CHAPTER 37

Thursday –
Gilles Requests Search Warrants

Gilles got to the office early and reviewed the forensics report to ensure that his memory was correct. He called the Identité judiciaire division with the hope that it had identified the maker of the shoe that left the bloody footprint. They hadn't.

Gilles's next phone call was to Manon Tremblay, the crown prosecutor. He gave her a brief rundown of the case he had and asked her to get warrants to search the homes of both François Royer and Denis Stevens. He gave her the addresses.

"Based on what you told me," Manon explained, "I'll be more likely to be successful if you specify what you are looking for. I anticipate a problem if you want an open warrant, allowing us to take anything and everything that may or may not be suspicious."

"In this case that's not a problem. I'm looking for four things: bloody clothing, shoes with a distinctive pattern on the bottom, I'll send you a photograph. Bullets or anything else related to the firearm we found that was used in the murder of Felix Nergal. And finally, Axnor, a medication used for the treatment of COPD. You can claim that I need the warrant for Stevens in order to eliminate him as a suspect, if that helps."

"Clever," Manon said. "But is that all you're looking for? No computers, cellphones or iPads, that kind of thing?"

"No. That stuff may be required later but by that time I will—I hope—have pressed charges against someone."

Manon asked for a few details concerning the gun, which Gilles provided.

"I wish all the requests I received were that specific. I don't anticipate a problem. I'll get to a judge as soon as they start their day and get back to you," Manon said.

Gilles next made a full report to his boss and asked for two teams to serve the warrants. Captain Lacroix called Stéphanie Giroux into his office and told her to work out the details for serving the warrants with Gilles.

They decided that Gilles would lead the team serving François Royer and she would take care of serving Denis Stevens. They reviewed the files and made additional copies of the shoeprint and had a coffee and chatted while they waited to hear from the crown prosecutor.

Just after ten thirty Manon called and told Gilles that she had the warrants. Gilles and Stéphanie agreed to pick them up on the way to the homes of Royer and Stevens.

Gilles and the two uniformed cops who accompanied him arrived at François Royer's apartment, a third-floor walk-up on Esplanade across from Jeanne-Mance Park. François answered the door wearing sweats. Gilles concluded from François's messy hair that he had been in bed. His suspicion was confirmed when he and the cops entered the apartment and saw Beth emerge from the bedroom wearing one of François's sweatshirts. "What?" she asked

"Cops," François explained. "They want to search."

"What? What for?"

"Let them." François looked at the copy of the warrant that Gilles had handed him and added, "They're looking for things that I don't have." He turned to Gilles and said, "You guys have harassed me for the last time. I'm calling Berg."

Beth went into the kitchen to make some coffee while François called his lawyer and explained what was going on. He read the warrant to him and received some instructions which he passed on to Gilles. "My lawyer has advised me to watch what you do and make certain that you don't take anything not specifically mentioned in the warrant. You can have one of my old fucking inhalers, I need to keep a supply of the new ones for my health. I'm quoting my lawyer." François confirmed that Berg had heard what he had said and hung up. He went to the bathroom and retrieved an old inhaler with a few doses left in it and tossed it to Gilles. Gilles slid it into an evidence bag and annotated it.

The main room of the condo, a combined living-dining room, was large. Gilles guessed that it was originally three rooms which had been renovated into one. It was big enough that there was room for a gaming area at the front of it. Typical of renovated condos in that area, one wall had been stripped down to brick. A bedroom and an additional room served as a study. There was a large-screen TV on the brick wall with a sound bar beneath it. Gilles counted half a dozen additional TV monitors in the apartment. An IKEA shelving unit in the study held some books and magazines.

Having brought François a cup of coffee, Beth retreated to the kitchen. She did not offer coffee to the cops. François followed them from room to room as they searched his condo. The cops were thorough and it took them almost two hours to complete their search; all they had to show for it was an almost-empty inhaler.

Gilles hoped that Stéphanie had had more luck at the Stevens residence.

As he was leaving Gilles said, "If I need to see you again, I'll arrange it with your lawyer."

"You do that," François said and made no effort to hide his smirk.

◉

As he walked to the squad car, Gilles called Stéphanie to get an update.

"Fais-tu des progrès?"

"It's slow going. The house is large and the maid wouldn't let us in until Stevens showed up with his lawyer. They're here and we've started. How about you?"

"We're done. Didn't find much other than some Axnor, which I knew would be there. So no luck. We're on our way to Stevens's house. We'll help with the search." Gilles gave the uniformed cops Stevens's address and they drove there.

The Stevens home was a large house on McCulloch Avenue in Outremont, a red-brick mansion with a large porch on two sides. It was situated on a large tree-filled lot. Gilles guessed that the house dated from the early years of the twentieth century. Denis Stevens's grandfather had built the house and Denis grew up in it. This was the prestigious area favoured by Quebec's ruling elite. More than one former premier of the province lived in the neighbourhood. The large homes on streets shaded with old and substantial trees had been built early in the twentieth century and would likely be there for another hundred years.

The maid ushered Gilles and the two uniformed cops into the dining room where Stéphanie was seated at the table with Denis Stevens. Another man, roughly the same age as Gilles but dressed in an expensive business suit, was standing behind Stevens. Gilles introduced himself to the man, who turned to shake his hand and identified himself as Pierre St. Marc,

Denis Stevens's lawyer. St. Marc asked Gilles if they could have a word in private and he agreed. St. Marc led him to a small room that held a TV set and a couple of two-seater sofas.

"Detective Giroux tells me you're in charge of the investigation," St. Marc began. He leaned against the back of one of the sofas. Gilles nodded. St. Marc pulled the warrant from an inner pocket of his suit jacket and went on, "Then I want to make it abundantly clear that we consider this," he waved the paperwork at Gilles but continued to speak in a calm voice, "to be harassment."

"Noted," Gilles replied. "Is that it?" He did not wait for an answer and walked out of the room to join Stéphanie and Stevens. St. Marc followed, still holding the warrant.

After a moment or two, Stéphanie got to her feet and motioned for Gilles to follow her to a corner of the room where they could not be overheard. "How did the other search go?" she asked.

One of the uniformed cops called Gilles using the walkie-talkie function of his cellphone. "Nous avons trouvé quelque chose dans la chambre."

"On my way," Gilles said and headed for the stairs. St. Marc and Stevens followed, as did Stéphanie Giroux. Gilles stopped everyone at the bedroom door and entered the room alone. The room was large, with a queen-size four-poster bed centered against the back wall. There were windows on the right and the usual bedroom furniture along with a couple of easy chairs and a dumb valet. A TV hung on the wall opposite the bed with closet doors on either side of it. One of the doors was open and the cop who called Gilles was standing in front of the open closet. The light was on in the large wardrobe and the cop was holding a shoe with a pen, "Show me the bottom," Gilles instructed. The cop lifted the shoe so that it was at Gilles's eye level. He studied the pattern on the sole and checked it against the photograph of the bloody footprint. "We have a match," he said. Gilles made certain that the shoe and its partner, which was still on the floor of the closet, were carefully placed in evidence bags and annotated. Once that was done, he examined the shoes, Air Birds, a brand he had never heard of, very carefully. There was no blood visible to the naked eye but Gilles knew that that didn't mean that there was no evidence on the shoe. He told the cop to show the evidence bags to St. Marc and Stevens. Gilles turned on the voice recorder on his cellphone and asked, "Monsieur Stevens, are these your shoes?"

Before Stevens could answer his lawyer said, "Not a word."

Gilles spoke into the voice recorder: "For the record I showed Denis Stevens a pair of grey Air Bird shoes, size eleven. He did not respond. His lawyer's is the voice on this recording." Gilles gave the date, time and location of the recording and turned off the voice recorder. "Get those to forensics, ASAP," he ordered. The cop with the shoes and his partner left the house.

Just as everyone was leaving the bedroom, the cops who were searching the ensuite bathroom emerged with an evidence bag that held an Axnor inhaler.

Gilles gathered the uniformed cops who remained for a quick meeting. "Have you covered every square inch of the house?"

"Sauf le garage," Giroux replied.

Gilles and two of the cops found the door to the garage was halfway down a flight of stairs that led to the basement. The garage contained some shelving high on the walls, about two feet below the ceiling. There were boxes on the shelves that would have to be searched. The uniformed cops found a ladder and got busy. Stevens and his lawyer watched from the doorway. The only other thing in the garage was Stevens's black Mercedes.

"Les clés, s'il vous plaît?" Gilles held out his hand.

St. Marc stopped his client from handing over the keys. "The car is not mentioned in the warrant."

"The car is on the property. The keys please."

St. Marc nodded and Stevens handed over his car keys.

There was nothing suspicious in the car. Gilles popped the trunk and poked around with his pen. Shoved into the corner behind an emergency kit he discovered Mickie's Michael Kors satchel. He took a photo of it with his cellphone and with a gloved hand he pulled it out and held it up for all to see. "Qu'est-ce que c'est ça?" he asked, staring at Denis Stevens.

"It's not on the warrant. My client won't be responding," he replied.

Gilles shrugged and returned the satchel to the trunk of the car. "That stays there. I'll get an amended warrant." Gilles slammed the trunk closed and placed the keys in an evidence bag.

Denis Stevens went white and stumbled. His lawyer had to support him.

Gilles turned to Denis Stevens and said, "Denis Stevens, I am arresting you on suspicion of the murder of Julia Sutton. Please turn around."

St. Marc again cautioned his client, "Do not say a word unless I am with you. Not one syllable."

Denis Stevens was rooted to the floor, paralyzed. Gilles gently put his hand on Stevens's shoulder and turned him around so he could put the handcuffs on him. The set of Stevens's jaw indicated stoicism but the look in his eyes indicated terror.

Stéphanie used her cellphone to call for an additional squad car to transport Stevens and his lawyer to the police station for questioning.

CHAPTER 38

Thursday –
Gilles Interrogates a Suspect

Gilles arrived at the shopping centre that housed the Major Crimes Division ahead of the squad car carrying Denis Stevens and his lawyer. Gilles waited at the elevator on the ground floor for them. They, along with the cops who had transported them, rode up to the police department in silence.

Gilles had decided that he would interview Stevens in the conference room.

He invited Denis Stevens and his lawyer to take seats opposite him. Stevens sat down but his lawyer remained standing. Gilles wondered if he did this to avoid putting a wrinkle in his navy-blue suit. Gilles had no desire to crane his neck every time he had to address the lawyer and said, "Maître St. Marc, please sit down." St. Marc was about to demur when Gilles added, "I insist." St. Marc pulled out a chair and sat next to his client.

"Merci," Gilles said. "I want to point out before we start that this interview will be recorded." He paused to indicate the microphones that hung from the ceiling. He turned to the lawyer and added, "You'll be given a copy before you leave."

"Je vais simplifier les choses," Pierre St. Marc stated. "My client does not intend to say anything. Someone from my office will be in court as soon as possible to arrange for bail for Monsieur Stevens."

"Oui, Maître, but that will have to wait until the charges are filed."

"Exactly my point. If you're going to bring charges then do so. If not, we'll be on our way. As I said, my client has the right to say nothing and he intends to assert that right."

Gilles inhaled and exhaled deeply. "As you wish. But I am not constrained to remain silent. I think it best to tell you where you stand."

Pierre St. Marc shrugged but said nothing. Denis Stevens whispered something to him and the lawyer shook his head. Denis Stevens faced Gilles across the table. Gilles leaned forward, rested his elbows on the table and said, "I was about to arrest a young man, François Royer, for the three murders I am investigating. The only reason I didn't was because I wanted to be certain that there was no other possible suspect. This was a lucky break for Royer because you, Monsieur Stevens, are as likely a suspect as he is. You both have access to the poison that killed Michaela Bédard, Axnor. But only you have shoes that have the same pattern as what we found in the bloodstain at the scene of the second murder victim, Julia Sutton."

Pierre St. Marc interrupted. "Without conceding anything I want to go on record as saying that first, my client is not the only person in Montreal with shoes that have that pattern, and even if he were, you have no idea when the imprint was made. It could have been after the murder had been committed by some other person, innocently walking down the street."

"Possible, but unlikely," Gilles replied. "Both of you have motives. In one of our earliest conversations you said something to the effect that Michaela Bédard was taking the firm in a direction you found to be fraught with risks and not part of your traditional business. As far as motive is concerned,

I would argue that in order to stop your partner from risking the future of your firm you poisoned her. Things would have ended there had you not discovered Julia Sutton at the scene of the crime. You grabbed the lamp and killed her. Later on, when you realized that Felix Nergal posed as much, if not more, of a threat, you walked the two or three blocks from your office to where he lived, waited for him and murdered him."

Pierre St. Marc grinned a lawyer's grin and said, "You say my client poisoned his partner. Are you suggesting he went to her residence first thing in the morning and force-fed her the poison? C'est ridicule!"

"Not for a minute am I suggesting that. I am suggesting that Stevens slipped the poison into something that Michaela ingested and went to her condo to see if the poison had done its job. The murder of Michaela Bédard was premeditated, the murder of Julia Sutton was opportunistic, and the murder of Felix Nergal was done out of desperation."

"I'm not conceding anything and certainly not your fanciful description of events," St. Marc commented.

"Fanciful? I don't think so. We're here to determine whether or not your client should be charged with the crimes."

"As I said," St. Marc stated, "he should not. I overheard you talking to the other cop, the woman, and I know that you searched the premises of at least one other suspect. You can't charge my client if there is another suspect who is just as likely to have committed the crimes."

Gilles and the lawyer were staring at one another and neither man noticed that Denis Stevens had folded his arms on the table and rested his forehead on them. "Not just as likely," Gilles pointed out. "We searched the homes of both men and only your client had shoes that matched the print we found."

"And as I said—"

Denis Stevens lifted his head from his folded arms and said in a barely audible voice, "Je suis fatigué, tellement fatigué. I lost my beloved wife to a terrible disease." St. Marc put a restraining hand on Stevens's forearm and cautioned him to be silent. Stevens shook his hand away. "I know you're acting in my interest but I'm too tired to go on. I lost my wife, the woman I spent over half of my life with. I hoped working with Mickie, whom I, we, loved as if she were our daughter, would help to fill the void. She was as compassionate and loving as any daughter could be." Denis paused and his lawyer leaned close to him and whispered something in his ear. Denis waved his lawyer away.

"J'ai fait une erreur catastrophique." Denis paused and stared at Gilles for a moment. Gilles was struck by the sadness in his eyes. It was usually those close to the victims of crimes who looked that miserable—not the perpetrators. Gilles said nothing, hoping Stevens would continue. "I only intended to scare Mickie. I wanted her to stop, that's all. I meant her no harm."

"I don't follow," Gilles said. "Scare her, why?"

Again St. Marc tried to silence his client, and again he went on speaking.

"Mickie wanted to take our business, which had been in our families for well over a century, in a direction I didn't understand. I tried to convince her but she refused to listen. And when I did comprehend what she wanted to do, get involved in public offerings, I was even more opposed to it. It was full of risks and dangerous competitors. She was young and wanted to do what young people always want to do. Change things. Even if there is no good reason for doing so."

"I still don't understand what you meant when you said you only wanted to scare her," Gilles prompted.

Denis Stevens spoke as if he was confessing to a priest, hoping for absolution, not to a cop and a lawyer. "I knew, of course I knew, that Mickie suffered from asthma, and I knew my wife's medication was dangerous to asthmatics. I thought that if I put a bit of it in her coffee, she would have attacks, think that they were related to the stress of the financing she had undertaken, and back off. That's all. I hoped that she would return to a less stressful way of running our business."

Pierre St. Marc realized that his client had just confessed to murder. He pulled his legal pad closer to him and started making notes, preparing a defence. Clearly, his client was distraught and not in full possession of his faculties.

"But you went to her home the day she died. Why?" Gilles asked.

"I was worried about her. I knew she had ingested the Axnor I slipped into her coffee and I called her to see if she was alright. She didn't answer the phone and I worried that she had had an attack and passed out or something and needed help. I went to help her. But she was dead." Denis Stevens lifted his hands to his face, breathing heavily and moaning.

"Why didn't you call for help?"

Denis intertwined his fingers and rested his chin on them. "I was going to but then the other woman appeared on the scene. I hid and waited for her to leave. But she didn't. She poked around the apartment. I didn't know what she knew or anything. I did the only thing I could. I struck her with the lamp."

"What about Nergal? Why did you kill him?" Gilles asked.

"That awful man," Denis sighed. "He pushed himself on me. He expected me to pick up where Mickie left off. What else could I do? If I hadn't got rid of him, he would have muscled his way into the business my family had built up over generations."

Pierre St. Marc broke the silence. "It's clear that my client is distressed and not in full possession of his faculties. I think it best if I take him home. I'll make him available for further questioning after he's seen his doctor." St. Marc stood up and motioned for Stevens to do the same.

Gilles got to his feet and said, "Not happening. Sit down." St. Marc sat back down.

Gilles looked at St. Marc. "I understand that your client is upset. Most people who confess to murder are. But he's not leaving. You know as well as I do it is my duty to charge Denis Stevens with the murders of Michaela Bédard, Julia Sutton, and Felix Nergal. Please stand, sir."

Stevens and his lawyer got to their feet. Gilles used the intercom to call a uniformed cop into the room. He explained that he was about to charge Denis Stevens with three murders and once that was done, he was to be taken to jail.

Once Stevens was officially charged and taken away, Gilles went to the cabinet on the back wall of the conference room, opened one of the doors, and removed two CDs from the recording device. He wrote the details on both of them and handed one of them to St. Marc. Gilles accompanied the lawyer to the elevator and waited until he saw by the lighted numbers above the doors that it had reached the ground floor and did not return. He then went to his desk to write his report and give it to his boss.

The last thing he did before he left the office was to call Annie and invite her to dinner.

CHAPTER 39

Thursday –
Gilles and Annie at the Burgundy Lion

"Let's go somewhere noisy and fun," Annie suggested when she got into Gilles's car.

"How about burgers at the Burgundy Lion?"

"Works for me," Annie agreed.

They pulled up in front of the pub about twenty minutes later and got the last table. They ordered cheeseburgers and fries along with a couple of beers. As soon as the beers were delivered Annie asked, "So who did you arrest, the young guy or the banker?"

Gilles smiled and said, "The banker, Denis Stevens." He described the events that led to the arrest of Stevens and concluded by saying, "I might not have taken a closer look at him at this point. I was pretty certain that François Royer was the murderer, so it's thanks to you that I re-evaluated my conclusion."

"You've got to consider *all* the symptoms—I mean evidence." Annie emphasized the word "all."

"Absolutely. The pattern on the shoes clinched it. It's not like Stevens had the only pair in town but the brand is not all that well known. It might have been harder to close the case if the print in the blood had been made by Nikes, for example. And we found the victim's satchel, as well."

"What about the bloody clothing?" Annie asked.

"The what?"

They were quiet for a moment or two while their meals were delivered and for the time it took to take the first bites of their burgers.

"From the way you described the murder of the woman, the one who had her head caved in, there would have been blood all over the murderer's clothing."

"Yeah, I wondered about that," Gilles said. "When we didn't find anything, I assumed that he'd destroyed the evidence. I guess he hadn't noticed the footprint and there was very little blood residue on the shoes. Forensics rushed their tests so I know there was a small amount but not noticeable by the naked eye. We'll be searching his office and anywhere else he had access. If there is any additional evidence, we'll find it."

"All in all, you must be pleased to have brought the case to a close," Annie said.

"Yes, that's true. But you know, I take no pleasure in it. Four people were killed over a business deal and Stevens is going to die old and alone in prison. It's sad."

Annie covered Gilles's hand with one of hers and gently stroked his cheek with the other.

After a brief silence their conversation turned to other things. He asked Annie what her day had been like and she told him about how busy it had been in the ER. By the time the empty dishes had been cleared and they were drinking their second beers talk turned away from the quotidian and to a plan to spend a long weekend in New York, leaving their daughters at home.

It was nine thirty when Gilles and Annie left the pub. While on the drive to Annie's house Gilles called his daughter to explain that he would not be home until the next morning. Annie had to be at the hospital at seven thirty and Gilles told Émilie that he would be home in time to have breakfast with her.

EPILOGUE

A month following the arrest of Denis Stevens, an interdepartmental envelope with a DVD in it found its way to Gilles's desk. Gilles could tell by the originating information and the signatures on the envelope that it was from the Computer Crimes Division. The memo that accompanied the DVD was from Suzanne Rigaud and explained that they had received it from a developer that was constructing a building in Griffintown.

"It will be clear from the DVD," the memo explained, "that there was suspicious activity at the building site, but the developer was not missing any tools or other equipment." The Computer Crimes Division was asked if the person seen in the video had a connection to any investigations.

Gilles took the DVD to the office player and slid it in. He marvelled at the quality of the images. Most security cameras were not all that good. He guessed that they used such good recording equipment because the equipment and materials on construction sites had a very high street value.

The date stamp on the video was the day of the murders of Mickie Bédard and Julia Sutton. Gilles clearly saw a man wearing a black hoodie and dark slacks carrying a garbage bag to the construction site. There was a pause of a couple of minutes and then the same man walked away without the bag. The camera caught a clear shot of Denis Stevens's face as he passed the camera on the way off the site.

"The missing bloodstained clothing, I'll bet," Gilles mumbled to himself, realizing that it was now part of the foundation of a condo development in Griffintown.

He ejected the DVD, returned to his desk and called Manon Tremblay. The DVD was insurance that Denis Stevens would not change his plea.

ACKNOWLDGEMENTS

Maggie Quinsey again, as in the first book in the series, *A Stab at Life*, served as my role model for Annie Linton. Maggie is a nurse in the Emergency Department of the Jewish General Hospital in Montreal. Under normal circumstances she is a caring, compassionate person and a sharp diagnostician. We are living in the age of Covid, a period that is far from normal, and Maggie and her colleagues, indeed all those who work in the health-care system, are called upon to work long hours and perform miracles of care under extremely difficult conditions. We owe them a debt of gratitude that can never be repaid.

Over the years that I've known Maggie I've come to admire her enormously and I am proud to be able to call her my friend.

Also working in the Emergency Department of the Jewish General Hospital is a young man, Chris Palmer. Chris is a unit agent in the ED. He is always calm, efficient, and eager to please. An example of his caring nature is that he tends to show up early for work so that he has time bring a coffee to, and spend some time with, his mother, Rose, a nurse in the ED. I want to thank him for allowing me to use him as a model for the fictional, eponymous detective in this novel.

Deirdre King read an early draft of the book and made invaluable suggestions for its improvement. I am indebted to her exceptionally keen editorial eye.

Elise Moser applied her excellent editorial skills to *Banking on Life*. I'm grateful to her as all her suggestions served to improve it.

I want to thank Blossom Thom for the extraordinary work she did to copy edit the novel. Her corrections and suggestions were, at all times, thoughtful and very much appreciated.

I am fortunate to have Robin Philpot as a publisher. His understanding of the creative process and his decisive style make working with him a delight. No other publisher would hand deliver books to readers when, owing to the Covid pandemic, bookstores were closed.

John Aylen makes himself available whenever I want to discuss anything and everything including plot points, grammatical problems, and potential cover designs. I am thankful to have him as a friend and advisor.

Mary Reinhold provides more support than I have any right to expect. She is patient when, instead of paying her the attention she deserves, I am lost in thought thinking of ways for my characters to commit heinous crimes. As I've been happy to say on previous occasions, she provides me with both emotional and nutritional support.

I also want to thank my friends Denis Bédard and Michael Stephens for allowing me to use their names in a mixed and matched fashion. The characters in the book are fictional and in no way represent their namesakes.

My brothers, Joel and Norman, and my son Nicholas are a constant source of joy and support. They bring me unimaginable happiness and I can't imagine life without them.

This book is lovingly dedicated to the memory of my parents, Laura Schecter King and Arthur King.

MIX
Paper from
responsible sources
FSC® C100212

Printed by Imprimerie Gauvin
Gatineau, Québec